Love Is Like Ice Cream

To Martha, with love and thanks!
JoAnne 2012

Praise for *Love Is Like Ice Cream*

Love Is Like Ice Cream is a joy-filled story which draws the reader into the lives of the inhabitants of a small mid-western town as they welcome the boys home from World War II. The many memorable characters lived with me for days after I'd finished reading the book and I found myself wishing for a sequel so that I could find out what happens to them next!

Charmaine Lindsay, teacher of English Literature

The immense world issues of World War II are carefully interwoven among the rich and complex lives and loves of the inhabitants of an American small town farming community as they try to adjust to the changes brought about by the war. *Love Is Like Ice Cream* was a very satisfying read that left me with a strong feeling of wanting to know what will happen next to these characters. The character development held my interest and I developed a liking for them so that I wanted to know more about them. I was also curious about what comes next because what comes next, rather than being predictable and unimaginative, is fresh and original.

Thomas More O'Meara,
Psychotherapist, Songwriter, and Musician

The years when the young men were beginning to come home from the battles of World War II was an era that later would be called the Greatest Generation. As one of those who lived through that war, I would never have dreamed that one day we would be called great. We were just ordinary people doing our best to help win the war. This novel delves into the lives of one of those families. Laird Nordstrom arrives home after being at war for three years. When he encounters problems with his fiancé, Jan, he is helped by her sister, Carla, as he works through his pain. I enjoyed the way their problems are resolved. It's an excellent book.

Carol Grier,
Author of *Choices, A Memoir*
and *How to Recognize a Good Man When You Meet Him*

Love Is Like Ice Cream

JoAnne Nordling

Copyright © 2012 by JoAnne Nordling
All rights reserved.

All characters appearing in this work are fictitious.
Any resemblance to real persons, living or dead, is purely coincidental.

ISBN: 978-0-9885184-0-7

Cover photo: On main street of Cascade, Idaho, July 1941
Russell Lee, photographer. Library of Congress Collection: Farm
Security Administration/Office of War Information Color Photographs.

Printed in the United States of America
Book design by raqoon design

Acknowledgements

Many people gave valuable advice and editing during the writing of this manuscript: June Cassimer-Howell, who shared with me the experiences of her own polio dominated childhood; Susan Perry, who kindly allowed me to read the letters her father wrote home during WWII and who introduced me to the memoirs of Paul Fussell, a young soldier in Europe during WWII; Jacqui Burri, whose father carried shrapnel in his body from World War I wounds; Craig Nordling, who contributed to the book's historical accuracy concerning the war; Viola Donkel and Carol Grier, who shared some of their experiences as wives of servicemen during WWII; Roy Lindsay and Harrison Platt, who helped with the math; Jewel Lansing, who waded through my first awkward draft and gave me priceless feedback; Janet Murphy, Duane Swenston and Gail Rupp, who read early drafts and gave advice; Tom O'Meara and Charmaine Lindsay, who gave generously of their time and expertise in the final editing.

I thank them all…especially my sister, Carla Rae, whose life inspired this novel, and my husband, George, who, along with many other veterans of World War II and their wives, have shared their personal stories with me.

Chapter One

Laird looked out the train window at the familiar, flat expanse of farm country rushing by. The young wheat showed green against the prairie soil under a familiar robin's egg blue sky decorated with only a few puffs of clouds, as clear and clean as he remembered. It surprised him to see how untouched everything seemed, except that the farm houses and barns seemed better maintained than when he'd left, mute testimony to the prosperity resulting from huge markets and bumper crops during the war years. Laird leaned back, closed his eyes and let himself be lulled by the steady rhythm of metal wheels rolling against steel tracks.

He straightened up and looked out the train window again. Italy and Germany had good farmland, too, although what he'd seen of Italy wasn't as flat as the Dakota prairie, nor the soil as deep and rich, but by the time the armies and the tanks had mucked around in it, the land changed into either a sea of mud or a cloud of dust. Mud or dust, it got into every damn pore and crevice of your body. When the rain wouldn't quit, your clothes started to rot off, even your shoes, and sometimes your feet. The mountains in winter offered up a different problem; instead of rotting away, your feet as well as your fingers and face, were in danger of freezing. He was lucky he still had good feet. He told himself to stop thinking about it…the war was over.

Laird checked his watch as the train began to slow down on the outskirts of town. He'd purchased the watch for twenty cartons of cigarettes from another soldier who'd bought it while on leave in Switzerland. Every week, the army gave each soldier one carton and one pack of cigarettes and, because the German mark wasn't worth a plugged nickel, a lot of people were eager to barter for cigarettes. The fact that Laird didn't smoke made him prosperous by GI standards; he smiled wryly at the thought he'd probably never be that rich again.

He watched intently as more familiar landmarks came into view: the football field on the outskirts of town looked the same as ever with its two spartan sets of bleachers. Many people brought their own chairs to the games, or just stood as close as they could to the line of scrimmage. There were never enough seats for the spectators, especially during the big games with Molalla and Langley.

He spotted the grove of trees on the old Harrison place where he'd had his first kiss, a milestone shared with another sixth grader named Diane. A couple of his buddies had discovered them in mid-kiss, and the next day they told everybody at school which caused Diane and Laird to be mercilessly teased for weeks. After that, Diane wouldn't speak to him for nearly a year. Laird smiled, thinking that Diane had been plenty eager to kiss him again for real when they were sophomores. He'd been smitten with gorgeous, red-haired, funny Diane until they were juniors, when suddenly Janice Swanson had popped up on his radar screen, and from then on, all he'd wanted was Jan.

Diane had been hurt and angry when he'd told her he was leaving her for Jan, but it wasn't long before Diane met Conrad Oberst at a football game and fell for him like a ton of bricks. Conrad was a vibrant, broad-shouldered defensive back on the rival Langley High School team who, more than once, had brought Laird face down in the mud. Whether to cheer for the home team or the rival Langley team had been a frustrating dilemma for Diane, until finally she'd decided not to cheer for either side, and instead sat hugging herself tightly, bouncing up and down on the bleacher seat, grinning wildly whenever Conrad stopped the Breton team's advance down the field.

Diane and Conrad had two months of marriage before Conrad was shipped out and killed a year later fighting in New Guinea. Laird closed his eyes and slowly rubbed his forehead, remembering Diane as she walked out the door of the Lutheran Church, one hand clutching her bridal bouquet, the other hand tucked firmly under Conrad's arm as she looked up at him, her emerald eyes shining, her lips parted in a huge smile. She was bound to resent Laird for coming home alive. Laird knew it was a crazy kind of hit or miss luck why one person lived and another one died, but he couldn't blame her if she didn't understand there was no logic or justice to the insanity of war.

As the train drew into the depot and slowed to a hissing stop, he saw a battered pickup and a green Ford parked out in front of Larson's feed store. Oscar Olson's police car was parked on the street beside the depot, the same old black Ford Laird remembered from his high school days, with "Breton Police" neatly lettered on the side of each front door. Evidently, not even the town cop could get a new car during the war.

Laird set his jaw as he got up from his seat, took his duffel bag down from the luggage rack, and slung it over his shoulder. He walked down the aisle, and stood impatiently waiting for the porter to open the door and let down the train steps, wondering if he should call his mother and tell her he was home, or just walk in unannounced. It might be better to just walk in and surprise her, otherwise half the neighborhood might be there to greet him.

He dreaded running the gauntlet of townspeople who would want to shake his hand and ask him what he'd done in the war. When he'd boarded the train in Chicago and gone to the club car for something to eat, he'd been besieged by men in civilian clothes, all eager to slap him on the back, buy him a drink, and hear what he'd done "over there." In the dining car the waiter had said with a broad smile in his black face, "No charge sir. The gentleman over there in the green shirt already paid your bill." Laird had acknowledged the man in the green shirt with a smile and a brief nod of his head. He knew they meant well, and he appreciated everyone's attempts to welcome him home, but it made him uncomfortable. The guys without arms or legs, and all those who weren't ever coming home, they were the ones who deserved the free drinks.

Laird knew Janice wouldn't be in town to greet him, but that was okay. He and Jan could wait one more day. A day was nothing compared to the three years of absence they'd already lived through. She was in Minneapolis finishing up her nurse's training at St. Mary's Hospital, but she'd written that her supervisor had cleared her for a week off as soon as Laird arrived home.

Jan's sisters would probably run over to see him the minute they heard he was back in town. His face relaxed into almost a smile, remembering teen-ager Squirt's bubbly personality and her mass of curls; Jan's youngest sister, Martha, had been in kindergarten when he'd left. The image of his brothers, his parents, and his beautiful Jan, with the sun accentuating the color of her auburn hair, waving goodbye to him when he'd boarded the train headed for boot camp flashed through his mind…it seemed like such a long time ago.

As he stepped down from the train, he saw the familiar mustard yellow train depot with the sign BRETON STATION carefully lettered above the door. He stood still a moment watching a man in a US postal worker uniform load cardboard cartons of cheeping baby chickens onto a baggage cart and, he could see, through the small round airholes stamped into the sides of the cartons, the noisy yellow balls of fluff moving around inside. He'd nearly forgotten the early spring farm ritual of ordering baby chickens from the Montgomery Ward catalog. Laird slowly shifted the khaki duffel bag into a more comfortable position on his shoulder and started walking towards the station door. Probably the best thing would be to call Dad down at the blacksmith shop to come pick him up.

Every noon, and some nights if he was free, Oscar Olson, the town cop, swung by the train depot to see who was leaving town and who was coming in. He told himself that in his line of work it made sense for him to keep an eye on things, but the truth was that he got a kick out of watching the locomotive hiss to a stop, and the conductor hop off the train to go through the ritual of pulling out a timepiece from his vest pocket to reassure himself that the train was on schedule.

Oscar, too, always checked his watch. He knew the schedule as well as the conductor. The train was supposed to roll in everyday at 12:05 pm but today it was ten minutes late…probably it had been slow to change cars in Chicago. Maybe he'd go kid the conductor about being behind schedule.

Oscar got out of the car slowly because the damn hip was giving him trouble again. At age sixty-four, it was probably time to think of retiring. Thank God spring was here, and he'd have a break from shoveling cars out of snow banks, driving through blizzards answering calls from frantic wives trying to calm down drunken husbands, and rescuing people who were snowed in with a sick child who needed to get to the doctor.

Oscar saw Laird just as he stepped off the train. It was Laird all right, and sure enough, there was a slight limp when Laird started to walk but it didn't seem too bad. Oscar had heard the knee injury was permanent, but Laird was alive and looked healthy otherwise. He'd filled out, put on more muscle, and carried himself with more authority, and Oscar recognized the same strong-boned face, clear eyes, and confident body posture of the born athlete.

Laird never drank or smoked in high school, probably because Coach Kimberly made all the boys promise: no drinking and no smoking, or they wouldn't play sports, and Coach Kimberly always kept his word. Not all the boys kept theirs, although Oscar was pretty sure Laird had kept his part of the bargain, at least until track season ended in the spring of 1943. He'd no doubt broken the no-drinking pledge the night before graduation when he and his buddies got the bright idea to plaster "1943" in red paint on practically every flat surface in town, including the sides of Mrs. Munwiller's cows. Someone, probably Laird, had climbed up 130 feet to paint "1943" on the water tower. Lots of people were outraged, but most townspeople agreed with Oscar that it was nothing to get so upset about. Many of the older men laughed together privately, and tried to outdo each other telling stories of their own past pranks including the Halloween in 1918 when some of them had taken apart the Carlson's new buggy and hoisted it up onto the roof of the barn where they'd reassembled it.

So maybe Laird and his buddies got a little drunk and did something crazy the night before graduation, but they had good reason to kick up their heels. Most of them were scheduled to leave the next day or two for boot camp. Oscar knew the army entrance drill from his own experience in the First World War. It was exciting to be heading out into the world, but scary as all shit. You held up your hand and swore allegiance to the good old USA, they gave you a dog tag and a new set of clothes, and from then on they owned you. From then on you needed three things…guts, patience, and luck.

Oscar waved his arm and shouted, "Laird, over here! Welcome home, kid!"

Laird turned and a smile transformed his face, his eyes sparkled and for a moment he looked almost mischievous. "Oscar…you haven't changed a bit…still checking on the train schedule, are you? Still keeping the town kids in line? Anybody shot at you lately?"

"Nope, no shootings, thank God…things are pretty quiet around here."

Years ago Oscar had been shot in the chest with a 12-gauge shotgun. Henry Slayton, who had just killed his wife, shot right through the front door after Oscar went up on the front porch and tried to reason with him, "Come on out now, Henry. I think we better talk." The town doctor later told Oscar he was one tough bird and the only thing that saved him was the thick frosted glass in the front door plus the heavy leather jacket he was wearing. Oscar always regretted he hadn't gotten there in time to save Mary Slayton, and he often complained to his friends about the damn drunks. It would be so much easier being a town cop without the drunks.

"Need a lift home, Laird? I guess your folks didn't know you were coming in on the train today." The two men shook hands and stood there grinning at each other.

"Thanks, I'd appreciate a ride…no, the folks won't know until they see me. I didn't even know myself until day before yesterday….that's the army for you…wait until you're bored out of your mind, then the shit hits the fan and you don't even have time to make a phone call."

Laird threw his duffel bag into the back seat thinking what a pleasant surprise it was to have Oscar be the first person to welcome him home. Oscar had been the town cop since before Laird was born. He was fearless and he was fair; every kid in town looked up to him. Oscar made sure to give every boy a tour of the town jail at least once. No lectures, no speeches, just a non-committal tour that included unlocking the two barred jail doors with a huge key and then closing them with a loud clang.

"So," Oscar shifted the gears as they started down Main Street, "what do you think of the old town so far? Has it changed much?"

"Well, so far things look pretty much the same." Laird hesitated and looked out the window at the familiar buildings on Main Street. "That's not quite true. Things look strange, different somehow. It's so… untouched. I'm not used to places that haven't been bombed out, I guess."

Oscar nodded slowly, eyes straight ahead. He turned left down the tree-lined residential street where Laird's folks lived, and as they drove past the Anderson place, Laird saw the gold star hanging in the living room window. He stared hard at the gold star. Last year Mother had sent him the newspaper clipping about Carl, another childhood friend who would never be coming home.

Laird turned his head and, on the other side of the street, saw the familiar sight of Mr. Krestle and his old horse, Bess, plowing the side yard of the Canady house. "Looks like the Canady's are putting in a big garden this year."

"Yah, they're big for gardening, that family."

Oscar glanced over and looked at the campaign ribbons on Laird's chest. A few months ago the town newspaper had run an article about Laird's two Purple Hearts and his Bronze Star. Oscar noticed Laird wasn't wearing them, just a few campaign ribbons. "In case I don't get a chance to tell you later, Laird, I want to say thank you for what you've done these past three years."

Laird was quiet before he said, "I was just a little part of it, a tiny cog in a big machine."

"Maybe so, but you were a damned fine cog and we're all proud of you."

"Thanks, Oscar, but you went through pretty much the same thing in World War I, didn't you? Don't you still have pieces of shrapnel working their way out through your skin?"

"Not so often as when I was younger. I had one come out of my left thigh a couple of months ago. I used to go to the Doc to have him cut them out when they got close enough to the surface, but, now, I just sterilize my old pocket knife and do it myself. They're just slivers, but sometimes I feel like a walking junkyard." Oscar fumbled in his shirt pocket for a cigarette, "Care for a smoke, Laird?"

"No, thanks, the Red Cross and the Army kept giving me free cigarettes but I never smoked them. I used them for barter instead."

"The hell you did!"

"Yup, I exchanged them for stuff like cheese, dry socks, whiskey, even this watch, mostly just stuff I happened to need at the time, whatever somebody else wanted to trade for." He held up his wrist to show Oscar his watch. "I got this and another one for my mother, too."

Oscar pulled over to the curb outside a neat, two-story white house that sat well back from the street. The well-tended garden and fruit trees at the rear of the house were mostly hidden from the street view.

"Here you are, kid."

Laird got out and lifted his duffel bag from the back seat, hoisted it in onto his shoulder and slammed the car door shut. He bent down, looked through the car window at Oscar, gave him a quick smile and a vague salute. Oscar tipped his cap in return and drove away slowly, still watching Laird through the rear view mirror, "Thank God," he said aloud, "Another one home safe."

Laird's three kid brothers were playing fort in the tree their dad had planted for shade twenty years ago. Aged eleven, twelve and fourteen, they came hurtling out of the tree like three big squirrels.

"Laird…" They all shouted at once, "You're home…you're home…you're home!" David and Johnny ran across the yard, throwing their arms around him so quickly he barely had time to brace himself against the onslaught. Duane brought up the rear, showing more restraint as befitted the oldest of the trio, but his face was alight and his grin as big as those of his brothers.

"Why didn't you call?'

"We didn't know when you were coming…"

"Mama's been baking pies and cookies steady but she won't let us eat the fresh stuff."

"She says we have to wait until you got home!"

"We don't mind, the day-old stuff is good, too," Duane laughed as he stuck out his hand to shake Laird's.

Johnny watched Laird's face anxiously and hung onto his arm. "Can we see where you got shot? You look okay."

"You look okay…"

"Are you okay?"

Laird blinked to clear away the moisture forming in his eyes and gave Johnny, who couldn't seem to let go of him, another squeeze, "Yes, you can see I'm okay. I'm okay, guys…I'm okay."

"Tell us about your decorations, Laird." Johnny reached up and touched the rows of campaign ribbons arranged on Laird's wool khaki dress jacket. "Which ones are for getting wounded? What's this one for?" he asked as he pointed to a small circle with a flying eagle in the center.

"That one's called a 'Ruptured Duck' and it means I'm officially no longer in the army."

"What a funny name." Duane grinned, "Who thought that one up?"

"I haven't got a clue, probably some GI," Laird smiled. "But that and the Victory Ribbon are my favorites." He put his finger on a bright red, white and blue ribbon, "This one means the war is over."

David frowned, "But where are your medals? Where's your Purple Hearts?"

"And where's your Bronze Star?"

"They're in my bag…I can show them to you later."

"I'll carry your duffel bag." Duane bent over to hoist it up. "Wow! It's heavy. It can't all be medals…what do you have in here, bricks?"

"Well, I did bring you home a few gifts, but three Swiss army knives don't weigh that much." Laird put an arm around each of his younger brothers as he followed Duane up the walkway.

His mother, Ellen, was in the kitchen, kneading a fresh batch of bread. She wore a freshly-ironed apron over a cotton housedress, and her hair was pulled back in a sedate bun that accentuated her fine-boned face with its calm eyes. The minute she heard the door open with its accompanying commotion, Ellen guessed that her eldest son was home. Not stopping to scrub the flour from her hands, she ran through the house, threw herself into Laird's outstretched arms and began to sob. No one spoke or moved. Every one of her sons was startled to see their reserved mother in tears. Finally, Ellen took in a long, shaky breath and whispered, "Could one of you boys find me a Kleenex or a hanky?"

"Here, Mother," Laird pulled a khaki handkerchief from his back pocket and tried to smile, "I guess the army knew what it was doing when they told me I should carry one of these at all times."

"Thank you, Laird," Ellen wiped her eyes and blew her nose, taking in small, staccato involuntary breaths. She looked up at Laird but couldn't see his face clearly. "I'm sorry to be such a cry-baby." The tears continued to flood silently down her cheeks and she hid her face against Laird's chest, both of her hands pressing the handkerchief against her mouth. Laird tightened his arms around her and closed his eyes. He rested his chin on the top of her head, and noticed she was smaller than he remembered.

"Go ahead and cry, Mother. It's okay, go ahead and cry." He was very near to it himself.

Ellen drew back, reached out to her youngest sons and ruffled the dark hair on each of their heads before drawing herself up straight and saying, in a determined voice, "Well, enough of that…I'll go call your dad and tell him to come home right away. You boys take Laird up to his room and I'll go put the coffee on."

Galvanized into action again, the boys rushed up the stairs ahead of Laird, Duane going a little slower, bumping the duffel bag along behind him. Laird's face broke into a grin, remembering the many times he'd heard his mother complain to Dad, "Can't you do something about these boys? They run around here like a herd of elephants!" And Dad slowly shaking his head back and forth saying, "I think we'll just have to wait until they grow out of it."

Laird's old room was smaller than he remembered, maybe because now there were three excited boys milling around him. Duane swung the duffel bag up on the bed, pointed to the wall above the bed and said, "Look, Laird. Look at our map."

"Yah, look Laird. We kept track of wherever you were. We listened to the news…"

"…And the radio…"

"…And we read the newspapers every day so we could follow you around."

"…To see where the Fifth Army was. We knew you had to be there somewhere."

"…And see those two little flags?"

"Those are for where you were wounded."

Laird stopped and looked. He knew they'd been following the Fifth Army on a map but he hadn't realized the map was hanging in his own bedroom. He'd envisioned it hanging in their room or in the back hallway somewhere. As his eyes focused on the flags in Salerno and northern Italy, all the old memories came flooding back, the insanity of the brutal slog up the boot of Italy into Rome and on up to the Brenner Pass…

Duane's eyes were on Laird's face. "Oh," he said and stopped talking. "Mama said maybe we should ask you if you want to keep this in your room…but we liked to be in here…"

David suddenly noticed Laird's smile had vanished. "We felt kind of like you were here when we were in your room," he explained.

Johnny, unaware there was a problem, turned and asked with a bright smile, "Do you like it? Dad says we've learned a lot about history and geography."

Laird was staring at the map. "It just brings back some bad memories."

All three boys stood stock still, their now serious eyes displaying differing degrees of comprehension.

"We'll move it right away," Duane said. "Is it okay if we put it in our room?"

"Oh, sure…sure, whatever you want. I'll see you guys downstairs." Laird turned suddenly and walked quickly back down the stairs.

The two older boys looked at each other with dawning understanding. Only Johnny was puzzled, "What's the matter? Doesn't he like it?" His older brothers didn't answer, but stood looking with new insight at the map of which they were so proud with its careful record of the Fifth Army's movement through Europe.

"We take it down…now," Duane said, and David nodded his agreement.

Johnny protested, "But why doesn't he like it?"

Duane bit his lower lip and paused long enough to look sternly at Johnny, "Because it makes him remember all the pain and killing during the war. He wants to forget it and we've got to help him."

David nodded, "Maybe we shouldn't put it up in our room either. We could roll it up and keep it under my bed."

Duane solemnly agreed, "Good idea."

No one said anything as they took the map off the wall, rolled it up and carried it off to stow under David's bed. Their trip downstairs was much slower and quieter than coming up. They found Laird sitting at the kitchen table waiting for the coffee to finish perking, and watching his mother fixing something for him to eat.

"He hasn't had a decent thing to eat yet today," Ellen told her three youngest sons as they hesitantly came into the kitchen and stood silently looking at Laird. They watched as their mother cut two slices from a loaf of her homemade whole wheat bread, generously spread on the egg salad mixture, cut the sandwich in half, put it on a plate and set it down with a small flourish in front of Laird.

"There you are." Ellen looked at her oldest son with satisfaction, "I've been worried you'd come home thin as a stick, but I have to say you're looking more filled out than when you left. I guess the army at least fed you." She raised her eyebrows slightly, wiping her hands on her clean and pressed apron.

"Believe me, army food was never half as good as your cooking, Mother, and that's the God's honest truth." He took his first bite of home-cooked food, chewed slowly, and gave a little sigh for his mother's benefit. "Just as good as I remember," he pronounced to a beaming Ellen.

"The coffee will be done in a minute, and your dad should be here soon. He had a customer with him but he said he'd get here just as quick as he can."

Laird waved his brothers over to the kitchen table, "Come on and sit down you guys." He smiled affectionately at them. "Thank you for following me on your map. It always made me feel good to read your letters and know you were here at home, figuring out where I was."

The boys' faces began to relax and Duane said tentatively, "I always wondered what the censors blacked out of your letters."

"We knew which division you were in so eventually we could figure things out from reading the newspaper articles and listening to the radio," added David.

"You did a good job, guys."

"I guess we should forget about it now, though, right Laird?" Duane was watching him intently.

Laird reached out and ruffled Johnny's hair, "Yup, that's what I'd like to do."

"Well, of course," Ellen said, "that's exactly what we'll do. It's time to forget about the war and praise the Lord it's over. Here's your coffee, Laird. Do you still like cream and sugar?"

"No. Thanks, Mother, I've learned to take it straight."

They heard the back hall door open and close and turned to see Emil Nordstrom standing in the kitchen doorway.

"Laird," he said. The two met midway, two pairs of hazel eyes locked together, right hands gripped in a tight handshake, their other hand firmly pressing the other's shoulder.

"Dad…"

Emil's eyes were lit from deep within, "You're home, son…at last, you're home."

At age fifty-six, Emil had a full head of dark hair, and, like his son, not one ounce of unnecessary flesh on his bones. Thirty years of working the forge and hammering metal in his blacksmith shop had kept him lean and tough. He took a handkerchief out of his back pocket and blew his nose, then let out a sigh he'd been holding in for three long years. As he pulled out a chair and sat down at the table, he said again, "You're home."

Laird took a deep breath and felt his body begin to relax. He studied his father's face, and found those familiar, thoughtful eyes looking gravely back at him. "It's so good to see you, Dad."

"And you, too, Laird…I think maybe you've grown up some."

As far back as Laird could remember, Emil had never said, "I love you," to any of his sons, and for that matter, neither had Ellen. They were both old country Swedes who believed it wasn't good parenting to give verbal praise to their children, although one time when Laird was in the fourth grade and brought home a report card with straight A's, Ellen had smiled proudly and said, "Pretty good for a blacksmith's son."

It was a Swedish axiom that, if you praised your children, they would grow up proud and self-indulgent, which was the worst thing that could happen to a child. Swedish children instead learned to interpret non-verbal body language…a slight smile of approval, a lift of the chin, a parent's proud posture when they introduced you to a stranger, an extra cookie or sugar lump, a ruffling of the hair on your head, a warm glance, a worried bustling about in winter time, making sure you were warm and dry after you came in from outside with wet gloves and near-frozen fingers. You knew you were loved when your father arose early on freezing Dakota winter mornings as you lay in a warm bed listening to the clanking of the furnace door as he took out the clay clinkers to stir up a new coal fire before the rest of the family got out of bed. Even though Emil always banked the fire so it wouldn't go out during the night, the house was so cold by morning you could see your breath in the air when you woke up, and on Tuesday mornings, after Mother's regular Monday morning wash-day had filled the house with moisture, a thin sheen of ice sometimes formed on the bedroom walls.

Swedish parents showed their love by doing, not saying. The summer before Laird started his senior year, he'd hired out to work on Hilder's farm for the threshing season. The night before he'd left for the farm, Emil gave him a pair of good leather work gloves, "Here, son. You'll need these. Those cloth gloves aren't worth a damn when you're working in the fields. Cloth wears out in a week."

There was also a down side to this mostly non-verbal communication: the arched disapproving eyebrow, the cool stare, the turning away, the tight lips. Taken together it was a form of child discipline choreographed from birth, and all Swedish kids and parents knew the dance.

Ellen poured coffee for Emil and herself, along with glasses of milk for the boys before she sat down, put her hands in her lap, and said, "Well." She gave a deep sigh of contentment, looked around the table at her happy men and said, "I'd like it if you said grace, Emil."

Neither Emil nor Ellen were especially religious. Ellen had sent her sons to catechism classes to be confirmed, as she had been, in the Lutheran Church, but she never attended church herself. All Laird could remember from his confirmation experience was a new suit of clothes, plus stern advice from Pastor Manley that dancing was a vertical position for a horizontal desire. At thirteen, Laird hadn't quite known what to make of that remark except it always made him feel slightly uncomfortable at school dances.

Laird repressed a smile, remembering the time he and Emil had come into the living room to find a hellfire and brimstone preacher on the radio shouting, "Repent! Repent! Every sinner who refuses to take the blessed Lord Jesus as his Savior is going straight to hell and an eternity of suffering!" Emil had calmly walked over to the radio to turn it off and quietly said, "Horseshit!"

Emil looked around the table at his four healthy sons, and his beloved Ellen of the strong, beautiful face, then bowed his head to recite the familiar Swedish table grace,

"Some have meat, but cannot eat, some would eat but want it, but we have meat, and we can eat, and so the Lord be thank't."

"Well," said Ellen, and passed the plate of cookies.

Chapter Two

Janice Swanson stepped through the front door of St. Mary's Hospital into the early morning. It had rained during the night, leaving the grass and bushes bending under the weight of suspended drops of water. She closed her eyes and stopped to breathe in the odor of wet soil and the scent of lilacs drifting in from the hedge lining the south border of the hospital grounds. There was no breeze yet to stir the leaves on the box elder trees, but the birds were in full chorus, busily gathering nesting materials. She could hear robins, and a thrush, even a meadowlark; it was unusual to hear a meadowlark so close in to the city. She suddenly wanted to be home, out scouting the ponds and fields around Breton, hunting up birds to identify.

"Morning, Janice," said Dr. Lawrence Blakesly. "You look like you're asleep on your feet. Tough night?"

At the sound of his voice, Janice's eyes flew open, and she was aware of a burst of energy. Lawrence looked intently at her through his thick glasses and smiled.

"Hi, Dr. Blakesly, I didn't hear you coming…you're right, I am tired. We were really busy all night, but the Baker boy is doing better this morning, so it was worth it."

Lawrence cocked his left eyebrow and gave her a sympathetic look. He knew only too well how tiring working night-shifts could be. He was still weary from that god-awful emergency surgery yesterday, and now he was headed for another twelve hours on duty. "Go home and get some sleep, and will you please stop calling me Dr. Blakesly when we're off duty? Since I haven't signed in yet, and you just signed out, I think at least for a few minutes we can use first names, no matter what they taught you in nurses' training."

She gave him a smile before she turned to go. "That's just where I'm headed, home for a long sleep…you have a good day."

"Thanks, I'll do my best," he said. Lawrence hesitated for a moment and looked down at her with a serious expression on his face; Janice wondered if he was going to say something more, but he turned away and walked quickly into the hospital.

She had looked so beautiful standing there, head lifted, eyes closed, upturned face in the morning glow, those wonderful lips slightly parted, her thick auburn hair half hidden under the proper nurse's cap. He'd wanted to freeze the moment in time. Oh, God, he wanted her. In spite of the fact he knew she was off limits, he wanted her, permanently, as in a lifetime.

During his first year as an intern at St. Mary's Hospital, Lawrence had been in the middle of early morning rounds with the demanding Dr. Crawley when he'd seen Janice standing at the nurse's station earnestly listening to instructions from the head nurse. Even under the critical eyes of Dr. Crawley he'd stopped to stare, and, after a couple of weeks, Lawrence was in love.

It wasn't only her physical beauty that attracted him. Hidden under that graceful exterior there was a core of solid rock. In an emergency she was unflappable, and those wide compassionate eyes were a godsend whenever someone needed cheering up. Even the arrogant Dr. Crawley, who was well known for snarling at nurses and interns right and left, had never once barked at Janice.

St. Mary's wasn't a big hospital. Everyone knew everyone else's business, and the entire staff knew Janice was spoken for. Lawrence had tried to resign himself to the unpleasant fact that she was waiting for some war hero named Laird to come home again. He sighed as he hung up his jacket, put on the white coat and hung the stethoscope around his neck.

Lawrence was the right age to be serving in the military, but because of his eyes he'd been given a deferment from the draft. In spite of the fact he'd worn thick glasses ever since the second grade, when his parents finally figured out why their smart little boy could read all the Burma Shave signs along the highway but couldn't read the books in his lap, Lawrence knew he'd never forgive himself if he didn't at least try to enlist for the war effort. But after flunking the eye test, he realized that trying to join up was a bad idea because now he had to go through life stamped with the 4-F label. For many months after his rejection he'd felt like a cut of Grade "C" beef, barely good enough for dog food. But since becoming a doctor, he'd seen so much pain and sickness that the 4-F label didn't bother him anymore. Farsightedness was a very small blip on the wide radar screen of the world's hurts.

❋ ❋ ❋

As usual, Janice's landlady was waiting for her with a pan of steaming hot oatmeal and raisins. "You've got to have a good breakfast, dear. Even if you're going right to bed, you need a good breakfast."

Mrs. Johnson took good care of her three roomers, all nursing students at nearby St. Mary's. She called them her girls and didn't think of them as roomers, although she was grateful for the rent money that kept her financially afloat. She once confided to Janice that she praised the Lord her husband had left her this big house, all paid for, when he'd passed away nine years ago.

Janice wanted to go straight upstairs and fall into bed, but she was too tired to protest. She obediently sat down at the kitchen table and watched Mrs. Johnson spoon oatmeal into a blue crockery bowl. Mrs. Johnson had been up for hours and was fully dressed, her apron newly starched and ironed, her long braided, graying hair carefully wound and pinned in a thick wreath around her head. She had a sturdy body that looked almost tubular, probably because of the corset Janice suspected she wore. It was the same with both of Janice's grandmothers: even in hot weather it was obvious they wore those confining corsets. Janice often wondered how the corset manufacturers had convinced women of her grandmothers' generation to wear armored underwear.

Mrs. Johnson beamed when Janice said, "You're awfully good to me, Mrs. Johnson."

"It's nothing, dear. It's been such a pleasure to have you here these past few years, I'll miss you when you go and get married to that boyfriend of yours. I hope he appreciates you. You just send him to me if he doesn't treat you right! I'll straighten him out! "

"Thank you, but don't worry, Mrs. Johnson. Laird always treats me right. I've known him since we were kids."

The oatmeal was thick and steamy, with brown sugar and real cream fresh from the farm. Janice ate it quickly and asked, "If Laird calls, or if anyone calls with news about him, will you come wake me up?"

Mrs. Johnson smiled, patted Janice on the shoulder and said, "Don't you worry, dear. You just go get some sleep."

❋ ❋ ❋

Janice's bedroom was one of three that opened off the second floor landing. The two other bedrooms had been recently rented by a couple of first-year nursing students from Aberdeen who spent a lot of time studying and giggling together far into the night. Janice was grateful that whenever she worked night-shift duty and needed to sleep during the day, the girls were out of the house taking classes at the college or the hospital.

When she heard them stirring around in their room getting ready to go down for breakfast, she quickly stepped into her own room and closed the door; she didn't feel like talking to anyone right now. On her way to the closet to hang up her cap and uniform, she reached out and pulled down the room-darkening window shade. Once her uniform was neatly hung in the closet, she tossed her underwear on the floor, put on a lightweight nightgown and climbed into bed.

She sighed gratefully and pulled the sheet up under her chin. Maybe she could get some sleep before the room got hot. It was already a bit humid but not too bad, maybe it would turn out to be a fairly good day for sleeping. She closed her eyes, turned onto her side, and started to think. That was the problem with closing your eyes, you started thinking about things you didn't want to think about.

Laird would surely come home soon, maybe even today. He'd called last week from New York when the troop ship had docked, but there was so much static on the line, she didn't know much more about his schedule than before, although she did understand him to say that he wasn't certain how many more days or weeks it would take for the bureaucracy to officially make him an ordinary citizen again. Janice could see his face in her memory, as it had looked the last time she saw him almost three years ago. She loved that slow, hesitant smile of his, how it lifted up one corner of his mouth a little higher than the other, and she loved those dark eyes in his strong face. Laird couldn't have changed that much, could he? She knew in her heart that three years and a war must have changed him. His letters didn't give much of a clue. They were always short, and mostly lighthearted; they were *don't worry, everything is all right* kind of letters. Laird had never talked about, or written to complain about, anything that bothered him, but his face had never been able to hide a thing. Whenever he was upset, that stubborn jaw of his would set and his eyes would turn flinty. She'd just have to wait until they were face-to-face and she could look into his eyes before she would be able to judge whether he had changed or not.

Dr. Blakesly came drifting across her mind, unpretentious Dr. Lawrence Blakesly: tall, gangly, smart, hard-working, and humorous, with mysterious grey eyes half-hidden behind amazingly thick glasses. No, she wouldn't think about him. Janice turned over and curled up in a fetal position, set her mouth in a straight line and thought again, "No!" If Laird had been home these past few years, she wouldn't be giving Lawrence Blakesly a second thought.

What if Laird had been the one killed instead of Conrad? She would be in Diane's shoes now, struggling with the pain of his death. Everyone could see the change in Diane after she'd gotten the telegram about Conrad. Her cheery, mischievous demeanor had totally changed, like a perky balloon suddenly collapsed. Now she was a widow after only two months of marriage spent together stealing precious hours in a boarding house near the army base.

Of course, Janice and Laird hadn't married before Laird left, but wasn't the commitment almost the same? Janice raised up on one elbow, punched her pillow into shape, and reminded herself she'd made a promise to Laird, a promise she intended to keep. Daddy was always quoting Robert Service, "A promise made is a debt unpaid." She'd grown up with that philosophy, and she believed in it.

She lay down again and turned over, tugging at the sheet, trying to keep it from twisting around her. She remembered how indignant she'd been when the news spread through the hospital that Rick Bailey's girlfriend had written him a *Dear John* letter when Rick was fighting in the Philippine Islands. His girlfriend told him she was so sorry but she was getting married to a guy who worked for the railroad in Minneapolis, and she hoped Rick would understand. Janice heard that Rick had written home to his mother saying that he knew it wasn't anything personal. "He was there and I wasn't," was all Rick would say about it.

"Oh, my God," she thought, and turned over again. There had been all those times when she'd look over and catch Dr. Blakesly watching her; it was hard to decipher his expression. Sometimes his eyes crinkled up in a kind of smile, but more often his eyes were serious, almost sad. He wasn't looking through her, or even at her. It felt like he was trying to look into her. Every time she looked up and met his eyes, something like a little electric spark would jump across, and they would both look away. Janice was careful never to be alone with him. Whenever some of the staff were in the coffee room with him, she would stay, too, but if it was just the two of them, she quickly found a reason to leave; there was always a patient to check on, or a report to finish.

Janice flung off the sheet, sat up and leaned over to reach under the bed for the most recent box of Laird's letters. His last one was an ordinary airmail letter like so many of the others, written on lightweight, tissue-like paper. She had three years of his letters. She'd never thought to count, but there must be hundreds of them. Some of the letters written during the second and third year were in the new Victory-letter format, photocopied onto small pieces of photo paper, with the words shrunken so small you could hardly read them. A person couldn't say much on such a small piece of paper, but that suited Laird's style. The letters fit neatly into three shoeboxes, one box for each year. The censors had been letting the more recent ones go by without a single black mark. Janice hoped it was because the censors were out of jobs now that the war was over.

Dear Jan,

Hurray! I'm coming home!! This might be the last letter I'll write before I see you again. We're supposed to ship out from Bremerhaven, dock in New York, then go to Chicago for my discharge papers, then it's home again. I kiss your picture every night and wonder about us. I need to tell you I'm not the same person you kissed goodbye. I imagine you've grown up, too. Maybe we'll need time to get reacquainted, so don't worry if you're thinking similar thoughts. I'll call, if I can, from Chicago.

I love you, my dearest friend. Laird

Janice carefully refolded the letter. Was he having doubts? Did he think she wouldn't want him because of his leg wound, that she wouldn't want him because he had a permanent limp? He'd been adamant before he left that they were too young to marry, and said he'd never risk her being married to a man with his legs shot off. She shook her head slowly. No, surely Laird knew she wasn't that shallow, but it bothered her that he'd called her "dearest friend," not "dearest love," in this last letter. She smiled and remembered an exchange of letters they'd had early in the war, when he was somewhere in southern Italy. She'd told him how much she missed him and signed her name, "Your lover, Jan." His answer was one of the first letters in shoebox number two.

Dear Jan,

I miss you, too, sweetheart, and I wish we could say we're lovers, but we're not. We love each other but we'll only be lovers when we actually make love. I'm thinking now it was probably stupid not to have made love before I left. The only good thing about it is that at least I didn't get you pregnant. I thought I'd mention this because most people, if you tell them we are lovers, will think we've been making love and that would upset your family. Don't lay awake worrying about me. The fighting isn't a constant thing, it comes and it goes, kind of like the weather.

I love you. Laird

Janice had written Laird back with the argument that the dictionary defined the word lover as "one who loves," so, therefore, they were lovers and Laird was wrong. She'd hated knowing the censors were reading their letters; she hated the war and the constant fear Laird might never make it back. Janice turned over, pulled the sheet up as far as her waist and looked up at the ceiling. The war was over now, Laird had his 85 discharge points, and he would soon be home. She closed her eyes and told herself determinedly, "I've got to go to sleep."

* * *

Two hours later, the phone rang in Mrs. Johnson's dining room. She'd just finished baking some oatmeal cookies and was putting on her old shoes and garden gloves, getting ready to go outside to plant spring lettuce.

A young man's voice said, "Hello. You must be Mrs. Johnson. This is Laird, Janice's friend. I called the hospital first but they said she'd already gone home."

"Oh, my goodness, she wanted me to wake her up if you should call. Do you think I should? She's only been sleeping a few hours."

"No, no. Don't wake her, but will you ask her to call me at my folks' house as soon as she gets up? She can call collect."

"Of course I will..." Mrs. Johnson hesitated. "I don't know you, Laird, but if Janice loves you, you must be a wonderful young man. You be sure to take good care of her now."

"I promise." There was silence on the line.

"All right, then," Mrs. Johnson said. She hung up the phone and hummed to herself as she pulled on her gardening gloves, envisioning the look on Janice's face when she told her the good news.

* * *

Janice opened her eyes and watched the drawn shade and the white lace curtains sway gently against the window pane. She was glad she'd left the window slightly open when she went to bed; it hadn't turned out to be such a hot day after all. She closed her eyes and stretched out her legs and arms. She heard a robin chirping on the lawn, no doubt happy the worms were easy to catch after last night's rain. When she looked over at the alarm clock by the side of her bed, she threw off the sheet and sat up. This might be the day he came home. At this very moment, Laird might be over at his folks' house asleep on their living room sofa. That was how Virgil Nelson's family had discovered he was home: his mother had come downstairs one morning and there he was, sound asleep, his long legs hanging over the end of the sofa.

Maybe that's why Janice hadn't heard from Laird since that one phone call from New York; maybe he'd just decided to surprise everybody and head straight home as soon as he got his discharge papers in Chicago. Virgil had complained about the long lines of guys waiting to use the pay phones at every stop when he was on his way home. Janice swung her legs to the floor and ran her hand through her hair. If Laird came home this week it would be just a few days shy of three years since she'd seen him; only a week after he'd graduated from high school, he'd reported for duty. Laird said he didn't begrudge being drafted by "his friends and neighbors" as the draft letter had put it, but he didn't especially want to join the Army. He'd been hoping for the Air Force, or the Navy, but, unfortunately, the Army wanted him. When you're drafted, you take what they give you, and he got the infantry.

In basic training in Texas at Fort Hood, Laird wrote that there were 90,000 guys playing with guns and trying not to shoot each other. He said it was kind of like Boy Scout camp with grenades. But don't worry, he said, he'd been hunting rats with his twenty-two rifle at the city dump since he was twelve, and the M-1 rifle wasn't that much different, although it was a lot heavier and had a bigger kick. Less than a year later he'd written he was recovered "good as new" from the shrapnel he got near Salerno, and nearly two years later he assured her that the wound he got in northern Italy had left him with only a limp. It wasn't too bad, he'd said. He was lucky, and she shouldn't worry about it.

She wondered if he'd ever realized she worried about him so much she sometimes felt physically ill. She'd worried about the war, about Laird, and every one of the nineteen boys and two girls who were in the service from their small town of Breton, South Dakota. One by one, at a much slower pace than anyone expected, most of them were coming home. Wouldn't you think that once the war was over they'd put them on a ship and send them right back? But no, they needed them for the occupation or for watching the Russians or some such thing, and they couldn't come home until they had 85 points totaled up. Everyone she knew agreed with her that being wounded twice, as Laird had been, with two Purple Hearts plus a Bronze Star for bravery, should qualify any soldier to return home immediately.

Janice put on her green bathrobe, opened the bedroom door and called down the stairs, "Is the bathroom free so I can take a bath?"

Mrs. Johnson came to the bottom of the stairs. "The bathroom's all yours, dear. The other girls have left for school, and I have happy news for you. Laird called, he's at his folks' house and he wants you to call him."

※ ※ ※

An hour later, when Janice called her mother, her voice was almost a whisper over the line, "Laird's home, Mother. I just talked to him." Janice cleared her throat and in a firmer voice said, "He's at his folks' house. He says he's in great shape for the shape he's in."

Dora laughed, "That sounds like Laird all right."

"I know." Janice smiled. "It made me happy to know he's still got his sense of humor."

"When will you be able to come home to see him?"

"I can come tomorrow. I have to work the night shift tonight but then I can take a week off. Laird said he'll drive his dad's car to the Cities to pick me up early tomorrow afternoon. I think we can get home in time for supper. Do you think you could have his family over for supper tomorrow? Is that too short notice for you?"

"I'd love to have the Nordstroms over. It'll be like a holiday… it is a holiday! I'll call them as soon as we hang up."

"And, Mother, be sure to tell Carla and Martha not to bother Laird this afternoon. I know those two girls are probably crazy to see Laird again, but he said he's planning to get some shut-eye right now. He said he'd go over and see you after supper tonight." Janice's voice was suddenly small and tentative, "Mother… It's crazy, I know, but I feel really nervous. Of course I'm happy, but I'm kind of scared, too…"

"Oh, don't worry, honey." Jan could hear the concern in her mother's voice. "I'm sure it's very natural after so many years apart to wonder if the other person has changed. But you and Laird have known each other forever. I'm sure you'll soon be reacquainted and everything will be fine."

"Of course. I know it will." There was silence on the line and then, brightly, Janice said, "I'll see you tomorrow, Mother. Bye."

Chapter Three

Carla ran for the closet to put on her blue cotton bathrobe. Maybe today, she hummed to herself, maybe this would be the day Laird comes home. She wondered how Jan was feeling. If she felt this happy, her sister's feet must be barely touching the ground. Carla put the bathrobe on, and made a quick stop in the bathroom to check out her hair in the mirror.

As usual, her hair was a mass of curls. It seemed to Carla that her hair looked the same morning, noon and night. She tried to comb it into submission, but it always stubbornly bounced back. She regarded herself in the mirror and sighed, thinking it was too bad that curls went out of style when Shirley Temple grew up. The new fashion standard was hair done up in a pageboy style, like Veronica Lake, but a person needed soft waves like Jan's or straight hair to wear a pageboy. A pageboy was impossible with this stubborn bunch of curls; no movie star would even consider being filmed with a head of hair like Carla's. It was true Betty Grable had curls, but Betty Grable's curls were organized. Still, Carla had to admit that her curly, thick, chestnut hair and vivid blue eyes were her best features. Big Grandma once told her she was lucky to have Sister Edla's eyes. Everyone in the family knew that Big Grandma had always envied her sister Edla's eyes, reportedly a deep blue-violet color with a dark ring around the iris, set in a frame of thick lashes.

Carla gave herself one last, matter-of-fact glance in the mirror and hurried down the back stairs to the kitchen where her mother stood by the stove, pancake turner in hand, waiting for the bubbling pancakes to turn brown enough to flip. Dora Swanson was a handsome woman, with thick, black hair that curled even tighter than Carla's when the humidity rose. Strangers often took her for a much younger person until they got to know her better and saw the quiet resignation half-hidden behind her hazel eyes. Dora turned and smiled as her daughter burst into the room.

Dora's mother, Jeanette, whom her grand-daughters fondly called, "Little Grandma," sat at the kitchen table with her son-in-law, Verle, drinking a second cup of coffee. The plates in front of them showed faint traces of fried eggs and syrup.

Verle gave his daughter a cheerful smile. "Morning, Carla. You're up late! Not even dressed yet? Now that you've graduated high school, are you going to turn into one of those ladies of leisure who go around in their housecoats all day long?"

Little Grandma's brows creased into a frown. "You leave her alone, Verle. Don't fuss at her. Let her have some fun this summer; the Lord knows life has been tough enough for Carla so far..." She stopped, looked down, and pretended to take a sip from her empty coffee cup to give herself time to decide how to change the subject. How many times had Dora asked her not to mention Carla's handicap, and now she had gone and done it again.

"My life's not as tough as it is for lots of people," Carla said, flashing a sympathetic smile at her grandmother's predicament. Carla knew her family tried never to mention her withered arm and crooked back, but Little Grandma often betrayed her feelings at unexpected times by saying rather loudly to anyone in the immediate vicinity that the Lord was not to be totally trusted if he had allowed a three-old girl to suffer so. Little Grandma could never forget the dark days when Dora had worked herself to the bone, nursing Carla through the ruptured appendix and the subsequent polio. Penicillin hadn't yet been discovered, and there was the constant worry of the terrible infection and fevers. Even though Verle and Little Grandma had tried to help, Dora never got enough sleep. She was constantly having to exercise Carla's legs and arms and change her cold packs, plus coping with the emotional stress of having to refuse Carla's pleas for warm packs instead of cold compresses. Years later, thanks to Sister Kenny, the medical profession decided that cold packs didn't do any good at all for polio patients, and maybe did some harm, reason enough for Dora to caution Janice to be a bit skeptical of what she learned in nurse's training; it was often better to rely on what the patient wanted instead of unproven theories.

Little Grandma told anyone who would listen it was amazing Carla had lived through it all, and that God must have special plans for her. Dora and Verle replied that if God cared a fig about Carla, she wouldn't have had a ruptured appendix and polio in the first place.

Carla herself had decided that in spite of the crippling effects of the polio, she could at least try to look and act like everybody else. She clearly remembered the moment she'd made that decision at the beginning of her sixth grade year. She'd gone shopping for school clothes with Mother and Janice and was wearing her favorite dress, the one with little white polka dots and a white collar trimmed with lace. It was also sleeveless, which enabled the JCPenney sales clerk to see Carla's right arm hanging useless at her side.

"Oh, my poor child," the woman had said sympathetically, her eyes lingering on Carla's paralyzed arm. "But, never mind about your arm, you have beautiful hair. Does your mother have to brush it for you every morning?"

Carla had tightened her lips, narrowed her eyes and swallowed hard, reminding herself she was supposed to be polite to adults, even terrible adults like this one. "I brush my own hair!" was finally all she could manage to choke out in an indignant voice. Her mother tried to support her by saying, "Oh, Carla does everything for herself, she even ties her own shoes!"

Later, that night, lying in bed, Carla had complained bitterly to Janice, "How could that lady be so rude? How could she think I can't even brush my own hair for heaven's sake? Does she need two hands to hold the brush while she combs her hair? Is she stupid? Or just mean?"

Janice had tried to comfort her. "I don't think she intended to be mean, maybe she's just stupid. If she's stupid, there's nothing to be done about it. Try to forgive her and be glad you're not that dumb." Janice sighed, "Just forget about it and go to sleep, Carla. You know what Daddy always says, 'A hundred years from now you'll never know the difference.' With that comforting thought Janice rolled over on her side and was soon breathing quietly, leaving Carla staring grimly at the ceiling vowing never, never to let her arm hang out in plain sight again.

From then on, Carla had refused to wear anything outside the house that wasn't long-sleeved. At first Dora tried to talk her out of it, but finally she'd given in and helped Carla find long-sleeved clothes for school.

Finding long-sleeved winter clothes wasn't much of a problem, but it took more perseverance to find summer clothes that were both long-sleeved and lightweight enough to wear in the heat of a South Dakota summer.

Carla felt a familiar flush of love as she smiled down at Little Grandma. She loved her grandmother for many reasons, one of which was that Little Grandma was willing to scold even God in Carla's defense.

Carla sat down at the kitchen table across from her father. She loved her father but she was a bit wary of him. He was always teasing and she found it hard to separate his idea of teasing from downright lies, like the time he told her if you dug a deep enough hole, you'd end up in a country called China, filled with men who wore pigtails. She'd been only three years old so, of course, she'd believed him…it must have been just before she got the polio. She'd dug the hole deeper and deeper, and found nothing but dirt, and more dirt. Her father was working in the garden and came over occasionally to check on the hole. He kept on encouraging her, "Keep on digging. You'll get there."

Finally Mother had come outside and asked what she was doing, "I'm digging a hole to China. Daddy said I'd find lots of Chinamen with pigtails."

"Oh, Verle!" Dora looked over at her husband who carefully avoided her eyes and continued pruning the crab apple tree. Dora sighed. She'd endured Verle's idea of humor since the day she'd met him. "Carla, Daddy is just teasing you…you can't dig all the way to China, no one can dig that far."

"But he said I could."

"He's right that China is on the other side of the earth, but it's not true you can dig to China, it's too far. He's just teasing you. Don't pay any attention to your daddy when he teases."

Then there was the time when Carla was five and she'd wanted to know where babies came from. No one in the family seemed to be certain about where you could get a baby except to tell her she wasn't old enough yet and she'd have to wait. She had a rubber baby doll that wet its pants when you fed it water from a tiny baby bottle. She liked that baby a lot, but she wanted a real one. Finally, one day when they were alone, Verle had leaned down and confided, "People order babies from the Montgomery Ward catalog."

"Can I order a real baby?"

"Sure you can. You just have to save up enough money."

After much hunting through the Montgomery Ward catalog, Carla had found the pages that sold babies plus everything else you'd need for a baby, little knit hats and sweaters, bottles, sheets, blankets and diapers. Since she wasn't old enough to read all the words and interpret the prices yet, she went to her mother for advice on how much money she'd need to save up.

"Oh, my," her mother frowned. "Where on earth did you get the idea that people can buy babies?"

"Daddy told me."

"Oh, my," her mother said again, taking a deep breath and briefly closing her eyes. "He's teasing you again. It's true you can buy clothes for babies in the catalog, but nobody can buy a baby. Babies come from a mommy and a daddy, that's where babies come from. Don't you remember I told you that? First you have to grow up before you can be a mommy."

Carla had been so upset about this teasing episode, she'd avoided her father for days. Mother called it teasing but it seemed like lying to Carla. You weren't supposed to lie, ever. No one else in the family teased like that, why did Daddy? Once, when she was older, she asked her mother, "Why does Daddy do this? He's always teasing and telling jokes. Why can't he be serious sometimes?"

Mother had looked off in the distance, "I don't know, Carla. I think it's because he doesn't know how to talk to people any other way…maybe it's the only way he knows how to do. He doesn't really mean any harm, and he loves you. I hope you know that." Carla understood her father better now that she was eighteen years old, but she didn't trust him in the same way she trusted Little Grandma and Mother.

Carla looked across the table at her father and smiled, "Has anyone heard anything about Laird coming home? It's been a whole month since he got his 85 points. It shouldn't take that long to ship him home from Germany, should it?"

Verle winked at her, "Anybody would think you're the one he's going to marry."

Carla looked down as she tried to hide the surprising hurt created by her father's words. She knew, even if Daddy didn't, that no one would ever want to marry her... still, she couldn't help hoping that a person as special as Laird might one day come into her life...couldn't help hoping that maybe one day she would be as happy as Jan.

"Will you quit teasing her, Verle?" Little Grandma protested. "Of course she's excited about Laird coming home. Think how wonderful it was when my boy Kenny came back from the Pacific...well, he's not exactly home but at least he's back safe in San Diego with his little family, and I pray to God they will be coming back to Breton to live. Oh, my Lord, what if they decide to settle down in San Diego? I won't be able to bear it." Huge tears spilled down her cheeks as she pulled a well-used handkerchief out of her apron pocket and dabbed at her eyes. "I won't be able to see their little girl grow up," and she burst into sobs.

Dora was silent and rolled her eyes heavenward while Verle steadfastly looked into his coffee cup.

Carla reached over and touched her grandmother on the shoulder, "Now Grandma, be glad Uncle Kenny came back from the war alive and well, not even a wound."

"Oh, I know it, I'm just no damn good, always crying at the drop of a hat." Her tears suddenly dried up and she resolutely stuffed her wet hanky back into her apron pocket, stood up and started collecting dirty dishes from the table, "I'll just get busy and do the dishes."

"But Mother," Dora protested, "Carla and I haven't eaten yet. Just sit down, leave the dishes and visit with us. How can I relax when you're up clanking dishes around?"

"No, no. Just you never mind, Dora. Why shouldn't you relax? You've been working all morning, feeding Verle and all the rest of us, now it's my turn to do something useful." She took the metal dishpan out from under the sink, turned on the hot water tap full-bore, tossed in some Fels-Naptha soap flakes and watched with satisfaction as the suds foamed and the water thundered into the metal pan.

It was no use asking for peace and quiet so that Dora could relax over a final cup of coffee. Accepting that it was an old battle she could rarely win, Dora sighed as she put the eggs and pancakes on two plates, took them to the table, and sat down opposite her daughter. Dora closed her eyes, and sat quietly with her hands in her lap for a moment. Carla suppressed a smile; she knew her mother didn't care much for God, and if she was praying now, it was only for the patience to live peaceably with Little Grandma.

Verle got up to get himself another cup of coffee. "Did you hear about Virgil Nelson coming home the other day? It must have been quite a surprise to find him asleep in the living room when they got up in the morning."

"Good thing his folks never lock their doors or he'd been sleeping on the porch," Dora said.

"I remember you locked the door that time we went to Saskatchewan to see the cousins, Mother," Carla laughed, "and then you took the key and hung it in plain sight on a hook over the door."

"Well, someone might have needed to get in, and at least it kept the kids out."

"Anyway," Verle continued, "I was talking to Virgil's dad down at the gas station the other day. Evidently there were long lines of soldiers and sailors in San Diego waiting to make a phone call before they got on the train so Virgil said 'To heck with it!' and climbed aboard the first train headed for South Dakota."

"It's wonderful that anyone in uniform can travel for free, at least they don't have to stand in line for tickets," Little Grandma commented, her hands deep in sudsy water.

Verle laughed and said, "Virgil said every man not in uniform wanted to take him to the club car and buy him a drink, said the only problem with the train ride home was trying to stay sober. He got in about midnight and hitched a ride with Oscar. He didn't want to wake anybody up so he walked through the front door and stretched out on the davenport, said it was at least as comfortable as the ship's hammocks he was used to sleeping on."

"Maybe Laird did the same thing last night," Carla said.

"Maybe," Dora said, "but I think either Janice or Laird's mother would have called us by now if Laird had come home."

Verle took a last sip of his coffee and stood up. "Well, I better get down to the station and get to work. Gas rationing is due to end soon, thank God. I'd hate to have to deal with those government coupons for the rest of my life." His eyebrows lifted and lowered as he gave them his boyish smile and waved goodbye.

Dora watched her husband leave. He was such a handsome man, wiry and strong, but it was too bad he wasn't taller. Maybe if Verle had been taller he wouldn't be always trying to prove how tough he was, like the time he'd been laid up for weeks with back pain because of that fool stunt he'd pulled, showing everybody he could lift the front end of an old Model-T Ford off the ground.

"Bye, Daddy...."

"Bye, Verle...."

Dora took a bite of her egg and pancakes, picked up her coffee cup and thought about her husband. He was a great talker, but, to tell the truth, there were great talkers on her side of the family, too. She'd often thought it might be in her Welsh genes. But Verle talked more than any of them, and he came from a Swedish family. Verle's mother once said it was because Verle's ancestors came from Skane which was the southernmost part of Sweden. She said the farther south you went the more people talked until you got to Italy where they never stopped talking except to sleep.

The thought of Verle's mother caused Dora to sigh. Thank goodness she was staying with her sister out in Washington state this summer. Living full time with her own mother was hard enough without having to entertain Verle's mother whenever she decided to pop over for a visit.

Somewhere down the line, the girls had started calling Verle's mother, Big Grandma, and Dora's mother, Little Grandma. Dora had tried to convince her daughters to call their grandmothers, Grandma Jeanette and Grandma Ellen, but they'd continued to use the names Little Grandma and Big Grandma. Dora never really understood why they had come up with those names; both grandmothers were pretty much the same height and build. Maybe the girls thought of Verle's mother as Big Grandma because she never let her emotions show and thought she knew more than anyone else, resulting in frequent philosophical and political lectures at the dinner table; whereas Dora's mother, Little Grandma, read *True Confession* magazines, cried at every little thing, and had mood swings that made her happy as a jay bird one minute and down in the dumps the next.

The two women could disagree about the smallest things, like the time they were doing the dishes and Little Grandma had tossed the forks in the silverware drawer helter-skelter as usual, after which Big Grandma had unsmilingly demonstrated to the granddaughters how forks should be carefully nested one against the other in the drawer… then there was the continual ongoing controversy between the two as to whether flour or corn starch made the best gravy…and, if nothing else reared its head, they were always ready to disagree about interpretations of the Bible.

Dora felt a little guilty about it, but it was hard not to be thankful that Verle's mother was gone for the summer.

She got up to get herself another cup of coffee. She was disappointed in herself for eating so fast, but it was hard to relax when her mother was furiously washing dishes at the kitchen sink. Dora sat down at the table again, took a sip of coffee, and watched Carla eat. Carla was usually the last one to leave the table, and actually seemed to savor every mouthful.

Dora met Carla's eyes over her coffee cup and smiled. Dora had done her best, after that bout with polio, to raise Carla to be independent. When Carla was five, they'd given her a tricycle as a reward for having stopped sucking her thumb; Carla had loved that tricycle. She'd pedal as fast as she could along the cracking sidewalks in front of their house. One day Dora and Verle were standing at the screen door watching Carla practice sharper and sharper turns at the end of the sidewalk, when the tricycle tipped over and pinned Carla underneath. Her paralyzed arm had hung useless as she doggedly kept trying to wrench the bike away with her good arm. Verle had started to open the door to rush out to help, but Dora grabbed his arm, dug in her fingers and held him fast.

"No, Verle," she'd hissed. "Don't you dare interfere…she's got to learn to do things herself."

They stood watching the determined look on Carla's face as she struggled to untangle arms, legs and tricycle wheels. The scene played out in slow motion while Dora's knuckles turned white from the pressure of holding Verle back with one hand and the screen door shut with the other. Later that day, Verle walked up behind Dora as she was combing her hair in front of the bathroom mirror, and gave her a grin as he showed her the bruises she'd left on his arm. He'd gently turned her around and kissed her on the forehead.

One of the hardest things for Carla to learn had been to tie her shoelaces. Verle helped by nailing a shoe with laces onto a heavy wooden block. Every day for weeks Carla concentrated on learning to tie what Verle called "those blasted shoelaces." Day after day, she bent over the shoe, trying and failing, trying and failing, her seven-year-old jaw locked tight, her lips pressed firmly together. Dora had wanted so much to say, "Give it up, Carla, you can always wear slip-on shoes." But she kept her doubts to herself, and threatened the rest of the family not to interfere, until one day Carla's five fingers triumphed.

As far as Dora knew, the only thing Carla had ever given up on was the idea she might one day get married. The evening after a festive gathering to celebrate Laird and Janice's high school graduation and engagement, Carla and Dora were alone in the kitchen doing the dishes when Carla confided in a small voice, "No one will ever want to marry me."

"Well, why not, I'd like to know?" Dora said indignantly, "You are growing up to be a beautiful young woman, inside and out. Why wouldn't some fine man want to marry you?"

In a rare outburst of anger, Carla furiously yelled at her mother, "That's not true and you know it!" She'd thrown down the dishtowel and run outdoors, slamming the back door so hard the kitchen window rattled.

※ ※ ※

Dora looked thoughtfully across the table at her daughter and took a last sip of her coffee. Little Grandma, still washing dishes at the sink, started singing, "Amazing grace, how sweet the sound, that saved a wretch like meeeeee...."

Carla stopped eating and joined in with her clear soprano voice, "I once was lost and now I'm found, was blind and now I seeee..."

Dora added her own soprano voice to the group. They sang all four verses before stopping and were quiet for a moment. That's the Welsh strain in us, Dora thought. Nobody can sing the old hymns like the Welsh.

Suddenly Carla asked, "Where's Martha? Isn't she up yet? We need her alto voice."

"Oh, no, she's up and eaten long ago, she went over to see the Martin kids' new sandbox."

"I'm amazed any kid could care about sand. I always liked mud, nothing beats gooey, squishy mud after a good rainstorm," Carla said. "You can't make mud pies with sand."

Carla leaned her elbow on the table and propped her chin in her hand. "I don't remember you ever complaining about Janice and me playing in all that mud. I must have been a mess. Did you have to hose us off?"

Dora smiled, "Yes, actually, I hosed the two of you off quite a few times."

Little Grandma turned from the sink and snapped open her dish towel. "You were never strict enough with the girls, Dora."

"Yes," she said to Carla, "your mother had to strip you naked on the back porch before she could let you into the house and give you a bath. And then she had to wash all those extra clothes." She pointed a finger at her daughter. "You still aren't strict enough, Dora. The idea of you fixing a separate pan of plain kidney beans for Martha just because she won't eat chili like the rest of us! You'll spoil her rotten!"

Dora stood up, took her empty coffee cup over to the sink and carefully deposited it in the cooling dishwater. She was remembering her own childhood, having to eat every single thing on her plate or get a spanking. Not that her mother was mean-spirited or ever held a grudge; it was haul off and hit one minute, and sing a cheerful tune the next.

"It's no trouble at all to fix a little extra pan of beans, and you know perfectly well that none of the girls are spoiled." There was a hint of exasperation in Dora's carefully controlled voice.

"Hmmph," Dora's mother pressed her lips together and started wiping the dishes.

"Time to get dressed and get something done," Carla said, jumping to her feet. She grabbed a dishtowel to help her grandmother finish.

"What do you need done this morning, Mother? I'm going to the post office this afternoon to see if there's any mail. Will someone be here all day in case anyone calls about Laird?"

"I'll be around to catch the phone after you leave," Dora assured her. "I'm going to stir up a batch of bread and then do some ironing. Maybe I'll make some cinnamon rolls, too, and yes, I'd appreciate it if you could clean the bathrooms."

After the upstairs and the downstairs bathrooms were cleaned, Carla walked into the living room, sat down at the organ and took out the music book of simplified Bach pieces she'd recently borrowed. They weren't exactly easy, but the first piece was not too difficult and it was so beautiful...

Suddenly Carla was aware of Martha standing behind her. As she turned to smile up at Martha, she could see Martha's forehead was damp with a faint sheen of perspiration, not surprising since Martha never walked when she could run. Her hair was arranged in the customary two stubborn braids that never completely managed to subdue her wiry curls.

"Hi, Martha, how was the Martins' new sandbox?"

"It was okay, but I'm getting a little too old for sandboxes."

Carla nodded and asked, "Want me to switch to some sing-a-long music so we can do some duets?"

"No, I don't feel like singing," said Martha. She was quiet a minute and then said, "I've been standing behind you, wondering how you can look at those marks on the page and make the music come out of the organ."

Carla swiveled the organ stool around to face her sister. "That's a really good question."

Martha said, "I never really thought about it before, but that's a new book of music you're playing from, right?"

"Yes, I borrowed it yesterday from Susan Jennings."

"So, you've never seen those songs 'til today?"

"Some of them I've seen. Not this one."

"Well, how can you play it so good, when you've never practiced it before?"

Carla gave a small shrug, "Well, my brain has learned the basic rules of reading the musical notations. Not just the notes, but the rhythm, the timing, the dynamics, you know, things like loud and soft. Then my brain tells my body what to do. I can play the music better if I've practiced it, but, if the music isn't too complicated, I can sight-read my way through okay."

The two sisters were quiet for a moment, studying the musical notations on the open pages in front of them. Carla said, "A few years ago, Martha, you didn't know how to read, but now you've learned the basic rules of reading the English language, and you can sight-read your way through lots of books. It's the same with the language of music except more of a person's body is involved."

Martha's serious eyes looked into Carla's, "So, sight-reading books must be a lot easier for you than sight-reading music."

Carla nodded, "Yes, that's true. My mind reads the music okay but if I had the use of my right hand, I could certainly play a lot better. Actually, that's why Mama and Daddy bought the organ for me, so I can use my feet to play the chords."

Martha impulsively threw her arms around Carla and squeezed tight. In a firm voice she said, "You play plenty good with just one hand, Carla!"

Carla put her arm around Martha's waist and gave her a quick kiss on the cheek. Smelling the soft fragrance of bubble gum and ivory soap wafting up from her sister's small body, Carla drew back and looked into Martha's clear eyes. "One more thing you should know: some people don't need to read music notations. They hear the sounds in their heads and they instantly figure out how to play the music on their instrument, they can do it without looking at music notes… I don't know how to do that, I've always wished I could."

"Do you think I'm old enough to take lessons so I can read the music?"

"I'm sure you are. We'll ask Mama. And when you've learned enough, we can play duets. I'll work the left hand and the pedals and you can do the treble clef, won't that be fun?"

After Martha ran from the room, Carla reached up and took down a book of more-familiar music. It was relaxing to play something you already knew, not like when her music teacher, Mr. Emory, would unexpectedly look up where she stood in the soprano section of the chorus and say, "Carla, could you come down and help me out? I need to get out from behind the piano for a few minutes and direct this bunch of opera stars."

Carla didn't like to accompany the school chorus, it was usually music she hadn't practiced before, and even though she knew the soprano part, having to sight read all four voices at the same time was stressful. Her left hand was too small to stretch one entire octave and she couldn't always reach the bass note at the same time as the high notes.

Mr. Emory had told her not to worry. It didn't matter if she couldn't reach all the notes at the same time. He didn't need her to play the whole accompaniment anyway, just the four voice parts, and he valued her help because she understood chord structure and how to accurately count complex rhythms. He thought that probably the reason Carla understood music theory so well was because music was based on mathematical principles, a subject for which she seemed to have an aptitude. Of course, they both knew it was more than that; you also had to practice, practice, and practice some more.

It was nearly eleven o'clock when Carla closed the music book, stood up from the organ stool, and went upstairs to change clothes for her walk downtown to the post office. Carla loved her bedroom. It had once been Jan's bedroom, too, but for the past two-and-a-half years, with Janice away at nurse's training, Carla had acquired sole proprietary rights. She and Jan had chosen the wallpaper many years ago, and she never tired of its tiny white lily-of-the-valley blooms set against a pale blue background. Daddy had painted the unmatched old furniture a creamy white, and the two grandmothers had joined ranks to coordinate the construction of two blue and white patchwork quilts. The sisters loved the fact that their grandmothers had taken the time to embroider local birds on every other square.

Carla opened the top drawer of her dresser and unwrapped a pair of silver-plated candleholders that nestled in one corner along with her underwear. She picked up and inspected one of the candle holders. The pair of candleholders had cost her fifteen babysitting jobs, but they were worth it. She planned to polish them before she wrapped them in a gift box for Jan and Laird. She often imagined them eating supper together at their very own table, their faces glowing in the reflection of the candlelight.

She wasn't sure if she should give the silver candleholders to Jan at her bridal shower, or whether she should save them for a wedding present. Jan might want something beautiful like the candle holders for a shower gift, or, on the other hand, maybe a shower gift should be something practical like pots and pans, or a toaster. Ever since the war had ended, Carla had tried to pump Jan as to what she wanted for wedding presents, but Jan was maddeningly reluctant to reveal any ideas about gifts. Now that Laird was coming home, people would want to know about wedding plans and gift ideas. Carla set her lips determinedly. She'd sit Jan down next time she had the chance and make her come up with a suggested list of presents; otherwise, people would give Jan a lot of wedding gifts she'd never even use.

"This is probably as close as I'll ever get to a wedding," Carla thought as she quietly closed the dresser drawer, "and I'm going to enjoy every minute of it."

Chapter Four

After his father had gone back to work, and after his brothers had raced off to the town swimming pool, Laird went upstairs to unpack his bag. He was suddenly seized by the urge to take his mother's advice and lie down for a nap. He'd learned in the army he could sleep for ten minutes at time if he was tired enough…a cat-nap was better than nothing, and it had been days since he'd had a good night's sleep. He threw himself face down on his bed and thought, "Just ten minutes…"

Four hours later, he was awakened by his mother calling up the stairs, "Supper's ready, Laird!"

Ellen had prepared all of Laird's favorites: pot roast, mashed potatoes and gravy, creamed peas, the ever-present home-made bread, and for dessert, apple pie. The Nordstrom men ate in appreciative silence, occasionally saying, "This is good." After the last piece of apple pie had been eaten, Laird pushed back his chair and said, "I guess I better go over and see the Swanson's. They're expecting me about now. I won't stay long."

"Can we come, too?" David asked.

"Can we…?" Duane looked expectantly at his mother.

Ellen shook her head, "Not this time, boys. Your brother needs to go by himself so they can visit without too much commotion."

"Oh, gee…" Johnny's face sent out a silent appeal to his mother.

Emil lit a cigarette and said, "It's almost time to listen to the 'Lone Ranger,' boys. You wouldn't want to miss that."

✳ ✳ ✳

After the dishes were put away, Carla went outside to wait on the screened porch for Laird. Martha had wanted to run the three blocks to the Nordstrom house to greet him, but Carla had decided that would be too childish, and besides, Laird might want some time to himself while he walked over. She sat down on the porch swing and rocked slowly back and forth; the birds had settled down and the crickets were starting to sing, sounding as happy as she felt.

Now that she was too old to play Kick-the-Can or Alley-Alley-In-Some-Free, and if the mosquitoes weren't too fierce, Carla often walked alone on summer evenings. Sounds were richer around dusk; in the twilight, even familiar sounds, like kids shouting and adults talking, or the creaking of the porch swing rocking back and forth, hinted at something mysterious, something she was never able to put into words.

She let her eyes go out of focus so she could listen better. She heard a screen door slam, and an occasional rustle of leaves; some evenings you could hear distant rolls of thunder, and when you opened your eyes, you could catch glimpses of far-off sheet lightning. She stopped rocking and listened intently, but nope, none of Nature's fireworks were anywhere near tonight.

Martha came running around the house with Mac, the Swansons' aging Scottie dog, at her heels. "Is he here yet?"

"No, Martha, not yet, but don't worry, I'll yell when I see him coming."

Carla stood up and started pacing. In a way, she knew Laird better now than when he'd left because she'd gotten to know him through his letters. Three years ago, Laird, like everybody else, had called her Squirt, a name she'd never liked. It was true she was short, a mere four feet ten inches, but almost everybody on Mother's side of the family was short. Mother said maybe it was because they were Welsh. Carla was willing to concede that Welsh genes could be partly the reason, but she also knew her crooked spine robbed her of a few inches. There was nothing to be done about her height, but she could certainly do something about people calling her Squirt.

On her sixteenth birthday, after she'd made a wish and blown out her candles, she announced that from now on she would not respond to anyone who used the name Squirt. "I have a perfectly nice name, Carla Rae," she told them, her chin up and her eyes blazing, "and Carla is the only name I'll answer to."

It had taken two weeks; day by day she'd perfected her ignoring strategy. As she'd anticipated, her father had been the hardest person to convince, but pretty soon everyone in the family was calling her Carla. It had taken nearly a year to convince the kids at school, but eventually the nickname Squirt faded into history. Only Laird still called her Squirt; his letters always began, "Dear Squirt," but she was certain she could change that once she was able to give him a face-to-face ultimatum.

She saw a shadowy figure whose face she couldn't make out coming towards her down the sidewalk in the dusk, but since the figure had a slight limp, it had to be Laird.

"Martha, Martha, he's here," she yelled and rushed down the porch steps, slamming the screen door behind her. Martha and Mac came dashing around the house close behind her. Mac, with his short legs pumping and his head held low, ran down the sidewalk following the two girls until all three came to an abrupt stop in front of Laird.

"You're finally here, welcome home." Carla's eyes started to brim with tears.

"Hi, Squirt," he smiled down at her, opened his arms and gave her an enthusiastic hug.

"Hi, Laird! Do you remember me?" Martha tugged at his shirt and grinned up at him.

"Of course I remember you, but, wow, how you've grown!" He picked her up and swung a giggling Martha around in a circle, her legs and skirt flying.

Carla took a step back, cleared her throat, and said, "Try my name again, will you, please, Laird?" She kept smiling but her eyes had dried and her jaw was set.

He laughed, bent down, picked her up by the waist and swung her around a couple of times and said, "Okay Carla, you win. I can see you're grown up enough for a real name." Putting her down, he said, "You both look wonderful! And how was your graduation, Carla? Sorry I missed it."

Carla, by now a little breathless, answered, "It was good, but I'm embarrassed to tell you I cried afterwards. Most of my girlfriends cried. How silly was that? There was no reason to cry, not like during the war when you and Janice graduated."

"Well," Laird said, "thank God for a place where girls can cry for no reason at all."

He reached down and gently placed his hands on each of her upper arms and experienced a small shock of surprise when he felt the withered muscles of her paralyzed right arm. Of course, he'd almost forgotten about the damned polio. Laird stood studying her face, thinking of the pressure of her firm breasts against him when she'd hugged him, taking in her delicious scent. His eyes were intent and admiring, "You've grown up, Carla. You're a beautiful young woman."

She averted her eyes and shook herself free. "Not really," she said.

"It's true. I read your letters and kept thinking of you as little Squirt, but now that I can see you in person, you really are Carla. No more little Squirt, Scout's honor." He held up his right hand in the old Boy Scout pledge and grinned at her.

Looking up at him with wide eyes, Martha grabbed his hand and said, "I've grown up, too." She pointed to her front teeth, "See, I've got my permanent front teeth in now, don't they look good?"

Laird leaned down to inspect Martha's teeth. "They're beautiful teeth, Martha, and they look strong enough to last you a lifetime."

Carla took his other hand and pulled him towards the house. "Let's go see the family. Little Grandma said she can't wait to clap her eyes on you. Mother said you're driving to Minneapolis in the morning to pick up Janice and they've saved some extra gas ration coupons for you to use. Gas is still rationed, you know."

She stopped, and looked up at his amused eyes looking down at her. "I'm babbling aren't I? Just babbling…it's because I'm so excited. I'm not usually like this." She stopped talking for a moment. "In fact, Mother says I'm the quietest one in our whole family, so if you think this is bad, brace yourself for when we get into the house."

Laird's grin got bigger, "Actually, I was thinking you sound just like your letters."

"Really? I know I ramble on when I write and can't seem to stop, but I always wanted to let you know what was happening here so things wouldn't seem so strange when you came home. I know we're just a little backwater town but it's all I know. Of course," she raised her eyebrows and looked questioningly at him, "Breton must not seem very important, after you've seen so much of the world."

He bent over to pet Mac, who was jumping around excitedly at their feet. "Oh, no, Carla, believe me, your stories helped keep me sane many times. Thanks for taking the time to write so often." He'd re-read her letters until they got lost somewhere in the chaos. He vividly remembered smoothing open those tissue-thin pages, grimy and dog-eared, and reading them aloud to his buddies who gathered, in silence, to listen.

"I loved writing to you, Laird, and I loved getting your letters. I feel like I know you a lot better now than when you left because of your letters."

Martha tugged at his hand. "Did you like my letters, too, Laird? And the pictures I drew for you?"

He smiled down at Martha as they walked up the steps of the front porch. "I loved your letters. I even showed them to some of the other guys and they loved them, too."

Verle was beaming as he swung open the front door to greet them. He grabbed Laird's hand, shook it fiercely, saying, "I thought I heard you talking out there. Welcome home, Laird." As he slapped Laird on the back, he added, "Have you figured out a way to make a million dollars yet?"

Laird grinned on hearing Verle's familiar million-dollar greeting, and reminded himself to tell Verle later about his brief experience with cigarette riches. "Not yet, sir. Good to see you again."

Verle waved his hand absently in front of him as if he were chasing away a pesky fly. "Please don't call me sir, that's strictly army stuff, it's Verle to you, son, plain old Verle." He clapped Laird on the shoulder. "Remember, we're almost family now." He took Laird by the arm and propelled him into the living room. "Come in, come in."

Laird could see Verle hadn't changed; he was still the same hyperactive man Laird had known from childhood. Verle's eyebrows had a way of moving up and down while deep in conversation with someone, and when the conversation got intense, he sometimes seemed on the verge of leaping out of his chair. Verle's mobile eyebrows had always reminded Laird of the bouncing ball at the Saturday movie matinee sing-a-longs.

The entire Swanson family engulfed Laird, and their questions and comments broke over him in rapid succession. "We missed you." "How long did it take you to get here on the train from Chicago?" "We worried about you." "Wait 'til you taste Mama's cake, it's got real butter in it." "You look great!"

Dora finally got them all to sit down at the dining room table while she poured coffee and milk, and set out her prize-winning white cake with the lemon filling.

Laird found himself seated directly across the table from Martha and asked, "How old are you now, Martha? Eight?"

Pleased to be noticed, Martha said, "I'm eight, but I'll be nine years in just seven more months." She swallowed a huge bite of cake and grinned at him.

"You're growing up, Martha. I like your braids, by the way."

Martha pulled on one braid and said, "Mama says these braids almost succeed in keeping my hair from flying all over the place."

After laughter about Martha's wild hair and a round of compliments for Dora's cake, Verle launched into an explanation of his latest, failed idea for a perpetual motion machine: "It worked on a gravity flow principle, but the problem was it had a water leakage problem, and if I got the seams tight enough to keep the water from leaking out, there was too much friction again and it would eventually slow to a stop."

Dora rolled her eyes heavenwards. "All I know is when you tried it, water poured all over the kitchen floor and it was a terrible mess to clean up. From now on," Dora turned to Laird, "I told him he could do his experimenting in the basement."

Little Grandma said, "I think his water-filled car bumper was a good idea, it was just too heavy to be practical."

"But his idea for defrosting a car radiator using a copper wire attached to the battery was a good one." Dora turned to Laird. "The Spengler Company was ready to buy that one, and then anti-freeze came out. So, that was the end of that."

Suddenly, Martha broke in and asked, "When are you and Jan getting married?"

Laird hesitated, "I'm not sure. I'll have to talk to Jan first."

Dora looked sternly over at her youngest daughter, "You shouldn't ask such personal questions, Martha. Laird and Janice haven't even had a chance to see each other yet."

"I just wanted to know." Martha looked at Laird to explain. "Big Grandma said she'd make me a special dress for the wedding and we already bought the pattern. It's a really pretty dress, with a ruffle around the hem. But we don't know yet what color material to buy until Jan lets us know."

Little Grandma steered the conversation away from the wedding and back to more of her son-in-law's crazy inventions, "The worst invention you ever came up with was your spring-loaded toilet seat. You men may like to have the toilet seat spring up every time a person stands up, but as I remember, it took a lot of work to get that darn seat to stay down long enough to turn around and sit down on it." She laughed her full laugh and her eyes twinkled; she had always regarded her son-in-law as a precocious and loveable child.

Verle joined in the general laughter around the table without any apparent embarrassment. A wide smile, revealing a distinctive gap between his front teeth, relaxed his face and calmed his animated eyebrows.

Martha looked at Laird and tried to explain, "Mama says Daddy has all the brains in this family and she has all the common sense, but I think Mama has plenty of brains, too."

The subject changed to what kind of crops the farmers were putting in this spring, and the prices Chicago grain dealers had paid for a bushel of grain last fall. "The farmers had bumper crops during the war years," Verle said. "Course, they'll never admit it. They're afraid the weather gods will send a hailstorm next year if they so much as breathe one optimistic word about the markets or the weather, but that's a farmer for you."

Little Grandma nodded her head in agreement; having been a farmer's wife, she knew all about the vagaries of the weather and the railroads. If you were a farmer, you had no control over the corporations or Mother Nature. Either one could take you down without a moment's notice.

Laird said, "The government will stop rationing gas and tires pretty soon. Now that they're switching back to making cars and appliances instead of tanks, the farmers will start spending their money again."

"Thank God for that," Verle said. He sat back in his chair and looked appraisingly at Laird. "If you want a new car or a used one, just let me know. A lot of people come into the gas station and tell me when they have used cars for sale, and Bud Torgelson down at the Ford dealership can get you a good deal on a new one."

"Thanks, I've been sending money home to the folks to save for me. I'd like to get a good used car if you can find one."

"I'll keep my eyes open," Verle promised.

Dora stood up and asked, "More coffee, anybody?"

"When gas rationing finally ends maybe we can take a trip again to Canada to see the cousins."

Carla sat in the midst of her family, intently following the conversation, contributing mostly smiles and nods. She loved listening to them, she loved watching them; her heart swelled with love for the people sitting around the table, including Laird, who would soon be part of the family, too. He wasn't talking much tonight, but that wasn't unusual. Like in his letters, his sentences were usually short but well chosen. Laird probably thought before he spoke, not like her family where people just blurted out the first thing that came into their heads.

Big Grandma once told Carla that Laird's family was less verbal and more reserved than the Swanson family because the Nordstroms' people came from northern Sweden, and northern Swedes didn't talk as much as southern Swedes. "Nothing wrong with not talking so much," she'd added. "You need both listeners and talkers to make a conversation." Carla hoped Laird didn't mind doing a lot of listening because in this family it was sometimes hard to get a word in edgeways.

One thing Janice's and Laird's families had in common was that neither set of parents had taught their kids to speak Swedish. Laird said his folks only spoke Swedish to each other when they didn't want the kids to know what they were talking about, and Big Grandma, Verle's mother, refused to speak Swedish in front of her children because she wanted them to be known as Americans, not children of immigrants.

Dora suddenly realized that Laird seemed tired. She stood up and started collecting the plates. "I'm glad you stopped by, Laird, but you need to go home and rest. You've got a lot of sleep to catch up on. We'll see you and your family for supper here tomorrow."

"Thanks, Mrs. Swanson, I'm ready to hit the hay all right." Laird got up and made his way to the door, trailed by the entire Swanson family, Verle shaking his hand and everyone telling him how good it was to have him home again, and how they hoped he'd have a good trip to the Cities tomorrow to get Jan, and did he need some extra gas coupons.

As the door closed behind him, Laird stopped in the silence to close his eyes and take a deep breath of the warm night air. He started to run, but gave it up. Damn, he'd forgotten he couldn't run with this bum knee. He settled for a fast limping walk along the old, cracked sidewalks as far as the football field where he sat on the lowest bleacher seat.

There were plenty of crickets out, their voices chirping loudly through the night air, but not many mosquitoes, thank god. The moon was just a sliver. He looked up for a long time at the wide expanse of the Milky Way flung across the sky, and felt sorry for all those people living in cities who never got to see the brilliance of a mid-western prairie night sky. There were no clouds tonight, which was a little disappointing because he'd been looking forward to seeing a good lightning storm.

Tomorrow he'd see his beautiful Jan. Three years was a long time, and he wondered if he would seem like a stranger to her. The phone conversation they'd had when he was in Chicago was frustrating. Her voice over the phone was warm and welcoming but the connection hadn't been good, and it was hard to make out all of her words. She'd answered his phone call from her boarding house and he supposed the landlady had been right there listening.

He closed his eyes, listened to the faint rustle of the nearby cottonwood trees, and tried to picture Jan as she'd looked the night at the golf course when he'd given her the ring.

Chapter Five

    Laird shifted his dad's old Chevy sedan into third gear and accelerated out of town, past the creamery and the cold storage locker, past the Farmer Co-op silos, past the Frostie-Freeze Drive-In, past the old Knudsen house with its fading Flowers For Sale sign, and out to the open, straight road that led to Minneapolis and St. Paul. He was headed east, driving into the sunrise. The miles rolled by as Laird watched the brilliant shades of pink and vermillion slowly change and fade into a pale blue cloudless sky. When the sun rose higher, he leaned over and groped in the glove compartment for the sunglasses his dad kept there.
    It was still illegal to go faster than thirty-five miles per hour. The speed limit imposed during the war did save on gas and tires, but the road was so straight and empty, and he hadn't seen Jan for three long years. Anyway, the war was over…to hell with the speed limit. He pushed down on the gas pedal and the speedometer crept up over fifty-five miles-per-hour before he eased up. Fifty miles-an-hour was probably all Dad's old Chevy could handle anyway.
    Back in Germany, guys had driven those unstable little jeeps full speed ahead, even over wet cobblestone roads, and, in Frankfurt, after the war was over, an average of thirty guys a month had died in jeep accidents, speeding around corners, some of them drunk out of their minds. The Germans had stockpiled huge warehouses of booze that were promptly liberated by the Allies and sold at a bargain price to the Allied soldiers. Beer and champagne had cost only five cents a cup, and whiskey, cognac and brandy were five cents a shot. Laird shook his head in an unconscious effort to forget the many hangovers he'd inflicted on himself with the surfeit of cheap booze.
    To hell with all that, he thought, in only a few hours he would see Janice again. He closed his eyes for a moment and could clearly see her

face with the delicate nose and mouth, her frank green eyes with the golden flecks, her honey brown hair shining in the sun, and those wondrous breasts gleaming in the moonlight. He took in a sharp breath, felt the nerve endings rustle along his body, and shifted his weight against the seat.

It was much harder to recall the sound of her voice. When he'd called from New York, with so much static on the line, she'd sounded almost like an old Caruso phonograph record. And it bothered him he couldn't conjure up the scent of her. He'd always wanted to ask her to send him a piece of her unwashed clothing, maybe her one of her blouses, but he could never get up the nerve to do it. The last picture she'd sent him showed her in her nurse's uniform, "That's just a student cap," she'd written. "I get an official nurse's cap at my graduation next September." She was finishing her education while he was just beginning to look forward to his. He'd have to accept the fact that Jan had a new life he knew nothing about. Well, he had a life she knew nothing about either.

In high school, Laird had sometimes thought about going to college, but back then it was pretty unlikely. College was for rich kids, and for doctors' and lawyers' kids, not for blacksmiths' sons; but now because of the GI Bill, Laird, son of Emil the town blacksmith, could go, too.

The government would pay his way, but the government couldn't make up for his lack of academic background. Laird's straight-A report cards had stopped in sixth grade after he'd figured out that you couldn't be both a straight-A student and one of the guys at the same time. The way to succeed socially at Breton High School was to excel in sports, and that's what he had done. Football, basketball, baseball and track, he'd done them all. Being captain of the football team, a first-string player in basketball and baseball, and top sprinter on the track team had resulted in a senior letter-sweater with four stripes and the big letter "B" for Breton covered with sports emblems. Laird had proudly given his athletic sweater to Janice to wear during their senior year.

He took one hand off the steering wheel to rub the top of his head. It all seemed so childish now. Was it Laird the sports hero Jan had fallen in love with, or thought she had fallen in love with, a big sports-hero-frog in a very tiny pond? He began to understand why his dad had never come to any of his games. Emil had always been pleased that Laird was good at sports, but he hadn't attended a single game. Laird finally had to agree with his father's unspoken message that sports were for kids.

There must be some reason he'd managed to live through the misery of the war, but there was no good reason he could see that he was still alive and Conrad Oberst wasn't. Lots of people from back home had written to tell him they were praying for him. Well, he was sure they'd prayed for Conrad Oberst, and for Carl Anderson, too, and for all the others who'd been killed. As far as he could tell, God didn't give a damn for human beings, probably with good reason. Laird clenched the steering wheel. Human beings as a species were insane. Maybe it was just during war that people went nuts, but they had to be crazy to go to war in the first place.

Even after the months of routine duty in Germany after the fighting was over, Laird hadn't been able to stop the sporadic invasion into his mind of battle scenes: the terror of the heavy bombardments, the bodies and parts of bodies, the stench of intestines hanging from trees and squishing under his feet, and the sounds of dying human beings.

On the troop ship coming home, he and fifteen hundred other guys had been packed together below decks like sardines in a can. If they weren't seasick, they were bored, so, when the weather was good, everyone who could sprawled on the deck to watch the horizon and get some fresh air. One day Laird had been sitting on the crowded deck leaning against one of the bulwarks, looking out to sea and clutching his coat around him to keep warm, when the soldier sitting next to him commented that you were less likely to get seasick if you kept your eyes on the horizon. They'd started a conversation about the lousy food on shipboard and the constant problem of vomit on the decks when the soldier stopped to light up a cigarette, stared into Laird's eyes, and matter-of-factly commented, "I'll commit suicide before I'll fight in a war again." He'd looked away, blown out the match and thrown it down on the deck with an air of finality. Laird had looked out at the empty horizon for a long moment before nodding his head in understanding.

Laird told himself to focus on the road and stop thinking about the war. He reached over to fiddle with the radio knob and found some

Big Band music. Maybe Jan would want to go dancing, not that Laird considered himself much of a dancer, especially with this limp, but he'd learned that if he got a little booze in him, he did all right.

Early this morning while his brothers were still asleep, Laird had eaten breakfast with his mother and dad. The kitchen hadn't changed much except his mother had a new oilcloth table cover with a yellow sunflower pattern, and he'd guessed the old red geranium-covered oilcloth must have finally given up the ghost. She had outdone herself with a big midwestern breakfast of bacon, fried potatoes, eggs and homemade bread.

"So," Emil had said, "I guess once you get your bearings, you'll be thinking about the best way to make a living."

"I'm planning to take advantage of the GI bill and go to college. I'm like you, Dad, I don't want to be inside working at a desk. I want to build things, bridges maybe. I was asking some of the officers at the Command Center about it, and they said I'd probably need a civil engineering degree to do big construction jobs."

His mother nodded her head approvingly but her eyes were thoughtful. "That will cost a lot, won't it?"

Emil's, "Yah," was accompanied by a quick intake of breath revealing the speech inflections of his Swedish childhood. "But the GI Bill will pay for as many months as Laird was in the service. How many years will they pay for, do you think?"

"I have three years of service…I think that will pay for most of it. If I run out of government money, I can always earn money summers working in the harvest fields. I'll also have that money I sent home, even after I spend some of it for a used car. I should be able to get through without help from you. Jan's dad said he'd try to find me a good used car."

"Yah," Emil said," you've got quite a bit of money in your savings account now. We made a deposit every month when we'd get your check."

With his right hand, Emil carefully tipped some hot coffee into his saucer, picked up the saucer with his left hand and pulled in a long sip through a fast-dissolving sugar cube which he held in his front teeth. Laird watched him over the rim of his own coffee cup, fascinated. He hadn't seen anyone drink coffee like that since he'd left home three years ago. First generation Swedes didn't saucer their coffee much in public anymore, but Laird had always liked seeing his dad re-enact the old-country ritual.

"I remember when you built that bridge across Harmon Creek over by Langlois," Laird said. "You took me along one Saturday, and I watched you weld…I loved watching those sparks fly."

"Yah, I designed that bridge, too. Of course, it's just a little bridge."

Ellen took a sip of coffee from the delicate English porcelain cup that was one of her few extravagances, and with a proud lift of her chin she smiled at Laird, "That bridge is still in perfect shape."

"I'd like to go over there with you one of these days and check out the bridge, Dad. I always envied the guys in the Corp of Engineers. They'd come along behind us and try to patch things back together after the army and the air force had smashed practically everything in sight."

Laird pushed back his chair and stood up. "Well, I better get going if I'm going to get to the Cities by noon."

He'd put his hand on his mother's shoulder. "Thanks for the great breakfast, Mother." He stood for a moment looking into her eyes. "I'm sick and tired of war… I'm sick and tired of all the wreckage."

"Yah," Emil said, "it's better to build than destroy."

Ellen still thought of Laird as just a boy, but she suddenly saw that his eyes looked old. As he opened the kitchen door to leave, she called after him, "You're a born builder, Laird. All the men in this family are builders."

※ ※ ※

Back at Mrs. Johnson's boarding house, the landlady tapped gently on Jan's door, "It's eleven o'clock, dear, time to get up."

Jan's eyes flew open. Laird had said he'd try to get there by noon. She looked at the clock and saw she'd had four hours sleep.

"Jan, dear, are you awake?"

"Yes, thanks, Mrs. Johnson, I'm wide awake." She sat up, threw off the sheet and called out through the closed door, "We're stopping for a bite to eat on the way back to Breton, so don't worry about fixing us lunch."

"All right, dear, just call me if you need anything," and Jan heard her footsteps going slowly back down the stairs.

The night before, she'd laid out her light blue dress, clean underwear, and white sandals; everything else she'd need for the week was packed in her suitcase. All that was left to do now was to take a bath and get dressed. Jan looked down at the diamond ring on her left hand and thought again, as she had so many times, that Laird must have spent almost all his savings to buy the ring, a diamond solitaire set in a broad platinum setting.

He'd given her the ring a few nights before he'd left for the army. They'd gone to the movies and afterwards driven out to the darkened golf course to engage in the inevitable frustrating necking session that always left them feeling dissatisfied and exhausted. You could go so far and no farther. No decent girl went all the way. Jan wasn't quite sure what all the way meant, except she knew for sure the place between your legs was off limits until you were married. Knowing Laird would soon be leaving made the necking sessions even more painful and, those last few weeks before he'd left, whenever they'd looked at each other their eyes had held the same unspoken question, "Will I ever see you again?" That night at the golf course, he'd pulled away from her after a lingering kiss, looked at her in that intense way that made her feel she was melting, and asked, "Is it all right if I unbutton your blouse… and look at your breasts?"

Shyly, Jan had nodded. She'd sat very still, holding her breath, her eyes never leaving his face as he reached over and carefully began to unbutton her blouse. The buttons were small and close together, and when he'd finally managed to open the blouse, her brassiere was in the way. He'd looked up at her and smiled a little, "Maybe you'll have to help."

Jan had solemnly reached back and unhooked her bra, then slowly pulled the straps off her shoulders. The three-quarter moon shone brightly through the open car window softly illuminating her firm, full breasts. Laird had drawn in a quick, involuntary breath, then reached over and gently stroked one breast. "You're so beautiful, so very, very beautiful." He'd leaned over and kissed each breast, cupping his hands under them, nuzzled his lips against her neck and ear, started to run one hand down her arm, and onto her thigh. Suddenly he'd pulled back from her, his eyes hidden in shadow. "I think we'd better stop, Jan. Maybe we should take a walk."

She'd felt his eyes on her but kept her own eyes averted as she rehooked her bra and re-buttoned her blouse. They'd gotten out of the car and walked along the narrow dirt road leading to the golf course parking lot, holding hands, and flirting. Sometimes Jan would laugh and try to run from him, knowing he could easily catch her, and when he'd grab her and press her close to him, she'd been aware of a mysterious hard bulge in Laird's trousers. The first few times that happened, she'd wondered if there was something wrong with him, but later she'd decided, since there was obviously nothing wrong with Laird in any other way, it must be something normal, although she wasn't sure exactly what.

They'd walked back to the car holding hands, neither one saying anything until Laird stopped, took a small jewelry box from his pocket, and, looking intently at Jan as he held it out said, "Will you marry me, Jan?"

Jan had opened the box and looked down at the ring, shining in the bright moonlight. She knew they were too young; she had three years of nurse's training ahead of her; he was going into the army during a war. Who knew how long he would be gone, or if he would ever come back? She'd looked at him in confusion. "I love you, too, Laird, and it's a beautiful ring, but we're so young."

"I don't mean for us to get married now. I know we're young, and anyway I wouldn't want to leave you behind pregnant and maybe with a kid who might have to grow up without a father. I'm talking about after the war. If I come home in one piece after the war, will you marry me?"

She'd thrown her arms around him, melting into the strength of his body closing protectively around her. She'd buried her face on his shoulder, and with a somewhat shaky intake of air, breathed in the mysterious musky odors of his skin. "Oh, yes, Laird. I'll wait for you."

Slowly, he put the ring on her finger, lifted her hands together to his lips and kissed one hand at a time. He'd seemed suddenly calm and certain in a way she'd not seen him before. They both knew it was settled… she had promised.

Janice sat on the edge of her bed and slowly took the ring off her finger, gravely inspecting her naked hand. It looked wrong and empty somehow, with no ring. She felt a flash of guilt and quickly put the ring back on her finger, stood up and began to dress with great care. She'd once seen a newsreel showing a matador putting on his clothing before entering the bullring. All his movements had been slow, deliberate, focused. She realized she was acting the same way.

She went to stand in front of the dresser and picked up her hairbrush. Big Grandma always said you should give your hair 100 strokes a day. Janice smiled, remembering that Carla always pooh-poohed Big Grandma's advice since Carla could hardly get a comb one time through her mass of curls, let alone one hundred. Janice appraised herself in the mirror as she brushed her thick, wavy hair that was so unlike Carla's tangle of curls. Janice wore her hair shoulder-length now and couldn't remember exactly what length it was when Laird left, but he'd always said he didn't care if her hair was short or long, it always looked good to him.

She picked up Laird's picture from the dresser and studied his face, that familiar face with the stubborn chin Big Grandma had warned her about, and his serious, thoughtful eyes looking back at her. She put Laird's picture down and leaned forward to inspect her own face in the mirror. She had smooth skin, full lips, and good eyes, maybe not striking eyes like Carla's, but good enough. People often commented that she had a beautiful smile, but Jan wasn't totally convinced of that since she couldn't see herself smile, and the couple of times she'd tried smiling at herself in the mirror made her look ridiculous. She inspected her two lipsticks, decided on the brightest red and watched her lips in the mirror as she carefully applied color, wondering what Laird would think when he saw her again.

She sat down on the straight-backed chair by the window and folded her hands in her lap to await Laird's arrival. When she closed her eyes, Dr. Blakesly's face came unbidden into view. She opened her eyes and shook her head but it was no use, she was not about to forget what had happened last night.

※ ※ ※

Lawrence had also worked the night shift last night. Around four in the morning, after he'd checked the patients on her ward, he'd said, "How about let's go get a cup of the worst coffee in town?" He'd smiled, but his grey eyes, magnified behind thick lenses, were serious.

Janice had hesitated, but he'd looked so worn out, she hadn't the heart to refuse. "All right, I'll let Bernice know I'm taking a break," and they'd walked together down the hall to the clean but ugly little coffee room, a space not much bigger than a large closet where the nurses and aides had been waiting five years for the administrative staff to replace the chipped wooden table with its six rickety metal folding chairs.

Lawrence had picked up the coffee pot before Janice could reach it and gestured with his other hand for her to sit down. "I'll pour. Nurses don't always have to be the ones to wait on doctors, no matter what they taught you in nursing school."

Janice liked the fact that Lawrence was somewhat obsessed with the injustices taught in nursing school about the superiority of doctors. The idea that nurses were supposed to stand when a doctor came into the room struck him as especially ludicrous, and Janice suspected his egalitarian streak was because his mother was a nurse.

He poured two cups of muddy coffee from the electric percolator, set one cup down in front of her, slowly folded his tall, lanky body onto one of the chairs, crossed his legs and said, "The only good thing about night shift coffee is that it makes all other coffee taste good."

Janice smiled, "I'm sure neither one of my grandmas would drink this stuff. They like it fresh, and weak as dishwater besides."

There was something so attractive about this man; maybe that was why she always felt slightly uncomfortable when he was near her. She probably shouldn't have come. Janice picked up her cup and avoided looking into his eyes.

"You've got a big day coming up," he'd said softly.

"Yes." She'd placed her left hand on the table so her engagement ring was clearly visible, and looked across the table at him. "Laird is coming to pick me up about noon. We should get back to Breton in time for supper with our combined families. It'll be quite a crowd."

"I hear you'll be gone for a week." Lawrence had hesitated and rubbed his forehead. "Janice, I've got to say this before you leave." He placed both hands on the table in front of him, his long, lean fingers spread flat: perfect surgeon hands. "I don't know how things will go between you and Laird now that's he's home, but if things should fall apart," he stopped, then continued, "I want you to know I'll always be here for you."

Jan's mouth had opened slightly and her eyes widened. She hadn't known what to say, but she wasn't able to stop looking into his penetrating grey eyes.

Suddenly, Lawrence pushed back his chair and stood up. "I know I'm probably speaking out of turn but I couldn't let you go without telling you." He walked around to her side of the table, picked up her right hand, the one without the ring, and still looking into her eyes, bent over to place a light kiss on her hand. "I think I've loved you since we first met."

Then he was gone, his soft-soled shoes retreating down the hall.

* * *

Janice stood up, looked out the bedroom window, and saw there were no cars parked on the street below. She hoped she'd given Laird good enough directions so he could find Mrs. Johnson's house. She smiled and thought Laird would probably wander around for an hour before he'd ask for directions. She was willing to bet the war hadn't changed that part of his personality.

She opened her suitcase one last time to see if she was forgetting anything. She wouldn't need many clothes for a week and there were odds and ends hanging in her closet at home. Actually, it was Carla's closet now. Janice closed the lid of her suitcase and snapped the locks shut just as she heard a car door slam.

She rushed to the window and saw Laird looking up at the house...it was him all right, but he seemed different somehow. She held her breath as she watched him walk slowly towards the front door. She'd known for nearly a year that he'd been wounded, but to see him limping startled her. He'd written that the bullet didn't completely shatter his knee and said not to worry about it, it could have been worse. She noticed that he seemed taller and larger than she remembered, or maybe it was just that he'd put on more muscle, and that he was more deliberate in his movements, but it was the same strong, wonderful face. During basic training he'd written, "One good thing about lugging around an M-1 rifle and a seventy-five pound pack is that it builds lots of muscle." That was so like him, never to complain about anything. Big Grandma said it was because Laird was a stoic... she'd said stoicism had moved into Laird's Swedish genes a long time ago and set up permanent housekeeping. Janice's brow creased in thoughtful lines as she continued to watch Laird's slow progress towards the front door, his somber face looking as though he was bracing himself for something unknown…

Downstairs in the front hall, Mrs. Johnson opened the door, put her hand out and shook his vigorously. "Well, you must be Laird, I'm so glad to meet you. Come right in, come in."

Laird automatically shook her hand but his first thought was, "Why is this woman here?" He'd been looking forward to this meeting with Jan for so long, and now there was a stranger in the way. When he looked past Mrs. Johnson, he saw Janice standing at the foot of the stairs holding a small black suitcase, her wide eyes riveted in his direction. Mrs. Johnson glanced at Janice and said, "Excuse me, I've got something cooking in the kitchen and I'd better go check on it." She turned and hurried off down the hall.

Laird held out his arms, "Janice?"

She'd been waiting for this moment for three years and now she wasn't sure what to do. Still carrying her suitcase, she walked slowly toward him feeling she was in a slow-motion film sequence. It was the same old Laird, surely, yet when she stopped and looked into his eyes, he seemed somehow unfamiliar.

He reached out, took her suitcase and set it carefully down on the floor beside her. "Janice?" he repeated.

"I'm so glad you're home, Laird."

Never taking his eyes from her face, Laird reached out and tentatively pulled her toward him. She put her arms around his neck, and laid her head against his shoulder as the dear familiar scent of him, the comfort of being held in his arms, all came flooding back. "I swore I wouldn't cry and here I am crying," she finally managed to say as she pulled a hanky from her pocket and tried to smile.

He took her handkerchief, and, as he tipped her chin up and carefully wiped her eyes, she couldn't see that his own eyes were wet. He kissed her gently on the lips, and still holding her handkerchief, wrapped his arms tightly around her. As Janice returned his embrace, she was flooded with the old feeling of being treasured and protected.

"I've missed you so much, Laird," she started to sob again and groped blindly for the handkerchief Laird was still holding in his hand.

"Here it is." He drew back and stood watching her with an expression on his face that Janice was unable to decipher, "Are you ready to go?" he asked.

Janice nodded, "My suitcase is all packed, but we should say goodbye to Mrs. Johnson."

They found Mrs. Johnson tactfully bustling about in her kitchen. "Here's a fresh batch of brownies for you to take home to the family, and you can bring the plate back next week, Jan." She reached out to shake Laird's hand again. "We're all so happy when you boys come home safe and sound."

"Thank you, Mrs. Johnson, I'm pretty happy myself."

She beamed up at him, glad to see a smile in his eyes at last. When she'd opened the door earlier, his face had been almost expressionless, looking, if anything, downright grim, and she'd felt a flash of uneasiness, but now there was a smile in his eyes and Mrs. Johnson caught a glimpse of what Janice must see in the boy.

Chapter Six

They stopped to eat at a little drive-in restaurant that Laird had noticed on his way into town. "Is a drive-in okay, Jan? Or do you want to go to a regular restaurant?"

"A drive-in is just fine. I've always liked drive-ins."

A jaunty teenage girl came up to the car window to take their order of hamburgers and chocolate malts. After the waitress left, Laird reached over and stroked Jan's hand for a moment before he shifted in his seat, leaned back against the car door and said, "I see we both still like chocolate malts."

Jan nodded and said, "Pretty hard not to like chocolate malts." They were both silent for a moment, smiling into each other's eyes, "Where do we begin?" Jan asked. "So much has happened to us in these past three years…there's so much to catch up on…letters just can't tell it all, can they?"

He thought she seemed different somehow, maybe a little more reserved, but that wasn't surprising. They had three missing years to catch up on.

"I missed the sound of your voice, Jan." He leaned over to touch her cheek. "Sometimes I thought I'd forgotten the sound of your voice, but here you are and you sound just the same."

"I've tried to imagine what you were doing and what you were going through during the war. You were so far away, it was like you'd dropped off the edge of the earth… we're all so glad you're alive, Laird."

He took both her hands in his and said, "It wasn't all bad; some of it was just boring, especially after the war was over, and it seemed like forever before I chalked up enough points to come home. Your letters were the best part. If it hadn't been for those letters from home, we'd all have gone nuts. Every so often a huge batch of mail would catch up with me…

some guys didn't get much mail so I'd read some of my letters to them."

Janice blinked in surprise and raised her eyebrows disapprovingly at him. "You read my letters to them?"

"Oh, I didn't read anything personal, just, you know, ordinary stuff from your sister, Carla, and from my mother…Sunday was Mother's regular letter writing day and my brothers used to add funny little notes to Mother's letters. My good buddies Virgil and Don used to write sometimes. I could tell Don felt guilty about being deferred to stay home on the farm to raise food for the war effort."

The jaunty waitress appeared again at the car window, fastened the tray loaded with food to the car door and handed Laird the bill. Laird took out his wallet and put some money on the tray. "You can keep the change," he said.

"Thanks. Just blink your lights when you're done," she winked at him and walked away, humming to herself.

Laird passed a hamburger over to Jan before he carefully unwrapped his own. "I've missed these wonderful Dakota hamburgers." They took the first bites in silence.

"These are good," Jan said.

"Yup, we didn't have anything like this in the Army." Laird reached for one of the chocolate malts, handed it to her and said, "Better have some before it melts." He grinned as he watched her try to suck the thick ice cream up through the straw."

"It's still too thick," she said and handed it back to him.

"Have I ever told you how much your letters meant to me? Letters from home were like gifts from heaven."

She laughed, "Yes, Laird, you just told me! And you told me in practically every other letter you wrote… it must have been lonely so far from home."

"It was that." He smiled into her eyes. "The guys loved Carla's letters. Do you know how chatty Carla is when she writes? She could make us laugh, and we needed a laugh."

"She loves you, you know," Janice said. "You're the big brother she never had." Janice felt a sudden rush of affection for Laird's constant, solid presence in her life, and profound gratitude that he was safely home. Her eyes sparkled, "And I love you, too. You're the wonderful big brother I never had."

Laird finished his hamburger and handed her the still frosty malt. His eyes were intense as he said, "I hope I'm more than a big brother to you."

She knew he was asking her a question, a question she didn't know how to answer. She looked away and began to sip through her straw, trying to block an image suddenly surfacing in her mind of Dr. Blakesly's face, with his magnetic eyes and his wry smile. Janice gave Laird a quick sideways glance and said, "I guess there are many kinds of love."

Laird nodded, turned away from her, and tried to concentrate on drinking his own malt, telling himself there'd be plenty of time to talk on the drive home. Although he'd consulted with the company chaplain about how to handle this first meeting, things were not going the way he'd envisioned…getting re-acquainted was turning out to be more awkward than he'd anticipated. He was beginning to realize that the best advice the chaplain had given him was that nothing ever turns out exactly the way you think it will and, the chaplain had added for emphasis, "Nothing."

Laird and Jan were quiet when they pulled out of the parking lot onto the main highway. As the car picked up speed, and as warm air rushed through the open windows and tousled their hair, they smiled hopefully at one another. By tomorrow, Laird thought, they'd be back on familiar ground and all this uneasiness would be over.

Suddenly, Janice knew this was going to be one of the hardest days of her life. She studied the road unwinding in front of them and folded her hands tightly in her lap. "Are you still planning to start college this fall, Laird?"

"Yes, but I don't know where or how to start the process so I thought I'd call Mr. Seglie over at the high school next week and see if he can help me figure out how to get started." He looked over at Janice, "Do you know where you'll be working after you graduate?"

"I have two job offers, one in Minneapolis at St. Mary's and one in Breton with Dr. Holliday." She chewed thoughtfully on her lower lip. "And you'll probably be going to the state college in Sioux Falls, so our schedules don't match up very well, do they?"

"We can always adjust our schedules," Laird said. "If we get married in the fall, you could maybe find a job wherever I go to school, and I'll try to get into the University of Minnesota so we can live close to St.

Mary's if that's where you want to work. Married vets get an extra stipend from the government so we could make it financially, even if you didn't want to work."

"Oh, I definitely want to work." Janice looked out the side window at the lush green farmland. It had rained hard during the past week, and she found it somehow comforting to see standing water in all the ditches in spite of the fact mosquitoes were probably busily breeding in them at that very moment. She closed her eyes, shook her head and said, "I don't know, Laird. I just don't know."

Neither one of them spoke for the next few miles. The road was empty of other cars, and it stretched ahead into the distance like a vast, grey conveyor belt. The only sounds were that of the engine and the rush of warm air on their faces.

Finally Laird asked, "Do you still want to marry me, Jan?"

Jan's voice had a desperate edge to it. "I don't know, Laird, I really don't know. We were just kids three years ago, I didn't think this far ahead." She turned and looked pleadingly at him. She knew her indecision was rooted in much more than the fact they'd been so young when they became engaged, but how could she tell him about Dr. Blakesly? She wasn't sure herself exactly how she felt about Lawrence Blakesly.

Laird kept his eyes focused straight ahead until he came to a wide spot in the road where he pulled over, turned off the key and ran one hand through his thick black hair. His eyes were dark as he turned to face her, "Look, Jan. I know there's a lot to think about, I know we need to get reacquainted, and I know we're not kids anymore." He stopped, uncomfortably aware of the pleading quality in his voice. A Nordstrom never asked for help and under no circumstances would a Nordstrom ever beg.

Janice's voice was almost a whisper, "It's not that, Laird. It's just that I'm not sure I'm ready to get married."

Laird reached over, picked up her left hand and slowly turned the diamond ring on her finger back and forth so that it sparkled brilliantly in the sunlight streaming through the windshield. "If you don't want to marry me, why are you still wearing my ring?" He looked into her eyes, his face an expressionless mask.

She looked unsteadily back at him, and her voice was almost a whisper, "Because I made you a promise."

He looked as if she'd hit him. He abruptly dropped her hand and clenched his jaw. "Then I guess that's it."

"No, Laird, I don't mean that we have to stop seeing each other, I just think we need time. I've loved you ever since we were kids, but I don't know if it's a marrying kind of love. Right now I feel like it's more of a friendship kind of love, or like I'd love a brother."

He leaned forward to turn on the key and pulled out into the roadway, still driving into the sun. "Will you get me those dark glasses in the glove compartment?" Silently, she handed them over to him.

"Thanks."

Pain and weariness surged through him. It was the same feeling he'd had sometimes when he'd come off the battle-line, dog-tired and weary to the bone. Lots of guys, even married men, had gotten *Dear John* letters during the war; some guys had read them while they were knee deep in blood and mud. At least Jan waited until he got home. He'd noticed a year or so ago her letters seemed different, not so teasing, a little more reserved. They were always affectionate, always ended with hugs and kisses or I love you. Laird supposed she hadn't been lying about the hugs and kisses or the love…she loved him all right, like a brother.

He finally asked, "How should we tell the family? Martha can't wait to get her new flower-girl dress sewn in time for the wedding."

Jan tightened her lips and frowned, "I know." How had this happened so quickly? She'd thought they'd have more time to gradually think it through and maybe come to some mutually friendly decision. She certainly hadn't planned to talk about this today, somehow it had just popped out. She fought against the small waves of nausea beginning to undulate through her stomach and the faint gagging reflex forming in the back of her throat.

They drove in silence for nearly an hour until they stopped in Fergus Falls to fill up with gasoline. In the men's restroom, Laird stood looking blankly at himself in the dirty mirror. He wanted to smash it…it was all he could do to keep from punching the mirror into shards of glass. He instead pounded his fist into his open left hand, and slammed the door on his way out hard enough to startle the old black Labrador dozing in the sun by the propane tanks.

Back in the car there was more silence. Janice felt a little better once she'd managed to vomit into the toilet bowl of the women's rest room.

On the edge of town, they passed a city park adjacent to a football field. Laird stopped the car, parked it under a maple tree, opened the door, got out and tossed the keys to Janice. "I'm going to take a few laps around the field."

Janice left the car, too, and walked slowly over to sit down at one of the picnic tables under the cottonwood trees. She watched Laird walk around the track as fast as he could manage with his bad leg and was stunned to see him limping. "Oh God," she thought, "how could I forget that Laird, the best athlete in the whole school, can't run anymore?" She laid her head down on her arms and cursed herself…she should have waited and given it more time, she shouldn't have blurted out how unsure she was, not on their very first day together. But if she hadn't told him how she felt, they'd have been right back at the golf course and he would expect more necking, which she wasn't ready to do, and now there was the added complication of what Lawrence had told her last night…although it was pretty far-fetched to believe that Lawrence loved her when she'd never even had a date with him.

She lifted her head and pressed her lips together… no, it wouldn't have been fair to Laird or herself not to be honest about her doubts. Janice realized she wasn't telling Laird everything, but there was no way she was going to tell him about Dr. Blakesly; she didn't even understand that relationship herself. She took off the ring and noticed that although her hand looked barren without it, somehow it seemed lighter, freer. She felt a deep stab of pain in her chest, and, as tears ran down her face, she watched Laird begin a second lap around the field.

By the time Laird returned to the car, her tears had dried and her face was composed. She was seated in the passenger seat when he got into the car and before he could start the engine, Janice held the ring out to him and said, "Here's your ring, Laird."

Laird shook his head and refused to look at her. "I've got no use for it."

"But I can't keep it, it's not mine."

He started the car and shifted into gear. "Deal with it." His voice was hard, "You can give it to the Salvation Army."

Aware of a hot surge of irritation, Janice carefully put the ring in her purse…didn't he realize this was hard for her, too? "Okay," she said, trying hard to keep her voice level, "but you don't have to be so hardheaded about it. You certainly don't believe I intend to keep it, do you?"

Laird stepped down on the gas pedal as the car accelerated out onto the highway. "I don't care what you do with the god-damned ring," he answered through clenched jaws.

Janice was stunned. Laird had never talked to her this way before; she'd never even heard him swear before. This wasn't the Laird she remembered. For an instant he seemed like an angry stranger. Her damned up emotions burst out of control and she began to sob. She couldn't seem to stop crying; between bouts of sobbing, and taking in short gasps of air in order to cry some more, she managed to blurt out, "Can't you respect the fact that I'm at least being honest?...Would you rather have me pretend to feel something I can't?"...

Laird maintained a stony silence as he drove on, looking only at the road.

Finally, between sobs, she asked, "...What shall we tell the family?"

Curtly, he answered, "Tell them the truth, that you changed your mind and don't want to marry me."

"But...it sounds so harsh to say it that way."

"Maybe so, but it's the truth."

They drove on in stormy silence, both of them looking straight ahead. As they sped by a series of Burma Shave signs, both Janice and Laird read the words silently to themselves, *Don't / try passing / on a slope / unless you have /a periscope /Burma Shave.* Those signs had been so much fun when they were kids, but there was no humor in anything now.

Janice stifled a sob and blew her nose. "We can tell them we've changed in three years, that we're different people now, and we need time to think things over and get reacquainted...they'll understand that marriage is too important to rush into."

"Tell them anything you want," his voice still held an edge of anger.

Janice gave a shaky sigh. "I suppose we don't have to say anything until someone asks, but Martha and Carla are sure to ask about the wedding date." She looked down at her left hand. "And someone is bound to notice I'm not wearing your ring."

"It's not my ring, I don't want it...look Jan, part of me understands your feelings, but mostly I'm so pissed that you strung me along all this time. Wouldn't it have been better for both of us if you'd written and told me earlier?"

Jan's voice was indignant, "But I didn't really know how I felt. How could I write a letter like that before I had a chance to look into your eyes…to see you in person…and actually talk with you about it?"

Laird sighed and hit the steering wheel with his open hand. "I wish to God we hadn't promised to have supper with the families tonight. You want me to tell everybody it's okay, that we're just waiting before we get re-acquainted again, but that's not true and you know it. You say whatever you want and I'll try to be gracious, but I'm still the same old Laird who is no damned good at pretending."

✳ ✳ ✳

They needn't have worried about how and when to tell their families. The minute they walked through the door, Laird's closed countenance, reinforced by Jan's still puffy eyes, forced smile, and missing ring, told the adults the wedding was off. Even Martha eventually realized the topic was off-limits after she was sternly shushed by Little Grandma when she tried to tell Laird's parents about the flower-girl dress she was planning to wear to the wedding.

Chapter Seven

The next morning Carla opened her eyes to the sounds of robins. Ever since she and Jan were kids, they'd looked forward to the robins coming back in the spring, loving the idea that you could make a wish on your first robin sighting if you licked your thumb and stamped it against the palm of your other hand. She'd seen her first robin back in April, and she'd made a wish that Laird would soon be home. In hindsight, she should have wished that once he was home, Jan would still want to marry him. She rolled over to see if Jan was awake yet, but Jan was still sound asleep. Carla turned over on her back and noticed she didn't feel well, almost like she was recovering from the flu. She closed her eyes and sighed, knowing it was the stress of the break-up causing her malaise, and that there was nothing physically wrong with her.

Before they went to sleep last night, she'd tried talking to Jan about Laird. All their lives they'd talked together in the dark about so many things. They'd made up stories about Little Orphan Annie; they'd wondered who was right about God: was Daddy right that there wasn't a God, or was Big Grandma right that there was, and would Mother ever convince either one of them they should stop arguing about it; and why did Little Grandma keep reading those *True Confession* magazines when they made her rock back and forth faster and faster in the old rocking chair and cry while she muttered darkly about those god-damn men. They'd talked about what would happen to you when you died, and were there really ghosts, and how could Amanda Leppert's family afford to buy her all those beautiful pleated skirts and cashmere sweaters. She and Jan had talked about how pleased their science teacher was when Laird brought a piece of coal from his dad's blacksmith shop with a fossilized lizard embedded in it, and they'd tried to guess how many fossils must get burned up every winter in people's furnaces. The night the tornado had destroyed the Robsons' farm, knocked it right down into kindling wood and killed Mr. Robson because he didn't make it into the storm-cellar in time, they didn't talk much except to discuss whether it was true, what Daddy said about the tornado sticking a straw right into a tree.

Then there'd been the night Carla had been so angry at Mama for lying to her. Martha was born on Carla's birthday and when in all the excitement, no one remembered to buy Carla a birthday present, Mama said Carla shouldn't feel bad about not getting a present because, after all, Martha was the best birthday present ever. In bed that night, Carla protested it wasn't fair that just when Martha was getting to the really fun stage of walking and talking, Mama had gone back on her word and said, "You don't own Martha. You have to stop bossing her around!"

Janice had turned over in bed to look at her. "Well, Mama's right, Carla. You don't own Martha, nobody can own another person."

Carla had stuck out her lower lip defiantly, "But she's mine. She was my birthday present!"

Jan had tried one more time. "Be reasonable, Carla, that was just a manner of speaking. Mama meant that having a new little sister was as good as any old birthday present."

In recent years, after Jan had gone off to college, there'd been fewer night time discussions, but when Jan did come home, their talks were as interesting as ever. One night Carla and Jan lay awake for hours discussing Jan's psychology professor who had insulted his entire class by telling his student nurses that they were too young to know what love was, and that it came in assorted flavors. "Really!" Jan had told Carla indignantly, "As though you have to be sixty years old to figure out there are different kinds of love!"

Yes, there had been lots of good discussions in this old bedroom. Carla sat up, put her feet on the floor and looked over at her sister, still asleep in the other bed. She sat quietly, watching Jan's even breathing, and thought about the events of last night. There hadn't been much conversation at all after she and Janice had gone to bed. The big celebration supper had turned out to be more like a funeral, and even though Daddy and Mama had tried to keep the conversation going, anyone could see that every person there, with maybe the exception of Martha, was miserable. The Nordstroms hardly said anything, and everybody sighed in relief when they finally went home; probably no one was happier than Laird and his family to escape.

Afterwards, while the women were quietly doing the dishes, Janice had said, "I just can't marry him. He's like a brother to me. I love him, but I don't want to marry him." She'd grabbed a wet plate from the dish drainer and wiped it furiously. "I feel terrible about it."

Dora had looked at her eldest daughter with compassion in her eyes and said, "Of course, you must do what you think is best, Jan,"

Janice threw down her dishtowel and ran from the room, and as they'd listened to her footsteps going swiftly up the staircase, the women looked at each other and breathed a collective sigh.

"Oh my," Dora said quietly, "this is going to be hard."

Martha asked, "But why aren't they going to get married?"

All the women shook their heads and were silent.

"But why not?" Martha persisted, "They've waited so long."

"Well," Dora said, as she continued washing the dishes, "that's probably part of the problem. They had to wait too long." Her hands still in the soapy water, she turned to look at Martha, "People change as the years go by, and maybe after a while they feel like different people. Remember three years ago when you were in the first grade? Do you still feel like you're the same person now that you're almost a fourth grader?"

"Well, no, of course not, but why didn't they say something earlier? We were all so happy for them."

"Maybe they didn't know 'til today," Little Grandma said. She started to cry and grabbed her apron to wipe her eyes. "Oh, I'm just no damn good. I'm just a damn cry baby."

Carla reached out and touched her grandmother's hand, "It's okay, Little Grandma, go ahead and cry, this time I think we all feel like crying."

By the time Carla had gone upstairs, the bedroom was dark and Jan was in bed. Carla undressed quietly, got into bed and lay there awhile before she whispered, "Jan?"

Jan's back had been turned and her voice was muffled, "I don't want to talk, Carla. I just want to try to go to sleep."

Carla wished there was something comforting she could tell her sister, but all she could finally think of to say was, "Goodnight then, Jan."

"Goodnight."

"I love you, Jan."

As Carla turned over, she'd heard Jan start to cry. She could tell Jan's face was pressed tight against her pillow as she tried to stifle her sobs, and Carla felt her own eyes spill over with tears. Eventually the room was quiet, and, for a long time, they both lay awake in the dark, listening to the sounds of crickets drifting in with the warm night air through the open window.

By Tuesday, everyone knew that Laird and Janice had broken their engagement. "Never mind the gossip," Carla told Jan. "At least you won't have to explain to every person you meet why you're not wearing the ring anymore."

"I suppose you're right, but the worst thing about living in a small town is that everybody thinks they have a right to know everybody else's business."

"I guess it's not like that in Minneapolis?"

"No, Minneapolis is too big, but the hospital is like a small town, a real gossip mill." Janice gave Carla a forced smile. "As soon as I tell one person what happened between Laird and me, the next day everybody, including the janitors, will get some version of the story."

The two sisters were walking along one of Breton's tree-lined streets, heading in the general direction of Main Street, going nowhere in particular. When they came to an intersection and saw the Nordstrom house on the next block, Janice hesitated, then made an abrupt turn to the right and said, "Let's go over a block."

Carla nodded and followed along without commenting on why Jan had changed course, but she hoped Jan wouldn't try to avoid Laird forever. After all, how could they expect to stay friends if they never saw one another?

"Jan? I've been thinking that maybe we could ask Mrs. Holliday to go birding with us in the morning. We haven't gone out birding with her for a long time."

"Sure. I'd love to do that."

"Do you think we could ask Laird to come along? He's still like our big brother, right?"

Janice didn't answer. As they passed the Ewing house, they encountered three small girls playing hopscotch on the sidewalk. Janice walked around the kids to the left and Carla went to the right. "Bread and Butter," Carla said and smiled at the kids who smiled back; Janice didn't feel like smiling at anyone. The children had triggered the grim thought in her mind that problems are a lot smaller when you're seven or eight.

"No, Carla," she finally said. "I absolutely do not want to see Laird. I'm so ashamed at having hurt him I can't look him in the face, and I doubt he wants to look at me either. I've ruined his homecoming. This was supposed to be such a happy time and I've ruined it for everybody." She turned and looked beseechingly at Carla, "I do love him, he's like my brother, but I don't want to marry him. I think I realized that as soon as I saw him again. It was a mistake to promise him, but he was going off to war and how could I possibly have said no?"

Carla reached out, put her arm around her sister's waist and gave her a squeeze. "Of course you couldn't."

She thought of the silver candlesticks tucked away in the corner of her underwear drawer and the image of their shining surfaces flashed through her mind. Well, there was no help for it…the candleholders would just have to stay hidden away.

Janice gave her a grateful smile, "I'm going to take the bus back to the Cities day after tomorrow. If you want, we can still go birding with Mrs. Holliday tomorrow morning, but after that I want to get away from here until the gossip dies down. I'll write Laird a letter later and try to explain."

She stopped and faced her sister. "Carla, will you check on him sometimes? And if the subject comes up, will you tell him how bad I feel and that I do care for him so much? Tell him my whole body aches from the sadness of it."

Chapter Eight

Laird woke early that morning to a quiet house, looked at his watch and realized he was probably still functioning in an earlier time zone. He stared up at the ceiling thinking about the night before. No wonder his head hurt and his stomach felt queasy. After the miserable evening with the two families last night, he'd walked down to the Hide-Away-Bar with the intention of getting good and drunk. He'd have preferred to buy a pint of whiskey and drink himself into oblivion under the stars at the football field, but the liquor store had closed at five o'clock.

He pulled the sheet up over his face and groaned, "Oh, God…what kind of an example am I setting for my kid brothers?" He vaguely remembered police chief Oscar Olson coming into the bar, talking with him, getting him to drink some coffee, and, finally, walking him back home. Laird yanked at the sheet that was twisted around him, trying not to think about the fact that Oscar had to sober him up some before he would let him go home.

Those damned recurring dreams had been especially bad last night, dreams in which Laird was in some kind of a workshop, with piles of body parts stacked on the floor around him, knowing with a terrible certainty that he was to blame for these dismembered human beings, and feeling a sickening guilt for having been the cause of all the butchery. He couldn't understand why he had done such a terrible thing, and he knew it was somehow up to him to make them whole again. The long table in front of him was like an operating table, but it wasn't white like an operating table should be, it was red, and thick with blood, so much blood that it dripped down and filled his shoes…and there was the stink of trying to stuff the mound of intestines back into the body lying on the table…it was impossible to fasten on both arms at the same time, they were so difficult to attach, you had to insert them just right and give them a little twist, like putting the arm back on one of those little rubber dolls the girls used to play with, and the intestines kept coming back up and out, no matter how hard he tried to push them back inside.

Laird threw the sheet off and sat up, swung his legs over the edge of the bed and stared at the long scar that ran down the outside of his right knee. He stood up and gingerly tested the bad knee, grateful that at least he didn't have to use a cane anymore. He was lucky; the first time he'd been hit the shrapnel hadn't hit anything crucial, and the second time the bullet got only part of his knee. It was a lot better than getting hit in the gut or the head.

After the second time Laird was wounded, the doctor had said, "You're young and healthy. The knee will heal somewhat, and it might even improve over time, but you'll probably have to learn to live with some reduced function." He'd studied Laird's chart and scratched his head with the stub end of his pencil. "You can't go back to the front lines with that leg, but you're not bad enough off to go home. Do you know how to type?"

Laird had kept his expression matter-of-fact in spite of his heart beginning to pound with excitement at hearing the good news. Knowing he wouldn't have to go back to the front triggered a flash of guilt because the guys out there probably needed him, but what the hell, most of the buddies he'd known from the old unit were either wounded or dead, and he was beginning to think that after so many battles and two wounds, his own luck was about to run out.

Laird had nodded to the doctor, "Yes, I can type," and silently thanked his high school typing teacher for working his butt off in typing class.

"Okay, that's it then. I'll send in a recommendation that you be assigned to some kind of office job."

Laird had been temporarily attached to his old company headquarters, but as soon as Germany surrendered, he was reassigned to the Command Headquarters in Frankfurt where he typed up decoded messages that came in for the big brass upstairs. It was almost like an eight-to-five job except they kept changing work shifts. You no sooner got used to being on swing shift then you got day shift, then they'd switch you to night shift. It didn't make sense to keep the staff groggy most of the time, but what else was new? There was a right way, the wrong way, and there was the Army Way, and at least it was better than being in the field with no sleep at all. He'd vowed that once he got out of the army, he'd never complain about anything ever again. Anything was better than army life.

Laird made up his bed carefully and tried not to think of Janice. The house was still quiet, even though his mother and father usually got up early, which made him wonder if they were sleeping late because he'd waked everyone up when he came home drunk last night. He wouldn't be surprised if Mother hadn't gone to sleep at all until she'd heard him come home. He shaved and dressed slowly. He couldn't seem to move any faster; his limbs were heavy and there was a lump of iron in his belly. It reminded him of an article he'd read in the *National Geographic* about the tremendous gravity on Jupiter. That was how he felt: crushed by gravity.

He went quietly down the stairs and out the front door where the sky was growing lighter in the east, and the birds were beginning their morning ritual of defending territory and advertising for mates. Jan had divulged the secret of birdsongs to him the very day she'd learned about it from Mrs. Holliday. "Can you imagine?" she'd written, "I always thought birds sang because they're happy, but, no! Only the males sing, and they're singing as loud as they can to scare off the other males and attract females to come build a nest with them!"

He walked slowly, partly because he was weighted down with the events of yesterday, partly because he felt a little hung-over, and partly because he'd wrenched his knee slightly while walking too fast around that damn field on the way home from Minneapolis, all the while uncomfortably aware that Jan was sitting at the picnic table watching him limp around the track and crying her eyes out. Oh, God, why hadn't she at least hinted to him earlier about her doubts? The chaplain in Germany had given good advice: nothing ever turns out exactly like you think it will.

When Laird returned from his walk around town, the family was dressed and sitting at the kitchen table, the boys drinking cocoa, his dad having coffee, and his mother frying bacon at the kitchen stove. She turned and gave Laird a wan smile when he came into the room.

"Sit down, son, and I'll get you a cup of coffee."

"Thanks, Mother, but I think I'll just have some water."

The Nordstrom men gave Laird a quick glance and mumbled," Hi," "Morning, Laird," then looked down again into their plates.

Laird sat down and sighed. As much as he hated to talk about it, he'd have to face it. "Look, everybody, I guess you know Jan and I broke up yesterday. It was Jan's idea and maybe she's right, maybe we're not ready to get married. She's right that we were just kids when we got engaged."

Johnny was the first to speak and his voice was indignant, "But she promised!"

"Yes, and she kept her promise to wait until I got back, but after three years, things change…she's a different person now…so am I."

Duane sat up straighter and stirred another spoonful of sugar into his cocoa. "Maybe after you get reacquainted you'll both feel more like your old selves."

"Maybe…"

Emil looked at Laird and said, "Can you come down to the shop today and help out? I've got more orders than I can handle today. I've got an extra set of coveralls that should fit you fine."

* * *

That was how Laird came to spend the first day of his new life without Janice: in his father's blacksmith shop down by the railroad tracks, shoveling coal, pumping the bellows, and hammering out white hot metal. He threw himself into the hard physical work like a drowning man lunging for a lifesaving rope. He liked the feeling of sweat trickling down his face and back, and he was grateful to have nothing to think about except the noisy, hot work of the forge. He had to reheat and hammer out some of the pieces twice after Emil inspected his work and quietly told him, "Sorry, son. You'll have to redo that one."

At the end of the day, Laird laid down his tools and watched his father begin the routine chores of closing up shop. Laird's shirt was soaking wet under his armpits and down his back, his thick hair hung damp on his forehead, and he was aware of being curiously pleased with the smell of his own sweat. He wiped his face and hands on one of the big, red, cotton handkerchiefs his mother always provided for shop use before he walked over to his father and held out his hand. "Thank you, Dad. I guess you knew hard work was just what I needed."

Emil took Laird's still-sweating hand in his own calloused one and looked into his eyes. "Yah, a man is lucky who has honest work to do." He reached out his other hand and clasped Laird's shoulder. "You've been through all kinds of hell, son, but you're going to be okay."

The next day, after news got around that Laird was working at the blacksmith shop, people started stopping by to welcome him home. His fourth-grade teacher came by with a plate of cookies and a hug; his mother's best friend brought him and Emil an apple pie; Laird's brothers and their friends stopped to watch him work, as fascinated as Laird used to be as a kid watching the sparks fly when the hot metal was hammered against the anvil, awed by the intensity of the blue-white acetylene flame. Late in the day, Laird's old girlfriend, Diane, stopped by.

He was surprised to see her. Diane must surely resent the fact that he was alive, and Conrad wasn't. She stood in the middle of the wide blacksmith door. The sun behind her highlighted her bright red hair and hid her face, but when she stepped inside, out of the sun's glare, there was no mistaking that her eyes were warm and welcoming. "I just stopped by to tell you how glad I am that you're safely home, Laird."

He stopped sharpening a blade on the whet-stone and walked towards her. She was still the same tall, beautiful redhead he'd known in high school, except the old mischievous sparkle had disappeared. "I'm too dirty to shake your hand, Diane, but thank you for stopping by." Laird hesitated before he added, "I want to tell you again how sorry I am about Conrad."

"Thank you for the letter you wrote after Conrad was killed. His mother and dad really appreciated it, too. Your letter made us realize that you must have gotten to know him really well because of all the football games you played against each other."

"It's true, you get to know a person when you play against him. Conrad always played by the rules, and he never held a grudge. I always liked playing against him, even when his team won."

"He was special, wasn't he, Laird?"

"He was indeed."

Diane impulsively reached up and gave Laird a quick hug despite his protests that he was too dirty to touch. "Nonsense, Laird, what's a little dirt when someone comes home safe from the war." She smiled up at him and, with a little wave, turned to go. "Come by the pool some night for the adult swim. It would probably be good exercise for your leg. I'm working at the pool just during morning and evening hours. I never could handle full sunlight on this darned light skin of mine. I have to leave the afternoon lifeguarding to Milton."

❋ ❋ ❋

The next day, Laird looked up from the forge to see his old friend, Virgil Nelson, standing there grinning at him. Laird reached into his back pocket for a sweat-stained handkerchief, wiped his forehead to keep the sweat from rolling into his eyes and wiped some of the grime off his hands before he extended one to grasp Virgil's outstretched hand.

"Hi, Laird, I stopped by the house and your mother said you were down here helping out at the shop."

"It's good to see you, my friend. How long has it been?"

"Pretty near three years." Virgil's eyes were dark with pleasure and his mouth widened in a warm smile.

"So," Laird grinned back at him, "Here we are, home again."

"Hard to believe, isn't it?" Virgil took his cap off, smoothed his hair and put the cap back on again.

"Sometimes," Laird said. "Sometimes it sure is hard to believe."

"Have you done any fishing since you've come home? The walleye are biting up at Clear Lake. Want to come?"

"I'd love to taste some fresh walleye again. When are you planning on going?"

Virgil's face creased in deep smile lines. "How about tomorrow morning? I've been holed up in my uncle Ralph's cabin at the lake for a week. You remember where the cabin is, don't you? You could come up tonight or in the morning early."

Laird wiped his forehead and the back of his neck. "I'll have to see if Dad or Mother can get along without the car tonight and tomorrow. Do you have a phone up there so I could contact you?"

"Yup, they got one installed a few years ago; I think the cabin is in the phone book, or you can just ask one of the operators. Those ladies still know everything that goes on in this town."

※ ※ ※

That evening Laird drove up to the lake, and as he pulled up alongside the dingy white clapboard cabin sitting close to the edge of the water, he turned off the engine and breathed in the thick humidity of the lake air. Swatting at the mosquitoes buzzing his face, he got out of the car, and, as he walked around in front of the screened porch that faced the lake, he caught a welcome whiff of wood-smoke and saw Virgil building a bonfire on the small beach between the cabin and the water.

Virgil looked up and waved. "I thought I'd better build us a smudge to keep the damned mosquitoes at bay. Glad you could make it, Laird."

"Need any help?"

Virgil gestured towards the back of the house. "You can bring some more wood for the fire, there's a stack of it over by the outhouse."

"That was one of the few good things about Italy and Germany," Laird said over his shoulder as he went behind the house to the woodpile. "Not as many mosquitoes."

Once the fire was dependably burning, Virgil walked to the edge of the lake and pulled out two bottles of Pabst Blue Ribbon. "How about a beer?"

"Never been known to turn down a cold beer." Laird grinned, squatted at the edge of the downwind smoke, and returned Virgil's silent toast as they both took a first satisfying mouthful of cold beer.

Virgil leaned forward to stir the fire with a stick. "I guess you heard about Carl Anderson? How he died on a prison ship headed for Japan?"

Laird stared into the fire. "Pretty ironic he'd die on a ship right after he'd survived the Bataan Death March."

Virgil nodded. "My mother sent me the article from the Breton paper. It said Carl was a medic." The fire popped and sparks flew into the night air.

"Those medics were amazing guys. I've seen them charge right into the middle of a firefight to get the wounded. They're supposed to be protected by those red crosses they wear, but I don't think the other side paid much attention to the crosses." Laird took a long sip of beer and said, "The medics hauled my ass back safe a couple of times."

Virgil studied Laird's face. "You had it a lot rougher than I did."

"I don't know about that, Virgil. Aren't you the guy who survived a torpedoed ship?"

"Well, that was rough all right, but after that first ship sank, I was assigned to a milk-run supply ship for the rest of the war. I think you had it harder."

"Maybe, I don't know." Laird got up and went over to pull another bottle of beer from the lake, "All I know is that we're both alive, and Carl's dead, and Conrad Oberst is dead, and there's six more guys from our little town who didn't make it home."

Laird threw a rock into the fire and looked across at Virgil's face highlighted in the flickering light, "We're a couple of lucky sons of bitches, aren't we?"

Virgil nodded solemnly and took a swallow of beer, "Yup, a couple of lucky sons of bitches." They sat quietly, looking into the fire and listening to the haunting sounds of a loon calling from across the lake.

Virgil broke the silence. "You know how I managed to get into the Navy instead of the Army, don't you?"

Laird shook his head, "No idea."

"My eighteenth birthday was in July so I rushed right down as soon as we graduated in May and volunteered for the Navy. Otherwise I knew they'd draft me into the Army the minute I turned eighteen." Virgil threw a bottle cap into the fire. "You guys with spring birthdays got stuck with the draft and no choice except the infantry."

Laird looked at Virgil and smiled, "You feeling guilty?"

Virgil glanced at Laird before looking away, "I guess so."

"Well, stop it." Laird gave him a friendly punch on the shoulder and said, "It was all the luck of the draw."

Virgil stirred the fire again. "What were the Germans like, Laird.? Did you ever get to know any of them? After the war, I mean."

"No, I didn't meet many Germans…there were the women who washed my clothes every week and they were honest, they never stole my clothes, always brought them back clean and pressed. Except for the fact we couldn't understand each other, they reminded me a lot of the ladies here in Breton. I once saw two women fight out in the street over who could pick up the manure from a horse who'd just passed by. They both needed manure for their gardens."

"Imagine that," said Virgil, "and here we are in South Dakota, loaded to the gills with manure! Too bad we can't ship them some."

"We had to keep a sharp look-out for the German kids or they'd steal you blind…a kid anywhere in the world will steal when he's hungry." Laird thought for a moment. "One time the paratroopers put on a parade and lots of German people came to watch. I was surprised they came at all, and surprised they stood there so quietly. There was never any kind of an insurgency, nobody ever took shots at us. I guess they were as tired of war as we were."

Virgil jumped to his feet. "God, I'm glad the war is over," he said. "I've got hot dogs in the cabin, let's roast 'em on a stick like when we were kids…you stoke up the fire and I'll get the hot dogs."

Four slightly-blackened hot dogs later, the conversation again returned to Carl Anderson. "Have you seen Carl's family yet? Or any of the other guys' families?" Virgil asked.

"No, I haven't seen any of them except Diane. She came into Dad's shop to say hi…I'm surprised she bothered to come see me… I thought she'd try to avoid me."

"Why would she want to avoid you?"

"Because I'm alive and Conrad isn't," Laird's voice trailed off and he sat staring into the fire. "I've thought about all those guys a lot, and their families. I go by Carl's house every day, but I haven't had the guts to stop in and face his folks."

"Same here," Virgil said. "How about if we go together to see them sometime?"

"Okay, we could do that. We could go together."

Next morning, the mist that had settled over the lake during the night muted the calls of red-winged blackbirds notifying the world that this space was theirs. A light mist still shrouded the surface of the water when Laird and Virgil rowed back to the dock with five big walleye in tow. The fish had been hungry and bit on every lure Laird and Virgil dangled in front of them.

"How many do you want to keep?" Laird asked as they ran the boat up onto the beach. "I could drive down to the Mom and Pop grocery on the old Sisseton Road before I head home, and bring you back some more ice if you need it."

"No, I don't want any of the buggers, go ahead and take them home with you, Laird. I'm going to stay up here at the lake for a few more days, I can always catch more. Will you drop off a couple at my folks' house? And tell them hi for me?"

Laird raised his eyebrows quizzically, "Can't take those big city lights yet?"

"Nope," Virgil shook his head and tried to smile. "Not yet."

❋ ❋ ❋

Back in town the following day, another of Laird's old friends, Don Cramer, showed up at the blacksmith shop, and offered to take him to lunch at Dee's Café.

"By God, Laird, you old delinquent, you're looking good," Don beamed at him.

"Delinquent yourself! And thanks again for working off our sins by painting Mrs. Munweller's house for her."

"That good lady hasn't really forgiven us yet." The corners of Don's eyes crinkled with amusement remembering the night before high school graduation when he and Laird, along with a few other of their high school buddies, had painted the town red. Don and Virgil had been the only two of the painting brigade left behind to face the outrage and make amends. Mrs. Munweller had been especially unforgiving, and still insisted her cows had stopped giving milk after the trauma of having their sides painted "1943."

Don was dressed in loose, pinstriped farmer coveralls, with metal-buckled straps holding things together. He took off his John Deere tractor cap and smoothed his hair back to reveal a horizontal line across his forehead, white above, tanned below. Even this early in the summer the sun was well on the way to burning in the characteristic mark on his forehead that separated farmer from town dweller.

Laird looked at him appraisingly. "You look really good, Don. Farming agrees with you."

Dee's Café looked the same except that the sign out front had been upgraded to modern neon. Once inside, he and Don walked a friendly gauntlet of smiles, handshakes, and waves until they found a booth in the corner of the room.

The waitress, Mavis Scheele, still as skinny and energetic as when Laird had left for the army, came over to the table to take their orders for hamburgers and fries. "I'm so glad to see you again, Laird. Welcome home." Her eyes filled with tears, and she patted him on the shoulder before she turned to walk away.

Don folded his hands in front of him. "I'm sorry to hear about you and Jan breaking up. I guess three years was too long to wait."

"Not for me. But for her it was."

"She's never gone out with anyone else. The whole time you were gone, she never even looked at anybody else. I've got a friend who works at St. Mary's and he says the same thing."

The hamburgers were as good as Laird remembered, and the coffee, too. They ate in companionable silence until their plates were empty and Don settled back to light up a cigarette. "So, what are your plans now, Laird?"

"I guess I'll go to school and see if I'm smart enough to get an engineering degree."

"Oh, you're smart enough, and you might as well get an education so you can get out of here. There's no work in this little town that pays a decent wage except farming and owning a store." He grinned, "I'm not sure farming pays so good either."

Laird smiled and raised his eyebrows at Don, thinking that what Verle had said about the farmers was true. They always denied they made any money even when they were awash in it, but Laird didn't argue because he knew the farmers' fears were rooted in reality. With good reason, no farmer wanted to tempt fate by being overly optimistic. Still, Laird found it amusing that farmers were incurably superstitious about the need to predict dire outcomes, believing that if they got too big for their britches either the corporations or the weather gods would strike them down. Farmers were forever telling each other how the hay crop would probably be ruined by rain the day after it was cut, and when a bumper wheat crop was ready for harvesting with grains hanging heavy on the stalk, they invariably made dark predictions about the likelihood of hailstorms, or worried that the price of grain this year would be low because there was so damned much of it.

Don said, "A lot of people went to the west coast to work during the war and some of them aren't planning to come back home."

"You can't blame them, why would anybody suffer through another Dakota winter when they could have all that California sunshine?"

Don started to sing, "How you going to keep 'em down on the farm, after they've seen Paree?"

Laird couldn't help but smile as he observed how untouched Don seemed by the war years.

"One thing I'm worried about is my math," Laird said. "Or, I should say, my lack of math. I did all right in grade school but when I hit high school, math took a back seat to being one of the guys. God, I don't remember anything about high school math, and I'll need it for engineering school." He shook his head. "I'm going to need a tutor, but I hear Mr. Adams is away for most of the summer with his wife's family in California. Is there anyone else in town who knows enough about math to help me get ready for college?"

Don raised his eyebrows and smiled, "Well, hell, I know a math whiz who just graduated high school and, as far as I know, she'll be around all summer."

"Who?"

"Carla Swanson. Didn't you know? She got a special math award at graduation. In fact, I think she's getting a scholarship because of her math."

"Squirt?"

"Yes, little Squirt, although don't you let her hear you call her that. She's Carla Rae now if you please. She won't even look at you if you call her Squirt."

Laird grinned, remembering his first encounter with Carla. "I guess she did mention the scholarship in one of her letters, but she didn't say anything about being so good at math."

"She's probably just being modest, or maybe she takes it all for granted. She probably just assumes everybody else is as smart as she is." Don flicked off a section of cigarette ash into the glass tray on the table between them. "I asked Jan why Carla wasn't the valedictorian of her class, and Jan said it's because Carla could never get better than a B in physical education."

"Well, that's not fair," Laird bristled. "How could Carla be expected to do physical education as well as the other girls when she's only got the use of one arm?"

"Life isn't fair, old buddy," Don said and took a long drag on his cigarette, "but you probably know that better than I do."

Chapter Nine

The next morning as Laird walked up the worn wooden stairs of Breton High School, heading for his appointment in the principal's office, it was apparent nothing had changed since he'd graduated three years ago. The elementary school was still located on the first floor of the old brick building, with the high school above it on the second story level. Leaving the bright sunshine of the playground, walking into the dim light of the wood-paneled halls and up the broad stairs, felt like coming through a time warp. There was the same smell of oil, dust and chalk permeating the wood floors and paneling, and the same after-school faint echo of teachers' voices wafting up from the lower elementary school level downstairs.

The principal's office was still located at the top of the stairs, and Laird was pleased to see that his old principal, Mr. Seglie, hadn't changed either. He was the same stout bear of a man, with deceptively lazy eyes that Laird knew could flash steel when he was roused; even his familiar striped blue and white tie was the same. Mr. Seglie rose and came around his desk to greet Laird with a warm handshake.

"I've heard you were back in town, Laird. I'm so glad you made it through okay." He paused, "Well, not totally okay, I hear." The lines around his mouth deepened a little.

"I'm fine, Mr. Seglie. I'm lucky it was just a leg wound."

"Well...have you been out to the Gulch to see the new senior class tradition yet?"

"No, I haven't been out there yet, but I've heard plenty about it."

"I called in a few of the boys from the class of '44 and asked if they could come up with something less destabilizing than literally painting the town red. We had to think of something." He chuckled, "George

Johnson came up with the idea of putting stones on the hill above the picnic area, painting the stones white and then putting the year on the stones. The seniors love it, gives them an excuse for another senior party, looks good, too. Every class thinks they have to find bigger rocks than the last class, so it's turned into quite a competition."

John Seglie pulled up one of the oak chairs lining the wall of his office. "Here, take a seat, son." He sat down again in his oak swivel chair behind the desk, placed his hands on the chair's worn arms and watched Laird as he sat down in the chair opposite.

"You were all good kids, Laird…every damned one of you." The two men sat quietly for a moment, looking at one another with somber eyes.

Mr. Seglie leaned back in his chair. "So, what can I do for you, Laird?"

"I came by to see if you can give me some advice about what college I should apply to for an engineering degree and how to go about the application process. All I know right now is that the government will pay most of the bills."

"Sure, I'd be glad to help, best place to begin is the college catalogs." He got up and walked toward the outer office. "We've got eighteen of our seniors heading off for college this year. Eighteen out of thirty two, not bad for a little school, yes? Most of the girls are going into teaching and nursing as usual."

He came back with a stack of college catalogs, sat down and looked at Laird. "What kind of engineering? Electrical? Mechanical? Mining?"

"I'd like to build things…bridges, roads, buildings. I think I'll need a civil engineering degree, but I'm not sure."

"That sounds about right, but I'm not positive. I've got a friend in the engineering department at the University of Minnesota. I'll call him this afternoon and see what he says." John Seglie's eyes sparkled with amusement and his face assumed the stern lines of a disapproving teacher, "Of course, there's that little matter of math."

Laird groaned, "Don't I know it. I was more interested in sports and being one of the guys than studying back then. Dumb. Like my dad says, 'We get so soon old and too late smart'." Laird sat up a little straighter in his chair and said, "I need a tutor this summer to see if I can catch up, and I was going to ask Mr. Adams if I could hire him, but he's going to be gone most of the summer. Is there anybody else you can suggest?"

The swivel chair squeaked as Mr. Seglie settled back to think. "Well, no, I don't think any of the other teachers have an especially good math background, including myself. Of course, some of the seniors are pretty knowledgeable." He looked thoughtfully into space somewhere behind Laird and said, "There's Carla Swanson, she'd be excellent. Would you feel comfortable working with Carla?"

Laird shifted uneasily in his chair as he realized that Mr. Seglie probably knew that he and Jan's wedding had been called off. Probably everybody in town had heard the news by now. "Of course I'd feel comfortable with Carla," he said. "She's kind of like a kid sister to me. I just didn't know she was such a whiz at math."

"Well, you know how it is," Mr. Seglie cocked his head and looked appraisingly at Laird. "Or, maybe you don't." The old oak chair creaked again as he sat upright and leaned on the desk. "The thing is, girls tend to hide some of their academic lights under a bushel so as not to outshine the boys. For some reason, they think it's okay to be good in English and History but not in Math and Science; somehow they learn from the cradle on up that math and science are for the male sex. It's too bad, but those old habits are like ocean liners, you can't turn 'em around very fast." John Seglie sighed, and Laird remembered that his old principal had two daughters.

"Anyhow, Carla would be my first choice. Why don't you see if she'd like the job? Of course she can use any of the school textbooks. She'll probably want to use Mr. Adam's copies since his teacher's edition has all the answers in it. Tell Carla I'll track down whatever she needs."

※ ※ ※

Home again, Laird stood in the dining room looking down at the black phone sitting in its accustomed place on the oak table in front of the bay window. He picked it up and dialed the operator, "Will you get me Mercury 0628 please?"

"Right away…is that you Laird? This is Charlene Borden here. I heard you were home again. Welcome!" Charlene Borden had been one of the town's six telephone exchange operators ever since Laird was old enough to talk on the telephone. He felt a rush of familiarity and the sense that nothing back home had changed.

"You've got a good ear, Charlene," Laird said. "It's me, all right. How are you?"

"Great, just great! Oh, oh…gotta go now. I've got another call." Her voice dropped off the line and he heard the one long and two short rings that signaled the Swanson home.

Dora picked up the phone, "Hello?"

"Hi, Mrs. Swanson, it's Laird. I'm calling for Carla, is she there?"

"Laird?" Dora's voice was warm, "I'm so glad you called. Yes, Carla's home, I'll get her." There was a long pause, "I'm so sorry about you and Jan."

"It's okay, Mrs. Swanson. It's just one of those things, I guess."

"Yes…well, I'll go get Carla."

When Carla picked up the receiver, he could hear she was out of breath. "Oh, my gosh, I came as fast as I could. I was out helping Grandma in the garden. I'm so glad you called, I was beginning to worry you'd never want to see any of the Swanson family again."

"For Pete's sake, Carla. Jan was the one who jilted me, not your whole family. Don't worry about it."

Maybe so, Carla thought, but he'd sure been avoiding them for the past two weeks.

"I'm calling with a business proposition."

"Really…what kind of a business proposition?"

"I need to hire a math tutor to get me up to speed for college in the fall, and you come highly recommended."

"You don't have to hire me, I'd be glad to do it for nothing, Laird."

"No, I want to pay you. How about double what you get for babysitting?"

"Absolutely not! You don't pay a friend for doing you a favor."

"Nope…I won't do it unless I can pay you."

Carla could visualize him shaking his head and squaring off his jaw. She was silent, trying to figure out the best way to convince him, when she heard him say with a lighter note in his voice, "That way I'll be the boss and I can work the daylights out of you."

She laughed and said, "All right, Laird, you win…but only if you actually learn something." She hesitated before adding, "I'm not sure I'll be very good at this. Even when Jan and I played school as little kids, she was always the teacher. I never could catch up, she was always three years ahead of me."

"Well, seems like you've caught up now."

After she hung up the phone, Carla whirled into the kitchen, spinning around twice before she came to a stop by the table where her mother was kneading flour into a batch of bread dough. "Guess what?"

Dora stopped kneading the bread dough, looked up and smiled, "I give up. What?"

"I'm going to teach Laird math. He said Don Cramer and Mr. Seglie both recommended me. Mr. Adams can't do it because he's gone this summer and I'm the next best math person in town. Imagine that, Mama, I'm going to be a teacher." She hugged herself and turned around again. "This is going to be so much fun! And with Laird, one of my favorite people!"

Dora smiled and resumed her kneading. "Well, I'm glad people realize how smart you are."

"Oh, it's not that I'm smart, Mama…it's just that math is easy for me." She suddenly stopped dancing around the kitchen and frowned, "But I don't have the faintest idea how to go about teaching."

"Don't worry, Carla, all you need is an intelligent, hard-working student, and now that he's got a reason to study, Laird will do just fine." Dora gave the shining bread dough one last satisfying whack, "And so will you."

At St. Mary's, it was a quiet night on Ward C: Mr. Harmon was feeling good enough to complain about the hospital food, Mrs. Cranston was due to be discharged in the morning, and Mr. Belton was finally stable. Janice preferred to be busy. Only three patients on the ward left too much time for thinking. She'd spent two days writing a letter of apology to Laird, and it made her cringe to think that she'd sent him a *Dear John* letter after all. As hard as she'd tried to avoid it, Laird would still get the final bad news in a letter. She'd spent so much time writing it, she could recite it from memory.

Dear Laird,

I don't know how to explain to you how I feel. I just know it would be a lie to tell you I want to marry you. I'm returning the ring and asking you again to please take it back. You're the one to decide what to do with it. I still think you're one of the kindest, smartest, best-looking, most honorable men I've ever known, but I don't think it would work for us to get married. I hope you can forgive me, and forget about me. On the other hand, I hope you won't forget me entirely. In time, I pray we can be friends again. Somewhere out there is a much better woman than me waiting for you to find her.
Love, Jan

P.S. I'll write a letter right away to my family and let them know. Will you be sure to tell your family, too, so they don't find out from some stranger?

When Janice had returned to the hospital, she'd been relieved to learn that Lawrence Blakesly was away on a three-week rotation to the Mayo Clinic in Rochester. She wasn't quite sure how to tell him what had happened between her and Laird. If only she could feel the same urgent surge of emotion with Laird that she felt with Lawrence. Jan was finally able to admit to herself that what she felt for Laird was the same flood of warmth and love she felt for Carla and Martha. Well, maybe it was something more than that, but certainly not the bolt of energy she experienced with Lawrence.

Lawrence had said he loved her, but how could he love her when he hardly knew her? They'd never even been on a date together. Maybe it wasn't love he felt; maybe it was just some kind of hormonal attraction. Janice's psychology professor had tried to impress his student nurses with the deceptive attraction of hormones. "Infatuation is not love," he'd said. "Infatuation is a biological urge fueled by hormones, and it will not last!" Professor Murdock had turned to the blackboard and written, "Infatuation will not last!" and underlined it before he turned to glare ferociously and shake his finger at them. "Love grows by surviving hundreds of interactions together, big and small. Love grows by gritting your teeth and sticking with the other person in spite of their aggravating little habits. Love grows by developing trust. Trust is the most important prerequisite of love, and trust can only be earned with time and shared experiences."

Professor Murdock had suddenly given a sigh, sat down on the corner of his desk and quietly said, "Oh, hell. You're too young to understand about love." He ran his hand over his balding head and added, "Well, if you can't remember anything else, remember this line from a poem my wife wrote on our fortieth anniversary…*Love is like ice cream, it comes in assorted flavors.* Your assignment for our next class is to figure out what that means. Class dismissed."

Jan thought Professor Murdock was probably right about the infatuation part. It made sense that Dr. Blakesly was just infatuated with her, and maybe she was just infatuated with him, too. One thing she was sure of, by now everyone on the hospital staff knew the gossip. The first day she'd returned to work, all eyes had checked out her ringless finger. When someone had commented on it she'd given a matter-of-fact explanation, "We both agreed we weren't ready for marriage, we were just kids when he went away." To her close friends she'd confided, "Laird's a wonderful person, but I love him like a brother. He's not someone I want to marry. I feel so bad about it, but what else can I do?"

After the first few days had passed, staff members refrained from asking her about Laird, but they couldn't help noticing that she seldom laughed and that she had stopped her customary cheerful banter with the patients.

It was two o'clock in the morning, break-time for the third floor night-shift, as Janice walked slowly down the corridor to the dreary little coffee break room, poured herself a cup of muddy liquid, sat down wearily and laid her head on her crossed arms. She had no more responsibilities for fifteen minutes. She sighed gratefully and closed her eyes, thinking she'd never get used to these night shifts. The hospital was quieter at night, but hospitals never really sleep. Even small sounds echo down the hard-surfaced corridors, and nurses wake patients continually throughout the night for blood draws or medications. No wonder patients could hardly wait to go home; they were desperate for a good night's sleep.

Janice heard soft-soled footsteps coming down the hall, and when they paused outside the coffee room door, she raised her head and picked up her coffee mug.

"Do you have any more of that terrible coffee?"

Her heart started to pound and she felt her face flush. "I think you can squeeze out another cup."

Lawrence smiled his slow smile as his grey eyes locked onto hers. He walked over to fill a coffee cup, came over to the table and folded his tall form into the too-small metal chair across from her. His eyes never left hers as he took a sip of coffee. "I heard about you and Laird."

She looked away. "It doesn't take long for news to get around in this place."

"I was working in the hospital over at Rochester so I only just heard."

Janice nodded and looked down into her cup for a moment. When she looked up at him she said, "I feel terrible about it. I feel like I've betrayed him. People probably don't understand, but I'll always love him. He's like a brother to me."

Lawrence reached out and covered her small hand with his big one. "I would be lying if I said I'm sorry."

Janice felt a flash of anger and jerked her hand away, "You can't possibly know what I've put him through."

His eyes never left her face. "I think I have some idea...loving you hopelessly from a distance for the last two years has not been a pleasant experience."

She frowned at him. "I just don't see how it's possible for you to love someone you hardly know."

His eyes crinkled with amusement, "I've worked with you for two whole years, Jan. I've been with you through countless surgeries, stopped hearts, broken bones, appendectomies, psychotic patients...not to mention our constant battle with the administrative staff to replace these damned metal chairs...and you can say I don't know you?" He raised his eyebrows and smiled at her.

She couldn't help but return his amused look with one of her own.

"Jan, is it too soon to ask you for a date? We could go to the movies, if we ever get the same work schedule, or we could just find time for a bite to eat someplace other than the hospital cafeteria, or maybe we could go for a walk over at Lake Minnetonka park?"

Janice fastened her green eyes on his grey ones and realized she never wanted to stop looking into them. When he reached across the table to take her hands in his, she nodded slowly and gave him a tentative smile. And this time, Lawrence was relieved to see, she didn't pull her hands away.

Chapter Ten

The windows of the school office were wide open and the ceiling fan spun slowly overhead as Mr. Seglie took off his jacket, loosened his tie and rolled up his shirt sleeves. "Today is going to be a hot one." He picked up three letters containing neatly folded college applications from his desk top and handed them to Laird. "You need to complete these plus write a personal letter telling why you think you'd be a successful college student; I've written my own laudatory recommendation." His eyes twinkled as he added, "Don't worry, I omitted any references to the red paint incident."

He went into the outer office and brought back a stack of books. "Here's the books you'll need for algebra and geometry. There are teacher editions for Carla and regular ones for you. Be sure to tell Carla that if she needs anything else, just let me know. I'll be here most of the summer. My vacation doesn't begin until August."

"Thanks, Mr. Seglie. You don't how much I appreciate all your help."

The older man nodded and stood quietly, studying Laird's profile as Laird slowly flipped through the pages of the teacher edition. Laird looked up and grinned, "I always wondered what these teacher editions were like."

"Yah, well, I've learned from personal experience that the answers don't do a teacher much good unless he can explain to the class how to arrive at the answer." Mr. Seglie settled himself in his creaky swivel arm chair and waved at Laird to sit down, "I guess you know the FBI came to town last year to check you out."

" I heard they quizzed nearly everybody in town about me." Laird put the books down on the principal's desk and pulled up a chair. "They probably even found out about the red paint, but they cleared me for everything: restricted, confidential, secret, top secret and top secret-eyes only." Laird clenched his jaw. "The war's over, for God's sake, and they're still obsessed with secrecy. Even the weather reports are restricted."

"Yah, now they're worrying about the Russians." Mr. Seglie slowly straightened up some papers on his desk and asked, "What was it like, working in the Command Center for the whole European theatre? Did you ever get to see Eisenhower or any of the other big brass?"

"No, I was pretty low on the totem pole. It was almost like a regular job; the de-coding center sent stuff up to us to type out for the top brass. We worked three shifts and every time we'd get used to working one shift, they'd switch us to another, so we were always a little groggy."

"I guess your years in the infantry must have been the hardest." Mr. Seglie waited to see if Laird wanted to say anything about the war, but Laird only nodded, stood up and reached across the desk to shake Mr. Seglie's hand. "Thanks again, Mr. Seglie, I'll let you know how things turn out."

❋ ❋ ❋

Tutoring sessions began the following Monday morning. Laird had been firm with Carla about where they would hold their study sessions. "It's got to be in my house, I want my brothers to see that I think school is important. I'm afraid they've got stars in their eyes about their big brother being a high school jock and a big war hero." He'd turned an impassioned face to Carla's and said, "I've got to show them getting a good education is what matters, not being captain of the football team."

"Maybe they can do both, Laird."

He'd looked away and didn't answer.

❋ ❋ ❋

Carla straightened her back and marched into the Nordstrom living room where a small table and two chairs had been set up in the living room next to the bay window which over-looked the elm trees in the front yard. She laid her teacher's text and notebook on the table, and seated herself in a chair as she watched Laird start to sit down in the chair opposite her.

"I don't like the chairs arranged this way" she said. "I think we should sit side by side so we can see each other's writing."

"Good idea." He picked up his chair and moved it beside hers, noticing how perky and how pretty she was. Sitting this close to her, he was aware of a faint tantalizing fragrance. It wasn't perfume, it was probably soap… or maybe this was just how Carla naturally smelled. He looked sideways at her. "Is this okay, teacher?"

"Yes, that's better," she said in a serious tone of voice. "Now, I've been thinking how to start this. I'm going to give you a pre-test so I can tell how much you already know. We'll start with Algebra I and go from there." She shifted in her chair so she could look directly at him and asked, "Do you remember what Mr. Adams said is the basic method of algebra?"

"No, not really."

"Well, he says algebra teaches you a problem-solving process. An equation is like a puzzle that's already been put together, and you have to take it apart to find out what the variable, like x or y, equals. Instead of putting puzzle pieces together, you work backwards and unravel it." Her eyes were earnest as she looked at him, "Does that make sense?"

"Kind of," he said. "To find the unknown variable I have to unravel a puzzle. No, I don't remember Mr. Adams telling me that, but it sounds interesting. I'll give it my best shot." He smiled and added, "You really like this stuff, don't you?"

"I do," she grinned at him. "Actually, I think math is fun."

While Laird took the pre-test, Carla sat in the kitchen munching on a cinnamon roll and drinking a cup of coffee with Ellen Nordstrom, "These are such good cinnamon rolls, Mrs. Nordstrom. Not even my mother makes them any better."

Ellen beamed at the effervescent girl sitting across the table from her. How could this child manage to be so consistently cheerful with only one good arm and a crooked back? Carla carried it off so naturally and was so matter of fact about it that after awhile a person forgot all about it. Ellen wasn't sure why she was noticing it now, and she felt a sudden rush of gratitude towards Carla for keeping Laird's mind occupied and off the problem with Janice.

Working through the algebra problems, Laird was aware of feeling uncomfortably like a kid back in grade school, but was relieved to find he remembered some of the basic concepts. Later, as he watched Carla correcting his pre-test, he noticed her lips sometimes looked almost pouty as she intently checked his answers.

Once, she turned to look at him and said, "This is good, Laird, you remember how to solve a linear equation." Another time, as she bent over the test paper with her lips pressed firmly together she said, "Yes, you do linear equations just fine. You fall apart on quadratic equations, but that's understandable." Finally, she looked up at him and smiled encouragingly, "You'll get the hang of this in no time." She straightened up, her face serious again, shook her head to flip a riot of curls away from her face, and opened the teacher's edition. "I think we can start at chapter nine."

Laird obediently opened his book to chapter nine and tried not to smile. He was torn between amusement at her determined teacher demeanor and respect for her intellect, and, at the same, he was keenly aware of his attraction to her intriguing scent.

When the session was over and Carla was gathering up her books and papers, Laird impulsively asked, "How about we go out to Dead Man's Gulch and take a picnic lunch? I've been wanting to check out the senior rocks. Maybe my brothers would like to come along."

Ellen came into the room. "Your dad called and asked Duane to help down at the shop, but I imagine David and Johnny would like to go."

"It's a great idea, Laird. I'll run home and get a hat. I'll bring my binoculars and bird identification book, too, although at mid-day we probably won't see too many birds. I'll pack a lunch and you can pick me up in forty-five minutes or so. Is it okay if Martha comes, too?"

Martha was at the swimming pool with her friends again, so it was just the four of them, Laird and Carla in the front, David and Johnny in the back. The day was warm and they opened the car windows and let the wind blow their hair around. They shouted out the words of a series of Burma Shave signs, and roared with laughter as though it was the first time any of them had ever seen a Burma Shave roadside ad: *Train approaching / Whistle squealing / Stop / Avoid that rundown feeling / Burma Shave.* Carla threw back her head and started to sing in a clear soprano voice, *"You are my sunshine, my only sunshine…,"* then abruptly stopped singing when no one else joined in. She turned to David and Johnny in the back seat. "Don't you guys know that one?"

"Sure, we know it…but we're not singers."

"But that's what you do when you're on a car trip," she protested. "Singing is how you pass the time." She swept a commanding look at them and said, "Come on, you guys, keep me company."

Reluctantly, they joined in to sing; *You Are My Sunshine, Highways Are Happy Ways, White Coral Bells, Tie Me to Your Apron Strings Again*, and, by the time David suggested they sing *Twenty Four Bottles of Beer on the Wall*, Carla's soprano was nearly drowned out in the din of male voices.

They ate their lunch sitting on the ground in the shade of a cottonwood tree. On the nearby hill, sloping sharply up and away from the picnic grounds, sat the senior stones for the years 1944, 1945, and 1946. It was obvious the 1946 stones were much larger than the stones from the prior two years. They ate their sandwiches and leisurely discussed where the next senior class should place its stones, and whether the class of '47 would manage to drag even bigger rocks up the hill.

They walked around the small lake and spotted a pair of mallards with seven newly-hatched babies paddling in a straight line behind their mother. They admired several red-winged blackbirds perched on tall reeds near the water's edge, and noticed that the blackbirds were located a respectful distance from one another, which prompted a discussion on the probable size of each bird's territory. Far off, from a nearby farmer's pasture, they heard the music of a meadowlark singing, "I'll tell teacher on you."

They competed to see who could throw a flat stone and make it skip across the water the most times. After Carla gave the worst performance with only four skips, Johnny said, "Don't feel bad, Carla, you just need more practice."

Carla put her arm across his shoulders and gave him a little hug. "That's the truth. I'm afraid girls spend too much time playing jacks and hopscotch and not enough time skipping stones. Why do you suppose that is?" She took her arm off Johnny's shoulder and stood looking straight into his eyes.

He shrugged, "I don't know, maybe girls like playing jacks better."

Carla frowned, "I remember one time when I was in the fifth grade, I bought a bag of marbles and tried to join the neighbor boys shooting marbles, but they wouldn't let me play. They said I couldn't play because I was a girl, and here I had a bag of good marbles they could probably have won from me. They said, 'no way,' and laughed at me for thinking girls could play marbles."

David said, "Well, you know, there are some things girls aren't any good at."

Carla lifted her eyebrows and asked, "But how can a person get good at something if she doesn't get a chance to practice?"

The two boys looked away and shuffled their feet uncomfortably. Laird grinned at them and said, "I think Carla wins the argument, you guys. We better come again so she can get in some practice time."

Carla laughed, "Well, I'm through practicing for today anyhow. I'm going to go sit on the dock, take off my shoes and put my feet in the water."

Johnny turned to David, "Let's go see if we can find minnows and some water boatmen."

Carla and Laird watched as the two boys moved off to explore the shoreline. "They're such good kids," Carla said.

"Yup, they sure are."

Laird followed her onto the old wooden dock that jutted a short way out over the pond where the water gave off the pungent odor of decaying vegetation, and where they could see small insects boating across the surface tension of the murky, green water. They heard one of the red-winged blackbirds calling from far off on the left side of the pond. As they sat down, took off their shoes and dangled their feet in the water, Laird said, "I wonder if there are still fish in this lake."

"I think there are croppies here. Daddy said that's all they're catching here lately."

They sat quietly together, watching David and Johnny who were wading on the fringe of the lake, bending over occasionally to inspect an interesting find.

Carla looked over at Laird and regarded him thoughtfully. "Do you believe in God?"

"What brought that on?" Laird asked.

"I don't know," Carla shrugged and looked across the pond. "I guess it's just being out here…"

Laird's face was somber as he looked down into the opaque greenish water. "I guess whether I believe in God or not depends on your definition of God."

Carla nodded, "That's a fair point…"

She sat considering how to explain as she watched the puffy fair-weather clouds beginning to pile up into the cumulus mountains they would become by late afternoon. "Well, I suppose my definition of God is of some greater being or power that made the universe, a power that can intercede and help when you're in trouble." She turned and looked at him, "Of course, God doesn't always help, but when help doesn't come, it's because we humans don't understand the whole scheme of things."

Laird shook his head in disagreement, "I don't believe in that kind of God, Carla." He looked at her with eyes as dark and unfathomable as the water of the pond. "But if you want to believe that, I won't try to talk you out of it."

She cocked her head to one side and studied his face. "So, what do you believe, Laird?"

He hurled a stone far out into the lake, and as they watched the stone fall with a plop and send out ring after ring of radiating ripples, he said, "My beliefs aren't very impressive, Carla. I sure never learned them in the Lutheran church." He was silent awhile and said, "I believe in clouds and red-winged blackbirds and rain and dirt… I believe in the phases of the moon…and the wind. "He swatted and flattened a mosquito that had just landed on his arm, leaving behind a tiny bloody mark. "I even believe in mosquitoes." He turned to her with a wry smile. "Everything people call God is just an interplay of cause and effect. I just can't believe there's some outside force checking up on things. I thought a lot about God during the war, and I just can't believe that stuff about his eye being on every little sparrow…"

Carla watched her feet moving slowly back and forth in the water and said softly, "Wow…believing what you believe must be hard."

"No, Carla…for me, believing what you believe is harder." He stood up abruptly and reached down to help her up. "We better keep moving or these blasted mosquitoes will eat us alive."

The drive home was quiet. They were all hot, tired and contented, but when Laird stopped the car by the Swanson house to drop Carla off, David still had enough energy to suggest, "Let's all go for a swim. The pool is open for us kids until 7:00 tonight."

"No, thanks," Carla said, "I'm not much of a swimmer, but you guys go and have fun." In spite of the fact that she often longed to go swimming with her friends, there was no way she was going to appear in public in a revealing swimming suit.

"Sorry, David, but I don't want to go swimming now, either," Laird said. "I told Diane I'd start coming to the adult evening swims, so I'll be going swimming later. She thinks swimming laps will be good for my bum leg."

Laird got out of the car and walked around to open Carla's door. She smiled up at him as she stepped onto the sidewalk. "Thanks for the great day, Laird. I'll see you at class tomorrow at 9:00 am sharp."

As Laird drove away from the curb, David leaned forward, hung his arms over the back of the seat and asked, "How come you opened the door for Carla? …because she's only got one good hand?"

Laird glanced back at David and suppressed a laugh. "No, of course not, you little barbarian, you better watch and learn some manners from your big brother. I opened the door for her because she's a lady."

※ ※ ※

That night Laird slept deeply for the first time since he'd come home. He had a weird dream about Italy but it evaporated as soon as he woke up. At least it wasn't a nightmare. Thank God there were no nightmares at all last night. He turned over on his back, looked up at the ceiling and thought about Sophia. Sophia had been the only good thing that had happened to him in Italy.

The first time he'd seen her, he'd opened his eyes and there she was, checking his IV tube. She was the most beautiful woman he'd ever seen, and Laird wondered if he was dreaming. He'd closed his eyes again and remembered the bombardment that went on for days until he thought he'd go crazy…? He couldn't remember what happened exactly…but, he guessed he was alive. His brain seemed to be working okay. The sheets felt clean. They were khaki colored, but they were real sheets. He recognized a Frank Sinatra song playing on a radio, *"I'm Going to Buy a Paper Doll That I Can Call My Own..."*

He'd opened his eyes again and looked up at her. Maybe he wasn't alive. Maybe he'd died and gone to heaven. She had dark-fringed sloe eyes, olive skin, jet-black hair and a body that hinted at perfect curves under the loose fitting regulation nurses' khakis. She looked down at him and smiled, "Allo, soldier."

When he'd tried to answer, but couldn't get any words out, she put her forefinger on her beautiful lips and said, "Shhh," while she stroked his forehead, said something soothing in Italian, and went off to look for a nurse.

Laird wondered if he'd been captured by the Italian army. Damn... well, at least they were taking care of him. From the stories he'd heard, it was better to be a prisoner of the Italians than of the Germans.

It turned out Laird was in an American field hospital on the outskirts of Salerno, Italy, and Laird's doctor was a tired captain from Topeka, Kansas. When it was time for Laird to be moved from intensive care to one of the recovery tents, the doctor sat on the edge of the bed, looked under Laird's bandages, listened to his heart, took his blood pressure, checked his eyes, rapped on the soles of his feet and on his elbows with a rubber-tipped mallet, then sat back with a sigh, "Well, for a while there you gave us a scare. Lucky we had lots of type A blood on hand and I'm pretty sure we got all the shrapnel out. You were lucky none of it hit anything vital."

The doctor fastened his weary eyes on Laird's face. "I'm afraid you're going to eventually be recovered enough to go back to duty with your old unit." He'd scratched his head and given a wan smile. "It's a hell of a thing to send you back to the front lines, isn't it? But I can recommend a three-week recuperation time for you once you're healed. You certainly deserve to have a little rest."

When the doctor stood up to leave he'd said, "Any sign of redness, or severe pain, let a nurse know and get your butt right back over here, *capisce?*"

The beautiful angel's name was Sophia. After the Allies had set up a hospital in a partially destroyed school near her bombed-out house, Sophia had volunteered at the hospital as an aide to the nursing staff. The language barrier wasn't too big a problem as long as she worked the same shift as Melanie Caruso who had grown up in a big Italian family in the Bronx. Melanie spoke rapid Italian that made Sophia's face light up like a Christmas tree. It wasn't regulation but the nurses needed the extra help and so no one objected. The staff repaid Sophia in food they smuggled out of the chow tent, plus bars of soap, cigarettes, chocolate, toothpaste, and whatever else they could scrounge from their Red Cross packages and boxes from home.

When it was time to transport Laird by wheelchair to a tent in the recovery section of the field hospital, nurse Melanie had been there to push him along the maze of wooden boardwalks. Laird said, "You must know Sophia pretty well. How does she get by in this bombed out hell-hole?"

"She lives on scraps. The nurses and doctors help her out some. The Nazis found out her husband was part of the Italian underground, so when they caught him hiding with a downed American flyer they stood him up against a wall and shot him. Her father and two of her brothers are dead, and another brother is missing somewhere with the Italian army. At least Sophia still has her mother." Melanie shook her head sadly. "These people have nothing… nothing at all." She handed Laird's wheelchair over to an orderly and gave Laird a snappy salute, "Good luck, soldier."

Laird spent the first week of his recovery time in a group tent with seven other soldiers who, like him, had been patched up and were waiting to heal before being transferred back to their units. The Red Cross provided books, chess sets, cards and the ever-ubiquitous cigarettes to help them pass the time.

As soon as Laird was given the go-ahead to walk around the grounds, he decided to hang out near the urgent-care entrance and watch for Sophia. The day he saw her leaving, he'd hurried over. "Sophia? Can I walk you home?" She'd smiled at him, nodded and kept on walking. Laird took the smile and the nod for a yes and fell in beside her. It was weird walking a girl home through this hell-hole. Debris from smashed buildings was everywhere, and the only access was where bulldozers had cleared paths through the rubble. Corpses were still hidden under the wreckage, and the smell of death hung in the air, but at least there were no more bombs dropping in this part of Salerno. Neither one said anything.

Trying to communicate in a foreign language took too much effort.

Sophia lived in one section of a partially-gutted house that had survived the bombing; the exterior walls looked stable, but one side of the roof had collapsed, and all of the windows were broken and boarded up. Unless the door was open, it was as dark as a tomb inside.

Kids came out of nowhere and followed them down the street, "Hi GI. Chocolat, cigareetes? Okay?" He wondered if Sophia knew the GIs called these kids werewolves. He'd learned from experience they'd steal anything that wasn't nailed down, but this was the first time he'd seen them up close. Sophia scowled and shook her head, scolding them in Italian. The first time it happened, she'd turned sorrowing eyes at him and tried to explain, "I…help…a leetle." She gave an anguished sigh, whether about the kids, the difficulty in communicating complex ideas in a foreign language, or both, he couldn't tell.

"How do they survive?" he asked. "How does anybody survive in all this destruction?" Laird waved his hands helplessly at the bombed out buildings and the retreating gang of kids. She tilted her head to one side and studied his face. He could see she understood his feelings, if not his words. She shook her head helplessly and said something softly in Italian.

After that he started bringing her everything he could scavenge from the Red Cross boxes and his packages from home. Like many soldiers, Laird had written home early in the war asking for packages of dehydrated chicken noodle soup. "Don't bother sending cookies, they're pulverized before they get here. Can you just send good old dehydrated chicken soup?" After the mail from home caught up with him at the hospital, he had lots of chicken soup packages to give Sophia and the neighbor kids.

They seldom tried to communicate in words, it took too much effort and got in the way. During the first week, they fell into a routine of taking turns telling each other about their lives, at least that's what Laird talked about. He never knew exactly what Sophia told him, but he assumed she told him about her own life. He talked about the little town he'd grown up in, his kid brothers, his dad's blacksmith shop, his mother's wonderful cinnamon rolls, the farmers and their pessimism about the crops, painting red '1943' numbers all over town, basic training, and the beautiful open-sky sunsets of South Dakota. He'd even told her about Jan, how kind and beautiful she was, how they intended to get married after the war, and that she was studying to be a nurse. He told her it was somehow comforting to know that the Milky Way and the moon they saw in Italy were the same Milky Way and moon people looked up at in South Dakota.

Sophia listened carefully to the tone of his voice, smiled if he seemed to think something was funny, and nodded her head solemnly if he sounded sad. His accent was so strange, the Italian language was much more beautiful. Ever since she'd started working with the Americans, she'd been struck with how flat and boring the American language sounded, but gradually she was learning to love the accents of Laird's even, unhurried, mid-western American speech.

He was fascinated with the sounds of her lilting Italian, and sometimes he'd recognize a word or two, but he'd learned not to get stuck trying to figure out what she was saying. Instead, he'd decided it was better to pay attention to how she was saying it. A few times she talked about her dead husband, Luigi, and once when she said his name the tears started to roll down her checks. Laird had pulled his khaki handkerchief out of his hip pocket and given it to her. Other times her voice was light, almost lilting, and he'd smiled along with her at the good memories.

The second week, she'd asked him into the dark little house to meet her mother. Angelica Rossi was tall, like Sophia, with the same olive skin and almond-shaped eyes; her hair was pulled back into a bun, accentuating her thin face. Mrs. Rossi politely put out her hand to shake his, although her dark eyes were guarded and cool.

Two days later, Sophia asked him inside again. This time, when Laird looked around the dimly-lit room he saw her mother was not there. He arched his eyebrows slightly and asked, "Mama?"

Sophia gave him a slow smile and said, "No…okay… Mama go… zio, Mama's brother."

Laird took a quick breath and kept his eyes fastened on her face. "You're saying Mama is with your uncle tonight?" He hesitantly reached out to gather her in his arms and she clung to him while he whispered into her hair, "It's okay with you?"

She nodded her head against his shoulder and said softly, "Okay." He'd felt a small pang of guilt afterwards but none of this fit into any of the rules he knew. He and Sophia needed each other in a way neither he nor Jan ever had.

Sophia had held out a condom for him to use. "Yes?" she'd asked quietly, and helped him put it on. The next night he brought his own. Condoms were easy to find in the army, especially in a hospital unit in Italy. The European army was flooded with what everyone called rubbers, and soldiers were encouraged to use them. Even in the barracks back in boot camp there'd been a sign urging everyone to remember, "Put it on before you put it in."

Late one night, cuddled together spoon fashion on Sophia's narrow mattress, he started telling her about foxholes, explaining that the little folding shovel every GI carried was almost as important a weapon as the M-1 rifle. When you stood up in a foxhole, only your head and shoulders could show; the first foxholes hadn't been dug deep enough and enemy tank commanders found they could drive over a shallow foxhole, rotate the tank back and forth and mash you flat, so when the battalion was on the move, most nights you had to dig a five-foot deep hole. If you were pinned down in your foxhole on rainy days, your feet would start to rot because army boots weren't worth a damn when they got soaked. He'd read in *Stars and Stripes* that they'd improved the new boots; maybe his next pair would be waterproof.

Laird was quiet until, as Sophia was drifting off to sleep, the anguish in his voice brought her wide-awake. "Sammy stood up for just a minute to look around, and his head exploded." Laird's voice was strangled and Sophia could feel his naked body pressed against hers begin to tremble. "It was a two-man foxhole…we dug it together." Laird's arms gripped Sophia so hard, he worried later that maybe he'd cracked her ribs, but Sophia never moved a muscle nor did she afterwards complain.

When he could speak again, his voice was controlled and even. "Sammy liked to sing dirty songs while he dug foxholes, he sang dirty songs when he was doing almost anything. He knew lots of them, funny ones. He said it made the work go easier. After he died, I wrote a letter to his folks to tell them, you know, comforting stuff…he was a good soldier, and a good friend." Laird was quiet for a long time, "Sammy isn't the only one I've seen die, but he was almost like a brother…"

Sophia moved her hand to stroke his arm, and stared straight ahead into the darkness. When they woke next morning, Laird realized they were still touching each other, and he told himself that what he'd written to Jan was true…you had to make love to someone before you were their lover. He'd been right about that.

The next night in bed they shared an episode of love-making so intense, that afterwards, as Laird sank into the womb of sleep, he had the thought that making love was life's way of shouting 'No' to death.

It was still dark when he was awakened by Sophia moaning the name, "Massimo….Massimo…"

Laird knew what had happened to Sophia's brother, Massimo. Nurse Melanie had heard the story from an Italian woman who worked in the mess hall, and the story had quickly circulated throughout the hospital. They told about the Nazis coming to Salerno, about the girls they'd raped, how ten Italian men and boys were lined up against a wall and shot in retribution for one German soldier who was found with his throat slit, his pants down and his genitals mutilated. One of the young Italian men killed had been Massimo. Sophia and her neighbors had been rounded up by the German soldiers to witness the executions. Sophia watched Massimo and the nine others die. One moment, he was alive and terrified, but very brave standing before the firing squad. The next moment, he was a heap of flesh and clothing being dragged away and slung into the back of a truck. The Germans drove the bodies to the outskirts of town where they threw them into a ditch and forced the Italians to shovel dirt over them.

Laird turned on his side and curved his arms and body around Sophia. He buried his face in her hair, gently stroked her arm and said, "It's all right, Sophia…I'm here…I'm here." He held her there, carefully, in the same way he used to experiment back home with keeping a snowflake from melting when it fell on his glove. He held her there until he heard her breathing slow and deepen into what he hoped was blessed oblivion.

On subsequent nights, he talked about how grateful he was to have found her, how the war would eventually be won and the world would go back to being at least somewhat sane, a world where it would be normal for kids to laugh and play and have enough to eat. He told her how he dreaded the time when they would have to say goodbye, and how frustrated he was that he was powerless to change events. He talked about the fact there was no use denying that war had its own inexorable rules, and that whether they liked it or not, he and Sophia were only pawns in a vast, obscene game of chess.

When the day of Laird's discharge from the hospital arrived, he climbed into the rear of an army truck with eleven other soldiers, all headed back to the front lines. As he found a seat on a bench on one side of the truck, he tried to keep Sophia in his sight where she stood with a small group of nurses who had gathered to wave goodbye. Laird looked into Sophia's eyes one last time before the wheels of the truck kicked up a cloud of dust between them, obliterating her image, and he knew that this goodbye was forever.

Laird was issued a new set of equipment and sent via the replacement depot outside Naples back to his unit where he took his place in his old platoon. It wasn't the same unit anymore, seven of the original platoon members were either wounded or dead: Billy Bo, the red-haired boy from Mississippi, had stepped on a mine and bled to death; Bob Reeges was killed by a sniper one morning when he was scouting the perimeter; and Charlie Greer hadn't come back from the hospital after they took him away with that shoulder wound; he was probably safe behind the lines now because he couldn't handle throwing a grenade or firing a rifle anymore. The other four guys had been killed by so-called friendly-fire.

Lars Thornberg, the platoon leader, who was unhurt and still in charge of the unit, greeted Laird somberly. "A couple of weeks ago our spotters built a smoke-fire line between us and the Germans…the wind was out of the east and our fly-guys were told to bomb on the clear side of the smoke, but before the planes got there the wind shifted and our own planes blew us to smithereens. We were lucky only four men from our platoon were killed; some units were totally wiped out. I don't know why I'm still alive. I have no right to be."

He clapped Laird on the back. "I should welcome you back, but I like you, you sorry son-of-a-bitch, and I hate to see anybody I care about come back to this mess." He lit up a cigarette and tossed away the match,

"I'm afraid we've got a lot of green replacements now who don't know their butts from their eyebrows."

Laird shook Lars' hand, pulled out his shovel and started digging the night's foxhole. "I'll do my best to help you keep us alive," was all he said.

Chapter Eleven

Carla burst into the house yelling, "Hi! I'm home!" Everyone in the Swanson family announced they were home when they first came through the front door. Years ago, Carla and Janice had noticed that no one in the Nordstrom family announced their arrival when they returned home. It always felt strange to walk into Laird's house with him because he just walked in and quietly shut the door behind him. Janice and Carla had discussed this strange behavior and put it down to the fact that the Nordstroms, like Big Grandma always said, were northern Swedes.

"I'm in the kitchen, Carla." Dora was standing at the sink peeling potatoes for supper and stopped for a moment to study her daughter's flushed and happy face. "Well, it looks like you had a good time."

"I had a wonderful time at the Gulch." Carla set the picnic basket on the kitchen table and started to clean it out. "Mrs. Nordstrom sent food along, too, so we had plenty." She shook her head and grinned, "and can those brothers of Laird's ever eat! Actually, Laird ate a lot, too, so there isn't much left. They especially wanted me to tell you they liked the braunschwager sandwiches and the brownies…they loved your brownies!"

Dora smiled and went back to peeling potatoes. "How is Laird doing?"

"He's doing great, he remembers quite a lot of his algebra."

"I didn't mean algebra, I'm sure he'll do fine with algebra. I meant does he seem depressed about Jan?"

Carla thought about it, "No, come to think of it, he didn't." She laughed. "I got everyone of them to sing with me in the car, and when we were out at the Gulch, Laird seemed happy enough." She turned to look at her mother, her eyes wide, "Maybe he was just so busy today, he forgot?"

Dora smiled and kept on peeling potatoes. "Maybe, or maybe he's just decided to accept what he can't change."

"Well, he did mention he was going to start going to evening swims with Diane to strengthen his leg. That'll be good for him and help keep him busy don't you think?"

"I'm glad to hear that. I know he's been working down at the blacksmith shop, and the more things he has to do, the less time he'll have to spend brooding about Janice. Maybe he and Diane will be good for each other. I hear Diane has started drinking since Conrad was killed. Alcohol is not a good way to ease the pain… I hope she hasn't started down that slippery slope."

Carla sat down at the table, propped her chin in her hand and watched her mother working at the sink. Dora was a stoic, in spite of the fact she was 100 per cent Welsh and English with not a Swedish gene in her body. Maybe that was the reason she'd been able to survive having two of her five children die. Carla's baby brother and sister were both buried out at the graveyard under small tombstones, each one topped by the figure of a lamb with the inscription, "Gone with God." It was a God Dora no longer believed in.

The first to die had been a boy, dead from whooping cough when he was one-and-a-half years old; the other child was a girl who'd died at birth. Big Grandma said the little girl had been perfect in every way, but died from a supposedly wonderful new anesthetic called Twilight Sleep which the doctor had given Dora. And, to top it all off, Carla had nearly died from a ruptured appendix followed by polio when she was only three years old. Carla knew that Daddy had started drinking to ease his hurt from the deaths and sickness of his babies. Only Dora had endured, like a rock.

Carla asked, "How have you managed to stand all the pain you've had in your life, Mama?"

Dora paused a moment before she answered, "I tell myself that this, too, shall pass." Carla stood up and went over to her mother's side to give her a little hug, "I love you, Mama."

Dora leaned her head towards Carla until the side of her face rested on her daughter's curly head. "Likewise, dear Carla."

After Carla finished sorting through the picnic debris, she put the picnic basket back in its accustomed place in the pantry, and said, "I think I'll write a letter to Jan to let her know Laird seems to be getting along okay. She feels so guilty about cancelling the wedding but maybe she was right." Carla glanced over at her mother. "Maybe they were both too young. They were my age, weren't they?"

Dora nodded, "Yes, they were eighteen, exactly your age."

Carla set the usual five places at the kitchen table, using the old blue Chinese print pottery, the mismatched forks and knives, and the heavy glass tumblers. Carla couldn't understand why Jan had stopped loving Laird. Didn't all the letters they'd written back and forth during the war mean anything? Of course his letters to Jan had probably been short, but all his letters were short, and if Laird's letters to Jan were anything like the letters he'd sent Carla, they always sounded exactly like him.

Carla closed her eyes and saw Laird vividly in her mind, his strong face, the steady open eyes, his rare sweet smile, and his muscular male body. She pushed her curls back from her face and frowned.

When she opened her eyes and stood back to survey the table, Dora smiled at her. "A penny for your thoughts, Carla."

Carla shook her head. "Nothing special, I was just thinking I'll go write that letter to Jan now if I've got time before supper."

"Go ahead, supper won't be ready for at least a half hour."

Carla went slowly up the stairs to her room and sat down at the little desk in the corner by the window. She took out pen and paper and managed to write, "Dear Jan," before laying the pen down and staring at the blank sheet of paper. She got up and went to open the top dresser drawer where the silver candleholders lay, exactly where she'd put them three weeks ago. She polished them carefully with the cloth they were wrapped in and tucked them away again.

Dear Jan,

I wish long distance calls weren't so expensive. I miss talking with you. You told me you feel guilty about Laird, so I want to let you know he's doing okay, at least on the surface. He told me he's going to start swimming laps during adult evening swim times at the pool. Diane talked him into it, she says it'll be good exercise for his leg but I think Diane is lonely and just wants him around. I've started tutoring him in algebra so I get to see him every weekday morning. He remembers a lot of the math and I think he'll do just fine when he starts college. Today after the lesson, we took David and Johnny out to Dead Man's Gulch to look at the senior stones and have a picnic. Laird seemed to have fun. He even sang in the car and laughed out loud at those crazy Burma Shave signs along old Hwy 23. He insists he's going to pay me double my babysitting fees for tutoring him, but I won't take any money unless he passes his tests. We meet in the Nordstrom's living room because Laird wants his kid brothers to see him studying. I like teaching a lot! Of course I probably have the best student in the world!! I'm so excited about your graduation this September and about me starting college! Oh, oh, Mama's calling me for supper.

Hugs and Kisses, Carla

After the supper dishes were done, Carla wandered around the house not knowing quite what to do next. It was hard to settle down after such an exciting day. She called to Mac, the Swanson's old Scottie dog, "How about a walk, Mac?" It always made her laugh to see his body morph from a small black blob quietly snoozing on the porch into a taut spring of energy complete with jaunty gait and alert ears and tail, at the slightest suggestion of a walk.

Carla loved walking through the ending of a long summer day with the sun reluctantly traveling ever lower in the western sky, casting long shadows across the lawns and streets of the town. Mac trotted along just ahead of her, busily sniffing at every tree and lifting his leg at most of them. She laughed, "You're amazing, Mac. How do you have enough urine to pee so often?" She waved to Martha and the other kids in the Henderson yard who were in the process of choosing the person to be "It" in a game of kick-the-can. She felt a twinge of regret that she was too old now to join them, to hide in the dusky magic of a summer evening, and experience the thrill of leaping from her hiding place, racing to be first to kick the can.

She hadn't planned to go by the swimming pool, but decided she might as well see who was there tonight. As she approached the six-foot high wire-mesh fence, she put her hand on the metal links and scanned the pool for familiar faces. Diane was there sitting high up in her life-guard chair, looking beautiful in her simple black swimming suit. There were several older women from church standing in water up to their necks, slowly moving their arms back and forth and chatting together. Two men were swimming laps. When one of them stopped at the end of the pool right beneath Diane's chair, lifted himself out of the water and flung his head back to toss the hair off his face, Carla recognized Laird. He stood and smiled up at Diane, saying something that made her laugh. For a few long minutes, Carla stood and wistfully watched them through the fence. Then, she turned to Mac and said, "Come on, Mac. It's time to go."

Back on the front porch again, Mac dissolved from his jaunty persona into a small black furry ball as he lay down, snuggled his muzzle under his paws, closed his eyes and eased into one of his frequent long naps. Carla bent over and petted him affectionately on his head. "You have a good rest, Mac," she said, "and thanks for your company."

Upstairs, after she'd undressed and put on her nightgown, Carla opened the bottom drawer of her dresser and took out the shoebox of Laird's letters. She put the box on the bed, pulled back the sheet, climbed in, propped herself up against the pillows, crossed her legs, and took out one of his letters.

October 21, 1943

Dear Squirt,

You said you were worried about me. Don't be… I'm fine. I'm getting my strength back and the doctor says he thinks they got out all the shrapnel. Pretty soon I'll be good as new…maybe better. The surgery part of the hospital is in a bombed out school building they managed to fix up, and the rest of it is in long rows of tents with board floors. We've got great nurses and doctors. The hospital food isn't too bad, but then, anything beats K-rations. Of course, we've got a lot better food than the local people…they're really hurting for food and shelter after all the bombing. Keep sending those packets of dehydrated chicken soup, will you? I'll sure be glad when this war is over, Squirt. Give Jan a hug from me when you see her?

Love, Laird

Carla read the letter twice, slowly folded it and put it back before choosing another.

January 19, 1945

Dear Squirt,
Things are pretty quiet here. I've had a bath and am wearing clean clothes for a change...feels good. You asked how often the mail comes. It's sporadic...sometimes we don't get mail for weeks and then it comes in a big bunch. When we're on the move I'm surprised they manage to find us at all, much less deliver mail. The mail is like a lifeline to home...keep those letters coming will you, Squirt?

Love, Laird

She folded the letter, leaned her head back against the headboard and closed her eyes. He sounded so lonely. She sat up again and reached for another letter.

March 20, 1945

Dear Squirt,
This will be short because we're moving out soon. I want to thank you for your letter about old Mayberry. Yes, he was a good dog. I learned a lot from him. I could tell him anything and he'd sit there, ears cocked, listening and watching my every move. Sometimes he'd put his paw on my knee, kind of like he was saying, "I understand, old buddy." Every kid should have a dog like Mayberry. I'm sad to know he won't be there when I come home. Mother wrote that my brothers gave him a good burial under the crab apple tree. She said you came, too...thanks for being there, Squirt. I know they must have appreciated it.

Love, Laird

He must have written this letter just before he got the bullet in his knee, the one that left him with the limp. Carla put the letters back in the box and sighed. His letters seemed kind of sad, but maybe she'd accidentally picked out only the sad ones to read. Well, why wouldn't he be sad? There wasn't much to be happy about when you were fighting in a war. She lay down, turned out the light and reminded herself that everything was okay, the war was over and Laird was home again. Well, that wasn't exactly true, not everything was okay. It was hard for her to accept the fact that Jan had changed her mind about marrying Laird. Why would any girl with any sense not want to marry Laird? Carla turned over on her side and closed her eyes, vowing that she, at least, would do everything in her power to cheer him up. Just before she drifted off to sleep, Carla had an uncomfortable flash of insight remembering how Laird had effortlessly lifted himself out of the swimming pool and smiled up at Diane.

Chapter Twelve

The following Saturday Laird got a phone call from Don Cramer. "Hey, you son-of-a-gun. How about meeting me for a beer tonight? And maybe Virgil would like to come along, too…I'll give him a call…we can walk up and down Main Street and flirt with the girls."

"Sure, I'm always game for a Saturday night, but I doubt if Virgil will come. I think he's still holed up at Clear Lake. Dad will probably park the car on Main Street early. Just look for our old Chevy when you get into town."

"Yah, you city folks always did monopolize the best parking spots… us farmers have to get those damned cows milked before we hit town."

Laird laughed, "Same old complaint, good to know you haven't changed, Don."

Breton's main street was two blocks long, and boasted the Bar-None Tavern, Quarves' Drugstore and Soda Fountain, JC Penney's, two restaurants, a liquor store, the hospital, the Wheatland Hardware store, the Red Owl and the White Front groceries, the post office, Lottie's Women's Better Clothing, the Egyptian Movie Theatre, and Bobby Weaver's Popcorn Wagon. The north end of the street was anchored by the Legion Hall and the Texaco gas station. At the south end was the Creamery, the food locker, the town swimming pool and the small but handsome Carnegie Library. The two-story brick school building housing grades 1-12 stood well behind the main street establishments in the midst of a huge playground consisting mostly of trampled grass and large expanses of dirt.

On Saturday nights, when the weather was good, Main Street was a hub of activity. On a busy night in the summer when most of the farmers came to town, the population swelled from 1100 to nearly 1300.

People parked their cars early to reserve a good place; all the cars parked diagonally, the optimum situation for squeezing in the most cars and having a good view for people watching. Some people rolled down their car windows the better to see and be seen and to carry on conversations with passersby who were welcome to lean on the car while they talked. If there was room, especially if a person was old and getting a bit stiff in the joints, acquaintances were invited to sit inside. Both men and women paid particular attention to their hair and clothing on Saturday nights, and even if they didn't shave any other day of the week, and many farmers didn't, all the men shaved for Saturday night. It was also a special night for kids who were given their allowances to spend on ice cream and candy; they could buy a double-dip ice cream cone at the Quarve Drug Store, or, if the featured film was about cowboys, blow their entire allowance on a movie. Like the adults, kids reconnoitered up and down the street checking on who was in town and who wasn't.

Laird and Don found an empty booth in the Bar-None Tavern where the air was already thick with smoke. They ordered a beer and sat grinning at each other. "God, it's good to have you home again." Don lit a cigarette and squinted through the haze at Laird. "You never took up smoking?"

"Nope, I used my cigarettes for barter instead." Laird smiled ruefully and said, "I'm afraid I hardly ever turned down alcohol, but for some reason I didn't get hooked on smoking. The Red Cross handed out cigarettes steady. I figure the cigarette companies were trying to get us all hooked so we'd be good customers after the war."

Don took a long drag on his cigarette and blew out a cloud of smoke. "It was damned hard to find cigarettes here at home…they were sending them to you guys overseas. Ironic, isn't it? Here I sit, a loyal consumer of cigarettes, and without any help from the Red Cross."

The bartender set down two mugs of foaming beer in front of them, and reached out to shake Laird's hand, "The treat's on me, Laird. It's good to see you home again, the whole town's glad to have you back."

"Thanks, Mr. Beardsley. It's good to be back, and thanks for the beer."

The bartender grinned and waved his hand as he headed back to the bar.

Laird took a sip from his beer mug and looked at his old friend. "Do you still like living on the farm? Ever miss living in town like when you were a kid?"

"Sometimes I miss it, and I suppose you and me wouldn't have been such good friends if I'd been a farm kid all my life. After Mother and Dad died, and I moved out to the farm to live with John and Flora, I always envied you and Virgil for sharing the projectionist job at the theatre. You guys got to see every movie that came to town."

"You didn't miss anything on weekdays. God, those midweek movies were lousy. I think the only people who came in the middle of the week came to see the newsreels."

Don squinted his eyes as he took another pull on his cigarette. "At least it wasn't dangerous like when we used to set pins at the bowling alley."

"Sometimes I think those guys deliberately tried to hit us, or maybe they were drunk."

"They sure didn't give us much time to leap out of the way before they rolled those balls down the alley. I hear some of the big cities have automatic pin setters now."

"Good thing. The job's too dangerous for a kid, and I doubt a grown man could get out of the way fast enough."

Don took a gulp of beer, "The trouble with beer is you've got to drink it fast or it gets warm."

"Maybe that's why the English drink their beer at room temperature, that way they can make it last longer."

"The hell you say…warm beer…?" Don's eyes showed suspicion and a hint of a smile. "You're not ribbing me, are you?"

"No, swear to God, that's what the guys who spent time in England told us."

Don set his smoking cigarette down carefully in the ashtray, cradled his half-full mug in his hands and regarded Laird with solemn eyes. "Are you pissed with me?"

"Why would I be pissed with you?"

"For being safe and cozy here at home while you were going through hell."

Laird looked down into his beer. "No," he said slowly, taking time to think of how to get the answer right. "Not you personally. I know there's no way Flora and John could have run the farm without you, and the country needed food."

Don was surprised at the sudden flash of anger in Laird's eyes. "But those sons-of-bitches behind the front lines who got bronze stars for taking food to the front for a few hours on Thanksgiving, yes, I'm pissed at them, and I'm pissed at all the politics that goes on in the army. And I'm furious at the officers that got so many of us killed because they didn't know what the hell they were doing." He sighed, "Sometimes it was just because they were scared shitless and froze. We were all scared shitless, but not everybody froze."

Don sat without moving, his eyes fixated on Laird.

Laird took a long drink of beer. "Our platoon leader was a big, unflappable Norwegian from Minneapolis named Lars Thornberg. I'll never forget the day we had incoming shells bursting all around us. Luckily there was a farmhouse nearby, and we knew a lot of those farmhouses had cellars so we raced up to the door, expecting to kick it in, but Lars stopped and knocked." Laird shook his head, "I still can't believe it. He actually knocked several times before a scared little old lady came to the door and let us in."

Laird gave a humorless laugh and slowly shook his head. "Lars got bitter towards the end, but he never lost his sense of decency. He deserved a Silver Star just for being such a damn good role model, but, as far as I know, he never got anything except a Purple Heart. And the big brass kept sending us those green kids as replacements. They didn't have enough training and, a lot of times, didn't even have the right equipment. Most of those kids got killed before they ever figured out what in hell was going on." Laird stared off into space and his voice was tight with anger. "Then this latest law they tried to get through Congress, to give veteran's benefits to factory workers who were paid a dollar-and-a-half an hour for a safe, eight-hour-day job, and we got fifty dollars a month for the privilege of trying not to get killed."

"It didn't get passed into law, though."

"I know it didn't, but I'm pissed they even tried."

Laird drained his beer and stood up, "Let's get out of here." He threw some money on the table. "Sorry to be so negative, Don, but you learn to bitch in the army. It's a survival technique, and I vowed I wouldn't do it once I got home."

Don nodded, "You've got a right, Laird." He stood up, leaving his beer behind him, half-finished, on the table. "You've got a right."

Back out on the street they took a breath of sweet, clear air, and strolled slowly down the sidewalk, on the lookout for friendly faces. Occasionally someone would stop to shake Laird's hand and say, "Welcome home, Laird. How's the family?"

When the Deebly twins raced towards them down the sidewalk, Don stopped and spread his arms out wide. "Whoa there, boys. You're going to knock down some little old lady."

"Sorry," they said in unison as they looked sideways at him and slowed to a restrained trot.

Laird put his hands in his pockets and smiled as they walked on again, "It's good to see carefree kids."

"Aren't most kids?"

Laird shook his head and looked down. "No, there are thousands of homeless and orphaned kids right now."

Don looked at Laird's impassive profile and said, "I guess it's hard for people like me to realize how bad it's been over there."

"I don't mean to be critical, Don, it's just that things seem kind of surreal here at home…no bombed out buildings…no kids begging for cigarettes or something to eat."

They stopped at the corner and leaned against the side of the Red Owl grocery while Don lit up another cigarette and continued to listen.

"After the war ended and I was stationed in Frankfurt, German women would come stand by the gate and pick up our dirty clothes…some of them reminded me of my mother. They'd wash and iron the clothes and bring them back all neatly pressed." Laird ran one hand through his hair, "I was worried at first they'd steal them, but they never did. All they wanted in payment was to keep the bar of soap I gave them." He sighed and shook his head. "One lousy bar of soap."

The sun had been down for half an hour, and in the fading light Main Street was alive with people. As Laird waved across the street to his brothers, whom he spotted leaving the movie theatre, he noticed a group of laughing young women heading toward him.

Don saw them too. He grinned and casually waved, keeping his smile and his eyes trained on them, and said to Laird out of the corner of his mouth, "Why is it girls go everywhere in bunches? They even need company to go to the bathroom."

Laird, his eyes also focused on the girls, said, "Hey, don't ask me, I grew up in a family of boys."

Laird first recognized Carla in the group of young women by her laughter. He slowly straightened up and shifted his weight back to both feet as the girls surrounded them like a wave washing up around two rocks on a beach. "Oh, look, it's Laird and Don!" Carla's coterie of friends took turns giving Laird little hugs and exclaiming in chorus, "I'm so glad you're home!" You look great!" "I bet you're folks are so happy to see you again!" and other welcoming noises. After greeting Don and Laird, Carla stood back and beamed at them from the midst of the impromptu welcoming committee.

Laird smiled over the girls' heads at Carla, thinking it was strange he didn't remember much about her when he was in high school, although that was probably normal since he was three years older than Carla, and, when you're a kid, anyone that far behind you in school hardly shows up on your radar screen. He did remember that Carla had been voted homecoming queen when she was a freshman. The townspeople had been surprised when the kids chose Carla. People allowed as how Carla did have striking eyes and a beautiful head of hair, but most had anticipated that school kids would want someone with a perfect body for their queen. Still, the kids had voted for Carla overwhelmingly. Laird wasn't sure if he'd voted for her or not, but he probably did, since she was Janice's sister.

They stood talking by the Red Owl store until one of Carla's friends, Lenore, suggested, "Let's go over to Quarve's Drug Store and split some chocolate malts. I'll treat for the cashews."

Three of the girls begged off, explaining they'd promised to meet their folks back at the car by 9:00 and they wouldn't have time. Laird, Don and Carla agreed to adjourn with Lenore to the Quarve Drugstore soda fountain

"What's this about cashews?" Laird asked as he stood back to open the door for the girls.

Lenore explained, "You take a small handful of the roasted cashews they have for sale here, and you stir them into your malt. Delicious!"

The four of them squeezed around one of the round ice-cream tables by the soda fountain, and ordered two chocolate malts to share, along with a quarter pound bag of roasted cashews. Lenore, her brown eyes and chestnut hair shining under the fluorescent lights of the drugstore, was delighted to catch Laird up on the local news. She had an uncanny ability to be the first to know if anything important was happening in Breton, and the others listened quietly while she proceeded to tell Laird who had gotten married, who had a new baby, who was home from college for the summer, and who had moved out to the West coast.

Laird's brothers came breezing into the drug store and clustered around the table. "We saw you coming into the drug store so we thought we'd come in and bug you," Duane said with a grin.

"How was the movie?"

"It was good, a real shoot-em-up cowboy film with Gene Autry." The two younger boys nodded in agreement. Cowboy movies were definitely at the top of their list.

"Anyhow, we'll see you later, Laird," Duane said. "We're going to walk up and down awhile, and see who we can find to talk to. "

"Okay, but remember, Mother wants you guys home by ten o'clock."

"Sure, we know." The three boys gave haphazard salutes and left as quickly as they'd come, pausing only for a moment to stand aside as Diane came through the door. Diane hesitated for a moment, then waved as she walked toward the group awaiting their malts and said, "Hi, can I join you?"

Laird stood up to bring another chair to the table for her. "Of course you can, I'll get you a chair."

Lenore smiled up at her. "We've just ordered some malts, do you want one?"

"Yes, thank you," Diane said as she gracefully squeezed into the tight circle of chairs. Her quiet green eyes scanned the table. "I'm waiting for my folks to come pick me up as soon as they get out of the movies."

"My brothers just came in to tell us all about the film, so I imagine your folks will be here soon," Laird said.

"Maybe you won't have enough time for a malt?" Lenore asked.

"It's okay," Don offered, "I've got my old pick-up truck in town tonight, so I can take you home afterwards if your folks want to leave before you do."

"Thank you, that would be nice."

"Are you okay with chocolate like the rest of us?" Don asked Diane as he got up to order.

"Yes, thanks," Diane leaned back, crossed her long legs and looked around the table. "I hope I'm not interrupting anything?"

"No, I've just been trying to catch Laird up on all the local news."

"Yup," Laird said, "Lenore is as good as the local newspaper."

"She's better than the local newspaper." Don sat down and grinned at Diane. "The newspaper doesn't know half of what we just heard from Lenore."

The malts were delivered in three shining metal containers along with five glasses and spoons; no straws were offered because straws were useless in the thick, almost stiff, ice cream. Lenore passed around the sack of cashews, first demonstrating to Laird how to stir the nuts into the ice cream. Then, leaning forward to eat, she rolled her eyes heavenwards in appreciation.

"So," Lenore turned to Laird and smiled brightly, "What have you been doing for fun since you came home?"

"Not a whole lot," Laird said, avoiding her eyes.

"Oh, sorry, I forgot…"

"It's okay, Lenore," Laird said. "I'll get over it."

Lenore busily resumed eating her malt and no one said anything in the uncomfortable silence that followed.

When the malts were half-eaten, Diane started up the conversation with a forced brightness, obviously determined to be sociable. What were everyone's future plans, she wanted to know, and how was the farming going? Did Laird know where he would be going to college? Once she had the conversation back on track, she pushed back her long red hair and sat in an apparently withdrawn silence, but when her folks came into the drug store to see if she was ready to go home, she told them she guessed she'd stay awhile yet.

Laird studied Diane's face and thought how changed she was compared to the girl he'd known when he'd left three years ago. The smile never quite reached those beautiful green eyes anymore and he'd noticed that sometimes her eyes had almost no expression at all, as though something was missing inside. The only emotion he'd seen in Diane's eyes was the day they'd met at the blacksmith shop when tears had welled briefly in her eyes. At the swimming pool for the last few nights, there had been only distant smiles and blank looks. After the first evening swim, Diane had invited him to join her for a drink at the Bar-None Tavern, but they hadn't stayed long because after taking a few sips of whiskey, Diane had suddenly stood up and said, "I don't think this was such a good idea, Laird. Will you take me home now?"

No one at the table mentioned Conrad's death, or Laird and Janice's break-up, and no one asked Laird any questions about the war. He wondered whether Diane ever wanted to talk about Conrad. Everybody was probably experiencing some degree of uneasiness about him and Jan, and no doubt the others were as uncomfortable as he was about mentioning Conrad's name in Diane's presence. Laird wouldn't really have minded if they'd wanted to ask about the war, but they were right in suspecting he didn't want to talk about Jan.

Laird looked around the table and tried hard to listen. Diane wasn't the only one who had something missing, sometimes he felt as though a part of him wasn't there either. It wasn't because of Jan. For the past couple of years, he'd been aware that a piece of him he couldn't identify would occasionally disengage and stand off to one side, observing what was happening. It felt sometimes like he was watching tropical fish through an aquarium glass. He wondered if it showed on his face the same way it did on Diane's.

They stayed to talk until ten o'clock when Mr. Quarve started to close up the drug store. Don volunteered to give Lenore and Diane a ride home in his pick-up. "I've only got room in Old Blue for the three of us." Turning to Laird and Carla, Don added, "But you two can walk home, right?"

"Sure," Laird said, "Carla's right on my way home and I need the exercise."

Diane looked at Laird. "Will I see you at the pool tomorrow night?"

Laird gave her a friendly salute. "Sure, I'll be there, Diane."

Laird and Carla headed down the sidewalk towards home. A block off Main Street it was quiet; the sidewalks were hushed and dimly lit under a canopy of maples, box elders and elms. The school sat back from the street, almost hidden in its wide expanse of darkened playground, and, as they passed the Presbyterian Church sitting solidly across from the school, lights shone out of windows from houses lining the street. They strolled in companionable silence listening to a roll of far-off thunder and glimpsed a faint flash of sheet lightning against the clouds to the south. Leaves hung silent in the still air, muffling the voices of parents calling the older children in for a late bed-time.

Carla listened to the quiet rhythm of Laird's uneven footsteps. She hoped the limp didn't mean it hurt him to walk. She hoped his hurt leg was like her arm and back: the handicap was always there, but there was no pain associated with it. She wanted to ask Laird how it was for him, but decided maybe he would rather not talk about it.

Laird was remembering walking Sophia home from the hospital through streets of rubble and death. It was so different here, so clean and peaceful; the only similarity was the warm glow he felt at having a beautiful woman walking beside him in the dark.

As they passed under a streetlight, he turned to look down at Carla. "What college are you going to? You never said."

"The University of Minnesota gave me a math scholarship so, since I won't have to pay tuition, I'm going there. My only costs will be books and dorm fees. The only bad thing is that it's an awfully big school, and no one else from here is going that I know of, but maybe Jan will stay in Minneapolis to work and I can see her sometimes."

He reached out and took her hand in his. "You'll meet people who'll love you wherever you go, Carla."

They held hands in silence, their arms moving easily back and forth as they walked along. Laird suddenly wanted to stop and touch her face and her hair...what did that mass of curls feel like when you touched it? He felt himself grow hard, and he stopped breathing for a second.

He abruptly let go of Carla's hand and kept on walking, looking straight ahead. *This isn't Sophia, this is little Squirt...What's happening here?*

Carla looked up at him and tried to read the expression on his face. When she spoke, she struggled to keep her voice even, "I wonder when you'll hear about your college applications."

"I've got three applications in, but I haven't heard anything yet. One of them is to the University of Minnesota, but Mr. Seglie thought I'd have a better chance at schools like South Dakota State or Northwestern."

"Oh," Carla felt an unexpected leap in her chest as she blurted out, "I guess it's too much to hope for but it would be wonderful if we went to the same college." She was silent for a moment before she added, "Then I could keep on tutoring you in math if you needed it."

"I'll probably need it all right."

She shook her head, "No, actually, you're going through the material so fast, we'll be able to start on Algebra II next week. I guess you know you're a very smart guy."

"Not so smart. I think it's that I've got such a good teacher." He smiled down at her and asked, "Is that what you plan to be when you grow up? A math teacher?"

She looked up at him, her eyes glowing. "Maybe, do you think I'd be any good at it?"

He laughed and impulsively reached out for her hand again. "You know what I think!"

She gave a rueful smile, thinking she seldom had any idea what went on in his mind…maybe if she'd had a brother…

He dropped her hand again as they turned up the sidewalk leading to the Swanson house. "Guess it's time to say good night."

"Do you want to stay and sit on the porch swing awhile?" Carla looked up at him, her eyes hidden in the dark.

Laird suddenly wanted to reach out, grab hold of her and kiss those full lips, or maybe just a kiss on the forehead would be better the first time? He blinked and put both his hands in his pockets. What in hell was happening to him? Was this what happened to someone on the rebound? Carla was just a kid. He wondered if she'd ever even had a boyfriend. She had lots of friends but he wasn't sure about a boyfriend. She'd never written to him about a boyfriend, and Laird certainly didn't need a girlfriend right now. Jan had given him a hard lesson that women could be the source of pure misery… all except for Sophia.

"Thanks, Carla, but I'll pass on it this time. I think I should get home. I better check to see if those brothers of mine got home okay. I told Mother I'd keep an eye on them."

"Well then," Carla forced her voice to sound light and cheerful, "I'll see you bright and early Monday morning." Holding her hand was just a friendly kid sister thing for Laird, but as she walked into the house, Carla was stunned to realize that for her, it had opened up a whole new world.

※ ※ ※

At the Nordstrom house, Ellen and Emil sat in the living room listening to music on the radio, waiting for Laird to come home. When he came through the front door, Ellen put her embroidery in her lap and Emil leaned back in his chair, smiles of welcome on their faces. Laird gestured at the noises of thunderous footsteps over their heads and the sound of the toilet flushing. "I don't have to ask, I can hear the boys beat me home."

Ellen inspected her embroidery before she looked up and said, "Seemed like they had a good time, but they never tell me much about what they do. I'd know more about what goes on if I had a daughter."

"Sorry about that, Mother. One of us should have been a girl."

Ellen laughed and said, "Never mind, Laird, I'll just have to wait for granddaughters." She bit off her embroidery thread and began to thread the needle with a different color. "Did you see lots of people you know tonight?"

"I saw lots of familiar faces but mostly I spent time with Don, He said to say hi by the way. We had a beer and then later we ran into Carla and a couple of other girls, nothing too exciting."

Emil reached over to turn down the radio. "Do you want to play a game of chess before you go to bed?"

"Sure, let's break in your new chess set." Laird went over to the buffet to get the hand-carved Black Forest gnomes he'd brought back from Germany, purchased, like most of his other homecoming gifts, with cigarettes.

All the Nordstrom males liked playing chess. It was a quiet, intense inner game that suited them. Ellen loved watching them play through long periods of thoughtful silence, and loved their occasional bursts of groans and laughter, but had no desire to learn the game herself. Although Emil had tried to teach her when they were first married, she soon gave it up, telling her friends she was tired of being chased all over the board and inevitably losing.

When Laird was old enough to learn chess, Emil had known he'd better change his teaching technique, so he insisted that Laird remove however many of Emil's chess pieces necessary to even up the game. By the time Laird was in sixth grade, he was good enough to play with evenly matched armies. Chess was the one game, other than the card game of Whist, that Emil often played with his sons.

❋ ❋ ❋

Emil and Laird pulled out chairs and sat down at the dining room table opposite one another with the chess set between them. Emil said, "If only all wars were as bloodless as chess."

Laird nodded as he studied the curious little gnome chessmen he was arranging on the board. "Maybe if soldiers looked this funny, people would be too amused to fight."

When Emil declared checkmate, Laird pushed back his chair and stood up. "Sorry, Dad," he apologized. "I'm not much of an opponent tonight. Let's try it again tomorrow."

❋ ❋ ❋

Upstairs in his bedroom, Laird opened the bottom drawer of his dresser and lifted out a wrinkled brown paper bag stuffed with letters. Most of the letters from home had been lost, but after the war and his permanent posting in Frankfurt, he'd managed to save some. Janice's letters were bundled in a neat packet tied up with a string, the others were mixed together in no particular order.

He sat down on the chair by the desk and started looking through the envelopes. He studied the packet of Janice's letters for a long time before he put them back in the bottom drawer. He sorted Carla's letters into a separate pile and, after arranging them by date, placed them on his bedside table; it would be interesting to read her letters again. He turned on the bedside lamp, got into bed, pulled up the sheet and reached for the first envelope which he noticed was dated the day after President Roosevelt's death. Almost everyone from home had written to him about FDR's death; the President's death had been like a death in the family. Laird opened the envelope and took out several sheets of tissue-thin letter paper, surprised at the pleasure he felt at seeing Carla's familiar open, looping style of handwriting.

April 13, 1945

Dear Laird,

I suppose by now, you've heard about President Roosevelt. They say he was sick for a long time, but he didn't want people to know about it, and I also heard he had polio, like me, except he was a grownup man when he caught the polio, and I was only three. People say he always had trouble standing and walking, but I never realized that either, he always seemed so cheerful and strong. Daddy and Mama feel really bad he's gone and Daddy said, "Why couldn't he have lived long enough to see the war won?" But Mama said it must have given him some comfort to know the end was in sight. I just wish it was all over and you boys were home again. This has been a very sad day.

Carla

Laird slowly folded the letter and put it back in its envelope. It was probably the shortest letter she'd ever written. The day President Roosevelt died was stamped indelibly in his mind: the disbelief, the sorrow, the uneasiness at wondering who would be able to take charge of such a huge enterprise as a war on two fronts. Roosevelt was the only President Laird had ever known. He'd never forget where he was when he'd first heard the news of the Presidents death; he'd been sitting on the ground with the rest of his platoon, eating Spam from his canteen tray, and one of the guys had said, "My God! Who in hell is Harry Truman?"

Carla's next letter took up three pages on tissue-weight paper.

April 23, 1945

Dear Laird,

I probably shouldn't even write when I'm in this kind of mood, but I think I need a Father Confessor today, and you're it. I hope you don't mind. A few weeks ago I went to a slumber party over at Beverly Mason's house. There were six of us giggling girls so we didn't do much slumbering. After Bev's folks were asleep, Lenore pulled three Lucky Strikes out of her purse (she snitched them out of her Dad's jacket) and everybody started puffing away, everybody except me. They kept after me to try one, but I said why on earth would I want to try something that I hated for my Dad to do?

Anyway, when they'd finished smoking the cigarettes, Gail showed us an English test some of the boys had stolen from Miss Colton's desk. Do you remember how Miss Colton always gives a pre-test in the fall and then a post-test in the spring to find out how much we've learned? This was the post-test. I wouldn't look at it at first...I even tried to crawl under my blanket to get away from them. Bev and Gail kept pulling the blanket off me and saying, "Don't be such a Pollyanna!" I finally looked at the test, and I already knew everything on it except the question about gerunds. (And who cares anyhow about a noun that has some characteristics of a verb? Anybody knows to say 'playing the piano' without ever knowing it's a gerund. Who invented the idea of a gerund anyway?)

Well, guess what happened today? Miss Colton held up my test paper, looked proudly at me and said, "This person got the best grade in the class." Everyone turned and smiled knowingly at me. I felt like a criminal walking up to get my paper. I want to confess to Miss Colton, but I just can't bring myself to do it. I'm too big a coward, besides, if I tell the truth, then I'd be ratting on everybody else. I came home and laid down on the bed and cried. I'm too ashamed to tell anybody. (I don't know why it's okay to tell you. Maybe it's because you're so far away.)

Well, like Mama says, 'Everybody makes mistakes...and the only thing to feel bad about is if you don't learn from your mistakes.' So I make a vow right now, that I will never again do something I know is unethical, even if the whole world tells me I should. I'm crying again, but I feel a little better, telling you about it. My next letter will be more cheerful. I promise.

Love, Carla Rae

Laird checked the date on the letter and saw it had been written in the spring of her junior year. He grinned as he folded the letter and put it back in the envelope; he hoped she'd forgiven herself by now.

August 12, 1945

Dear Laird,

This morning I went to church with Little Grandma and my Great-Aunt Flora. You've probably never been to a Methodist Church. I know your family is Lutheran. My mother and dad don't go to any church, they are still *mad at God for letting my little brother and sister die, and me to have polio and appendicitis and nearly die myself. Mother says God obviously doesn't care about her, so she is returning the favor and doesn't care about him either.*

But Little Grandma and Aunt Flora still trust in God and love to go to church. We dress up in our best clothes, put on hats and gloves and ride in Grandma's little car. She is nervous about traffic and whenever we meet another car, which isn't very often, she clenches the wheel and starts to swear, 'God Damn It, why does everybody have to go somewhere at the exact same time I do?'

We usually sit in a pew down front. When I was little, I felt so proud standing between them, all of us singing hymns at the top of our lungs, but as I've gotten older, to tell you the truth, I'm a little embarrassed. They really belt out those old hymns and drown out everybody around us!!!! Mama says it's the Welsh in us…Big Grandma says that in Wales, even the men join choruses and sing the night away in the taverns. I have no idea how Big Grandma knows all this, don't tell anybody but sometimes I think she just makes things up!!! I hope she is right because it makes me happy to think of all those men singing away, especially now that the war is over.

Well, I better sign off. I think of you every day, Laird, and pray you can come home soon.

Love, Carla Rae

Laird remembered reading that letter to some of his buddies at the barracks in Frankfurt. The guys had loved the part about Little Grandma swearing "God Damn It" at the traffic on her way to church, and they'd wanted him to read that part a second time. Laird carefully folded the letter and placed it back in its envelope before he picked up the next one.

September 18, 1945

Dear Laird,

I had such a good time today with your brother Duane and Bobby Weaver. If Duane wasn't so responsible, I wouldn't have gone with him, after all, he is only 13 years old, but I figured if Bobby who just had his twenty-third birthday trusts him to drive his nice Pontiac, I could trust him, too. (Is it true that South Dakota is the only state in the country where it's legal for kids to drive? Daddy says that in Minnesota, they have to be 16 years old.)

It was cold this morning, but the sun was out so it turned out to be a beautiful day for a drive. We saw lots of Canadian geese go by in V formations, heading south and honking away... I wonder why they honk when they fly, you'd think they'd be too tired to keep up so much honking. Mrs. Holliday says she thinks they honk to encourage each other, and I like to think of that when I hear them flying over.

Well, back to my story. So Duane asked if I'd like to come along to take Bobby for a drive. We walked down to Bobby's house, got him in the passenger seat, and me in back and took off (Don't worry, Duane stayed at the speed limit which, as you know, is still only 35 miles an hour.) Bobby has such strong shoulders and arms, he does a lot of the lifting to get himself in the car but still needs someone else, usually his Dad, to help. That spina bifida is such bad stuff, isn't it? I think of my own situation when I'm with Bobby and am grateful I had polio instead of spina bifida.

First, we drove up Main Street with the windows rolled down, and Bobby gave the wolf whistle to every girl we saw, and he had a mile-wide grin on his face the whole time. They all waved and smiled back at him. We saw Mary Lou Larson, Ellen Haggerty, and Virginia Olsen among others. Then we drove out to the farm where Uncle John and Don helped Bobby get into his wheel chair and the guys all went out to shoot cans off the fence in the west pasture. I watched from the porch with Aunt Flora. Bobby and Don are both really good shots. Shooting is something Bobby can do that I can't. When they gave the gun to Duane to try, Duane hit the can square on and you could see he was pretty proud of himself. There are no baby animals now on the farm...winter's coming on so they've all grown up or gone to market.

Well, time to close. I think of you often, and hope you are not too lonesome for Jan and your family. But now that the war is over, it shouldn't be much longer before you're home again!

Love, Carla Rae

Laird and Don had spent hours shooting at rats out at the city dump with their twenty-two rifles when they were kids. It had always been a real triumph to bag a rat because they were wily and hard to hit. Laird had loved his old twenty-two, but now he never wanted to pick up another gun, not even a relatively harmless twenty-two. Laird folded the letter and put it back in its envelope, glad Bobby had a car and the spunk to whistle at the girls. The only good thing about the damn spina bifida was that at least Bobby would never have to aim his gun at another human being.

November 4, 1945

Dear Laird,

    Today I've got some real news to tell you! My Uncle Kenny called long distance from San Diego to tell us he is discharged from the Navy, he finally got enough points to get out. (He probably got his points faster than you because he's married and has a little girl.) We all celebrated with ice cream and Devil's Food cake, but then Daddy had to get a bottle of whiskey so he could make a toast to the end of the war and all the boys who were starting to come home. He drank an awful lot and finally ended up smashing his empty whisky bottle against the side of the garage and making a vow he would never drink again… I sure hope so.

    I haven't told anybody about this before, but Daddy was awful upset during the war. He worried about Uncle Kenny being on a ship in the Pacific with torpedos and Kamakazie pilots all around, and sometimes I think he even felt guilty that he was too old to fight. He used to come home from the gas station drunk as a skunk, looking for Japs to kill. He used terrible language about the Japs, which I won't repeat here. Mama and Little Grandma could usually calm him down and get him into bed to sleep it off. One night he started fighting Japs down at the gas station and he threw car batteries through the front windows and tore up the place something fierce. Of course he felt really bad about it when he sobered up, so I hope he means it when he says he's through drinking.

    Little Grandma used to sit in her rocking chair after it was dark, holding Uncle Kenny's letters and crying. Even now, after Uncle Kenny is safe and sound in San Diego, she sometimes still sits and cries, worrying that his wife and baby won't move back here and she won't get to see their little girl grow up. We all worried during the war…we worried ourselves sick about all of you. It's so wonderful to know that even though you're still far away, the war is over. We're still lonesome for you, but there's a lot less worrying going on now.

    So that's my news, Laird. We're counting the days until you can come home, too.

Love, Carla Rae

Laird had heard the town gossip about Verle's drinking binges, but Jan had never mentioned her father's drinking. Remembering the many times over the past three years that he'd been stupid, staggering drunk himself, Laird figured he had no right to point a finger at Verle. He'd been lucky to come home with only a limp. The limp he could learn to live with, but he suspected the load of emotional shrapnel he'd dragged home would be harder to deal with. The chaplain had advised him to be patient with himself, and reassured him that after a while he'd feel normal again. Laird hoped the chaplain was right, but he couldn't ignore the fact that shrapnel from World War I was still leaking out of police chief Oscar.

Laird put Carla's letters back in the drawer, reached over to turn off the light and lay on his back in the dark, thinking. She always signed her name Carla Rae and he'd deliberately kept on calling her Squirt. He hadn't realized she'd grown up. She wasn't the kid he'd imagined when he'd read those letters the first time.

Still thinking about Carla, he turned over onto his side. She was so damned attractive. It was odd how the polio didn't take away any of her beauty, just sort of blended in with who she was…her cheerful, smart, spunky self. He turned over on his back and lay staring up at the ceiling. She'd be going off to college soon and she didn't know anything about men and how they'd try to take advantage of her. She was so innocent she didn't even know she needed to be protected.

Chapter Thirteen

Lawrence Blakesly pulled up to the curb in front of Mrs. Johnson's house and ran around to open the car door for Janice. His eyes glowed behind his glasses as he held out his hand to help her out of the car. "I'll be back in an hour to pick you up," he said.

Jan looked up and flashed him a smile, "I'll be ready."

It had been a month since she'd sent the ring back to Laird and given herself permission to love Lawrence, and, whenever she was with Lawrence now, she experienced a curious kind of floating feeling. She loved looking at him, his lean, intelligent face, his lanky body, his magnified grey eyes, and his long, slender hands.

When he got out of the car, he pulled her close and kissed her full on the lips, "Oh, Jan…"

She kissed him back, but quickly looked around and pushed him away saying, "No, we shouldn't be doing this out here on the street."

He grinned and slowly backed off. "How long do we have to wait before we get married? I can't take much more of this courting business."

Janice smiled and shook her head at him. "Lawrence, you've only been courting me for a month!" She ran up the walk and turned to wave as he drove off. She wanted to get married, too, she wanted to spend every day with him, wanted to sleep with him and wake up with him, she ached from waiting, and she knew Lawrence did, too. The uneasiness she had felt necking with Laird was minor compared to the fierceness of the frustration she felt when she and Lawrence were alone together, his lips on her neck, the exciting odor of his breath, his urgent hands stroking her body.

She wished their wedding could be tomorrow, but it was still too soon to tell Laird she was going to marry someone else. She and Lawrence would just have to wait. She didn't want to make things any worse for Laird than she already had. Maybe time wouldn't heal all wounds, but a little more time for him to adjust was bound to help.

"I'm home, Mrs. Johnson," she called as she ran up the stairs, "but I'm going out again as soon as I get changed."

Mrs. Johnson, her apron dusted with flour from rolling out pie crust for an apple pie, came into the front hall just in time to see Jan's legs disappearing up the stairway. "All right, dear. I guess that means you won't want supper tonight?"

"Right, we're going out to eat and to a movie," Jan's voice drifted down the stairs.

Mrs. Johnson smiled and shook her head. Well, she thought, this young man seems to be the one, anyone can see those two are crazy in love.

She stood at the foot of the stairs holding onto the banister with one hand and called up, "A letter came for you today, dear. It's here on the hall table."

Jan came out of her bedroom, her face flushed and happy, and stood at the top of the stairs. "Does it say who it's from?"

Mrs. Johnson tried to sound matter of fact, "Yes, it's from Laird Nordstrom."

Jan froze and took a sharp intake of breath. "From Laird?"

Mrs. Johnson picked up the letter and held it out. "Yes, see for yourself."

Janice went slowly back down the stairs eying the letter cautiously. Mrs. Johnson smiled, "It won't bite you, dear."

Janice gave her a tentative smile and went slowly back up the stairs studying the familiar handwriting; it seemed strange not to see the old APO military return address written in the corner of the envelope. She sat down in the chair by her bedroom window, held the letter in her lap, took a deep breath, closed her eyes and said, "Please God, don't let him still be hoping we can get back together."

July 1, 1946

Dear Jan,

It's been almost a month since I saw you. I can't deny it was a big shock when you tried to give back the ring and told me it was over. I've been thinking that maybe you are worrying I'm still angry and upset. Carla tells me you

are feeling guilty. Please don't have any guilt, Jan. You kept your promise, you waited until I came home and then you told me the truth. You were right that we were too young to make a commitment to marry. Yesterday I was thinking about you, and I realized that in some strange way, you seem like a dream I had all through the war. It was a good dream, but it's over and I'm awake now. So don't worry about me. I'm getting on with my life. And someday, when you find someone you really love, I'll come dance at your wedding.
Your friend, Laird

Janice leaned back in the chair and closed her eyes. She sat clutching the letter, trying to blink back the tears. "Oh, thank you, dear Laird… and I will invite you to the wedding."

Later, when Lawrence drove up to the house, Janice was waiting for him, a smile on her face as wide as a prairie sunrise. She ran down the front steps and reached in through his open car window to give him a big kiss. "How would you like to marry me as soon as I graduate in September?"

"What happened?" Lawrence asked as a huge smile lifted the corners of his eyes and mouth.

Janice held out Laird's letter. "This letter happened, this wonderful, lovely letter happened."

Later, after Lawrence had gone back to the hospital and she was in bed for the night, Janice started to wonder how to break the news to Laird. Even though he'd written that he hoped she would find someone else to love, she worried it was too soon. Laird probably had some future date in mind, or maybe he hadn't meant what he'd said at all. Maybe if it was Carla who told him about the wedding plans, Laird would be honest and tell her how he really felt.

July 2, 1946

Dear Carla,

I've been thinking and thinking about what to do. This is the third draft of this letter, and it always comes down to me asking you for a favor, a big favor, actually. I guess I'm beating around the bush so here goes:

I'm in love with a wonderful man, his name is Lawrence Blakesly and he's a young doctor finishing his second year of residency at St. Mary's. I've known him for two years now. From the first time we met, we were attracted to one another, but for Laird's sake, I always tried to avoid him. Now that I'm free, it's been like the opposite poles of two magnets coming together. Everybody at the hospital knows about us since we started going out together this last month. I feel terrible that I've kept it a secret from the family and from Laird. We want to get married. Oh, Carla, we want to get married!! And even though Laird wrote me a letter saying he knew our separation was permanent and wished me well, I still worry it's too soon. It seems like I'd be rubbing Laird's face in my happiness to get married so soon.

Will you explain to Laird and let me know how he'd feel if I brought Lawrence home to meet the family? I mean, I need to know how Laird would really feel. Will you do that for me, Carla? I know Laird thinks the world of you...you're the kid sister he never had.

Love you, Jan

Carla re-read the letter before she folded it and put it in her purse. It was a good thing she'd been the one to come to the post office today to pick up the mail, nobody else in the family needed to know about this yet. It sounded like Jan had known this Lawrence person for two whole years and never mentioned him even once. How could Laird not feel betrayed? Carla felt a flash of anger at Jan for asking her to be the one to tell Laird the bad news. Didn't kings used to kill the bearer of bad tidings? It might be pretty extreme to actually murder someone who gave you the bad news, but it was inescapable that the messenger was the one who would first see the raw feelings of humiliation and anguish before a person could save face by hiding his true feelings.

She bit at her lower lip and got up from the bench where she'd been sitting outside the post office. It was midafternoon and only a few cars were parked along Main Street; Mr. Dingle was out washing the windows of the Red Owl Grocery and the window of Bobby's popcorn wagon was still closed. Maybe Duane had taken Bobby for a ride in the car again. Carla was glad there was no one on Main Street to talk to, she needed time to think. A block from home, she had an idea.

July 6, 1946

Dear Jan,

    Okay. I'll be the one to tell Laird on the condition you give me a few weeks before I do. That time-line should work out okay because you have to wait to get married until after graduation in late September, right?

My plan is to find Laird a girlfriend before he finds out about Lawrence. You do see, don't you, that it's important for Laird to have a girlfriend before the whole town hears you're getting married, otherwise people will pity him, and it will be so humiliating for him.

As far as I know, Laird hasn't been going out with anyone, just hangs around with his brothers and me, Don, and sometimes Virgil Nelson. He goes to night swims regularly where Diane works, but as far as I know they've never had a date. Of course people say Diane isn't interested in dating, that it's too soon after Conrad's death, but I think they'd be good for each other, and I've got an idea to get them together. I'll also include Lenore, in the plan, just in case things don't work out between Laird and Diane.

There's a dance coming up at the Legion Hall this Saturday and I'll try to arrange it so we go to the dance together in a group. I'm pretty sure Diane still likes Laird, and Laird used to have a crush on Diane before you came along. There's no problem with Lenore, she's always liked Laird. I'll ask Don to come along, then after the dance we'll all go out together for hamburgers. I'll do my best to maneuver Laird into a next date with whichever one of the girls he likes best. After that it's up to him.

Wish me Luck! Carla Rae

Carla put down her pen and sat looking at the letter, satisfied that it was a good plan, but surprised to realize she wasn't feeling particularly happy about it. Well, it was just common sense, she would never be anything more than a friend. As she picked up the pen again to address the envelope to Jan, the thought occurred to her she'd better meet right away with Don because she would need his help to put her idea into action.

※ ※ ※

Don parked his battered pickup truck—Old Blue—in front of Dee's Café where Carla had said she'd meet him at two pm. The timing was good since he had to come to town anyway to pick up some shingles for the chicken shed. He wondered what she wanted to talk about, and why it had to be kept a secret from Laird; maybe Laird's birthday was coming up?

Carla was sitting in a back booth, wearing something deep-blue that intensified the color of her startling blue eyes. God, she was a beauty, it was too bad about the damned polio. Don noticed that she had a determined look on her face, a sure indicator that that she was hatching some scheme or other.

Don waved casually at Mavis, who was standing by the cash register, and took off his cap before giving Carla his big-kid smile as he slipped his six-foot-two-inch frame into the seat opposite her, "What's up Carla?"

She didn't smile back. "I need your help, Don."

Mavis came over to take their order. "Just coffee for me," said Carla.

"Hi, Mavis," Don said. "Coffee and a piece of rhubarb pie for me, if you still have any."

Mavis shook her head. "Sorry, it's too late in the season for rhubarb. We've got fresh cinnamon rolls, though."

"I never turn down a fresh cinnamon roll."

Mavis gone, Carla leaned forward, her voice almost a whisper, "You have to promise not to tell anyone my plan… promise?"

Don lifted his eyebrows, and his eyes sparkled as he leaned forward and asked in a low voice, "You're not planning to rob a bank, are you?"

"Stop that, Don!" She pressed her lips together and her eyes flashed as she slapped her open hand on the table with a bang. "I'm serious."

Don straightened up and did his best to look chastised. "Okay, I promise to keep whatever secret you're about to divulge." He held up his right hand, palm open, "Scouts honor."

Carla took a deep breath and said, "The thing is, Jan is in love with a doctor she met at St. Mary's and she wants to marry him, probably right after graduation in September."

Don's mischievous look faded away, "Mmmmm…"

"Yes, Mmmmmm," said Carla. "And Jan is afraid to bring this guy home to meet the family for fear she'll make Laird feel even worse than he does already. In her words, she doesn't want to rub his face in her happiness. She can't plan for a wedding until the family knows about it, but once the family knows about it, everybody in town, including Laird, will know about it, too."

Mavis set the cinnamon roll and two coffees in front of them, asked about Don's horse, Nelly, who was due to foal soon, and went back to the counter.

"I can see this could be a little hard on Laird, but you know," Don paused to light a cigarette, "he doesn't seem to be exactly mooning around about Jan. He seems pretty upbeat in general."

"I thought of that, too. He does seem happy enough when he's with me and his brothers, we've done a lot of fun things together this past month, but I think he's just putting on a good front. You know all those Nordstroms are stoics, they could be half dead and they'd never let on."

"Could be you're right." Don looked into her troubled eyes and asked, "But what can either one of us do about it?"

Carla took another deep breath, "Well, I have a plan. If we can get him a girl friend of his own before Jan brings her boyfriend home at the end of the month, he can at least save a little face. Otherwise everybody in town will say, 'Poor Laird, Jan sure left him in the dust awfully fast,' or some such thing. They'll all feel sorry for him, and Laird will hate that."

Don's eyes widened. "You want to get Laird a girlfriend?" He studied her face as though she were a strange creature on the dissecting table in high school biology class.

"Well, yes." Her voice was indignant, "Do you have a better idea?"

"I don't have any ideas at all. Are you sure you know what you're doing, Carla?"

"Yes," she said firmly. "Well, not exactly, but I've got to do something. Jan asked me to be the one to tell him and I don't want to tell Laird until he's in a situation where he won't feel so abandoned." She added in a quiet voice, "and humiliated."

"So, how do you plan to pull off this feat of finding Laird a girlfriend?"

"Well, I've thought of two girls I think he likes. There's my friend Lenore, she always makes him laugh, and there's Diane. Remember how he dated Diane in his sophomore year before he started going with Jan? And did you know he's been going regularly to the evening adult swims where Diane is the lifeguard?"

Don nodded, his expression dubious.

"There's a dance at the Legion Hall this Saturday night, Benny Wilson's Big Band. I'll ask Lenore and Diane if they want to go to the dance with you and Laird and me. With me along, it will be a group and not a double date so no one should feel uncomfortable about it."

Don raised his eyebrows and took a big bite of his cinnamon roll.

"And then, whichever girl Laird seems to want to spend the most time with, you offer to take me and the other girl home so Laird can take home the one he likes most." She stopped and pursed her lips thoughtfully. "Maybe he'll even meet somebody at the dance I haven't thought of, and then, of course, you can take all three of us home."

"What if I'm the one who wants to spend time with Diane?"

Her eyes opened wide. "Oh, I didn't know you were interested in Diane. Are you?"

"Carla, every unmarried guy in town is interested in Diane, but no, there's nothing special going on between us. In fact, a couple of months ago I asked her out to see a movie and she refused, said it was too soon." He stopped to concentrate on the cigarette he was lighting before he asked, "What if you're the one Laird wants to spend the most time with?"

"Who, me?" She shook her head, "He's not interested in me, I'm like his kid sister."

Don leaned his chin on his left hand and deliberated a moment before he spoke, "I don't think this is a good idea, Carla. Why not just let things happen on their own?"

"Just letting things happen on their own doesn't make sense to me. If you're so smart, Don, give me one good reason why my idea isn't a good one."

Don put both his hands palms down on the table and assumed what his classmates at school used to call his judge position. "The most important reason is I don't feel good about meddling around in other people's lives. Reason number two is that Laird has just come home from a war where everything was a total mess and he's still carrying around who knows how many terrible memories. Reason number three is he's lost the girl he loves, or at least thought he loved. Reason number four is he's not sure he can handle college academics, besides which, he's on pins and needles waiting for responses to his college applications. He's all up in the air right now, and you think you can fix him up with a serious girlfriend in the next couple of weeks?"

"Well, maybe not a serious girlfriend, but at least he'd have someone to go out with to take his mind off losing Jan, and it wouldn't be meddling," she said indignantly. "What's so unusual about friends doing a little match-making?"

Don said, "Believe me, Carla, girlfriends aren't always the answer to a guy's problems."

"Please, Don?" her eyes were pleading. Don shifted uncomfortably in his seat. She'd never before asked him for a favor.

He groaned, took a sip of coffee and buttered another section of his cinnamon roll. "I still think it would be better to let things work out in their own way and not interfere, Carla. But okay, I'll do it this one time." He held up both hands in warning and said, "But just this once."

Carla heaved a sigh, "Oh, thank you, Don. You ask Laird and I'll ask the girls. We'll all meet at my house about eight o'clock on Saturday night. Maybe you should leave your car parked at the Legion Hall and come pick us up in Laird's car? We girls can sit all three in the backseat… have you seen his new car yet? My Dad found him a good used Ford."

Don slowly stood up from the booth, and carefully put his cap on as he looked down into her upturned face. "Are you sure you want to do this, Carla?"

She looked away as she picked up her purse, and her voice was firm, "Yes. I'm sure."

Chapter Fourteen

Don and Laird heard the girls' laughter even before they knocked on the front door. Carla opened the door and smiled up at them, her hair a froth of shining brown curls and her long-sleeved green dress swirling around her as she led them inside. "Here they are," she said, "right on the dot!"

Verle came over to the two men and shook their hands vigorously. "Good to see you, Don. How's the new car running, Laird?"

"It's a great little car, thanks again for finding it."

"No thanks necessary." Verle looked Laird and Don over approvingly; they were an impressive pair of young men, lean and muscular, with casual straight-backed postures. Only the hands in their pockets betrayed any uneasiness at being in the midst of this dazzling group of females.

Carla wasn't the only one dressed in her best; Diane wore a shimmering short white and black polka dot dress with black patent leather pumps; Lenore was a vision in a full-skirted white sleeveless dress trimmed with large, sky-blue buttons. Verle watched Laird and Don staring at the girls, and grinned. "Dora and me will see you at the dance a little later. We never miss Benny Wilson and his Big Band when they come to town."

Little Grandma stood in the dining room archway admiring, but also feeling somewhat envious, of the young people. "I used to dance the light fantastic, too, when Grandpa was alive." She held up her arms and started to twirl.

Verle put his arms out and smiled, "You sure did, Jeanette. You and Grandpa were great dancers…how about a dance right now?"

Little Grandma stepped back. "No, Verle, about all I'm good for now is to be a baby-sitter." Her smile evaporated and her eyes started to spill over.

Martha came into the room and saved the situation by protesting, "I'm not a baby and I don't need a babysitter!"

"Of course you're not a baby, Martha," Little Grandma said. "Would I play Monopoly with a baby?"

Dora came out of the bedroom with a lipstick in her hand. "Of course you're not a baby, Martha, you're just not old enough to stay home alone."

Verle waved them out the door. "You run along, kids, we'll see you at the dance."

It was a typical Dakota summer evening, a warm eighty degrees with the sun still hanging low on the horizon, when Laird pulled the car into a parking spot two blocks away from the Legion Hall.

"It's going to be hotter than a firecracker in there," Don said. "I'm leaving my sport-coat in the car."

Carla and Lenore got out of the car and started chatting with a newlywed couple they met walking hand-in-hand towards the dance hall. Diane stood by the car and watched Laird and Don as they took off their coats and tossed them into the back seat. They were dressed like most of the other men in town that night, in white shirts topped by ties of subdued colors, brown leather dress shoes, and neatly pressed dark slacks. Men dressed in such plain wrappings, but there was something so mysteriously attractive about the way they moved, their easy carelessness when throwing their coats into the backseat… Diane abruptly turned away. It suddenly hurt too much to watch.

At the entrance to the Legion Hall, Laird and Don tried to pay all the entrance fees, but Carla lifted her chin and insisted, "No, this isn't a date, we're just friends going out together and we should go Dutch." As good manners dictated, the girls were first in line and easily managed to pay for their own tickets. Laird and Don looked at each other and shrugged. It was clear who was in charge here, and it wasn't them.

As they entered the hall, they held out their hands to be stamped with indelible ink. If anyone neglected to get his or her hand stamped when they first paid for their tickets, they couldn't get back into the building without paying again. The hand-stamp was important because no liquor was served in the hall, which resulted in frequent comings and goings of small groups of men, all headed for the glove compartments of their cars to take a swig of Jim Beam or Old Kentucky Bourbon. As the local proverb went, whiskey provided a little false courage for the fainthearted.

There was already a sizeable crowd moving around the floor to the music. Built after the First World War, the Legion Hall boasted a carefully-crafted oak dance floor, the best one in Cottonwood County. Benny Wilson's Big Band was holding forth from the stage at the far end of the hall which contained backless wooden benches lining both sides of the room. The walls on either side of the dance floor were interspersed with high, narrow windows, all opened wide to let in fresh air and, hopefully, to thin out the fog of cigarette smoke that permeated the atmosphere. The light coming through the windows was fading into the dusk of evening, and soon the mirrored, rotating ball that hung from the high ceiling would begin to cast its reflected, moving spots of light around the darkening room.

The band was playing, *Moonlight Serenade*. Looking up at Don, Lenore said, "Oh, I love that song."

"I'm willing to give it a go if you are." Don held out his arms and they shuffled off smiling at each other.

Laird, Diane, and Carla looked around for a place to sit. "There's a spot over there right under an open window," Carla said.

As Laird put an arm around each girl to steer them through the crowd, he felt the warm contours of their bodies under their thin summer dresses, and it made him suddenly aware of the difference between the two. Diane was tall and willowy. Laird's right arm and hand came naturally to rest on her waist. Once, to avoid a spinning dancer, she leaned ever so slightly into him and, when their hips touched, he felt the sleekness of her body, her muscles moving in perfect symmetry on either side of her spine.

Carla was a full foot shorter than Laird; consequently his arm came to rest higher up across her back, and for the first time he realized that Carla not only had a paralyzed arm, she had a crooked spine and a slight hump on her back. He looked down at her smiling profile and thought, damn the polio. He wondered why he'd never noticed her back before, and why it had never occurred to him that Carla was probably carrying around her own load of emotional shrapnel…probably because she was always so damned cheerful. Laird felt a surge of affection for her and gave Carla a little hug saying, "Here we are, best seats in the house."

Diane sat down, smiled at Carla, and looked up appraisingly at Laird. Diane had expected that Laird might come home from the war moody and depressed, especially now after losing Jan, but he seemed perfectly natural tonight. He had the same strong face, the same unruly shock of hair and, except for the limp, the same athletic, muscular body. The only significant differences were that his eyes seemed deeper set in his face, and he had an aura of distance about him.

Carla sat down beside Diane, and matter-of-factly lifted her paralyzed arm onto her lap as she gave them both a big smile. "Why don't you two dance?" Carla said, "I'll save your places."

Laird shook his head. "Let's wait until someone else comes by to talk with you, Carla. It's no fun for you to sit here all alone. There'll be plenty of time for dancing." He put his hands behind his head, stretched out his long legs and settled back against the wall to watch the dancers slowly shuffling around the room.

"I don't mind," Carla protested. "I know almost everybody here. I can always find someone to talk to."

Laird looked over at her and grinned. "You're an independent little cuss."

Diane said, "You're sure you don't want to dance, Carla?"

"No, you two go ahead."

Laird stood up and held out his hand to Diane. "My leg is only good for the slow dances so maybe we should take advantage of this one while we still can."

Diane hesitated, not sure this was a song she wanted to dance to; *Sentimental Journey* had been a favorite of Conrad's. The night before he'd left they'd cuddled in bed together, and just before she finally went to sleep he'd hummed *Sentimental Journey* in her ear and whispered, "I'm going to be singing that song on the train coming back home. Don't you worry, honey, one day the war will be over and I'll be on that train headed home to you."

Diane stood up and tried to smile at Laird. "All right, let's give it a try."

Carla watched them move away, thinking how beautiful they were together. She sat back on the bench, trying not to feel like a wallflower, and remembered a high school dance she'd attended when she was a sophomore. A new boy had been in town visiting his cousin during spring break and, at the Spring Dance, when he'd come over to introduce himself, she'd been sitting on a bench like this one. He'd sat down beside her and they'd started to tell each other about their schools, their families, and their hobbies. It was one of those magic meetings where two people instantly like one another, but when he'd asked her to dance, as soon as he realized her hand was paralyzed and her back was crooked, his body stiffened, and there had been no mistaking the look of shock, almost of horror, on his face. He'd bravely finished the dance with her, but that was the last she'd seen of him.

"Hi there, Carla, can I have this dance?" She looked up to see her father holding out his hand and looking down at her.

"I'd love to dance with you, Daddy...where's Mother?"

"She's over there gabbing with Myrtle Beamer."

Verle took Carla in his arms and with a practiced flair moved her expertly around the floor, trying hard to hide his feelings by concentrating on smiling down at her. Damn it, he didn't know whether to thank God or curse Him that he'd happened to see Carla sitting over there all alone, looking so abandoned.

Carla gave herself up to the pleasure of moving her body with the music, thinking it was nice of Daddy to ask her to dance. She'd grown up being danced around the house by her father to the sounds of the Big Bands on the radio. Whenever he was in a good mood, which was often, he swooped down on his women, as he called them, and took turns dancing them from one end of the house to the other, and sometimes, on those occasions when his staid mother came to visit, he delighted his daughters by coaxing even their Big Grandma to take a whirl.

Carla was not so engrossed in the music that she forgot to search the crowd for Laird and Diane, and finally glimpsed them on the far side of the dance floor where they had stopped dancing. Laird's left arm was around Diane's waist and he was saying something to her. They were blocked from Carla's view for a moment, and when she turned to see them again, they were leaving the dance floor, headed towards the privacy of the dimly lit hallway leading to the area back of the stage. It was impossible not to notice that Laird still had one arm around Diane's waist.

When *Sentimental Journey* ended, Verle walked with Carla towards the bench and stayed with her until Laird and Diane rejoined them. Diane seemed subdued, but Laird had a wide grin on his face as he approached and applauded, "You two are really good!"

Verle reached out and clapped Laird on the shoulder. "It's practice that'll do it, son, just practice."

Laird shook his head. "I doubt it…some people are born knowing how to dance and I'm not one of them."

"Carla can teach you," Verle said, hoping Laird would take the hint. "Well, I better go rescue your mother from Myrtle. Thanks for the dance, Carla."

When the band started to play, *It's Been a Long, Long Time,* Laird asked, "How about dancing this one with me, Carla? I do pretty good on the slow ones, but I still think I could use some lessons."

Carla saw Don going off to dance with Diane, and Martin Hensley, a longtime admirer of Lenore who had appeared out of nowhere, was holding his hand out to Lenore. Carla decided it wouldn't hurt her plan to dance with Laird just once. He and Diane were obviously hitting it off, everything was happening just as she'd planned…so, yes. Why not dance with him?

As Laird put one arm around Carla's waist and lifted her paralyzed hand, he was startled by its incredible softness. When she put her left hand on Laird's upper arm, she felt an uncomfortable jolt of intimacy at the movement of firm muscles under the thin material of his shirt. Carla wondered how she felt to Laird when he held her; she knew it couldn't feel nearly as good as when his arms were around Diane.

"You don't need lessons, Laird, you're a natural," she said.

As he looked down into her eyes, which were looking almost a deep violet in the dimming light, he felt an almost irresistible impulse to kiss her on the top of her head and call her Little Squirt, but he didn't dare, knowing she would hate it. He pulled her closer so that the side of her face rested against his chest, and he could smell her perfume, or her hair, or whatever it was that smelled so uniquely Carla.

The soloist slowly walked up to the mike, her sequined dress reflecting back the light from the rotating mirrored ball, and, in a soft, husky voice, began to sing a familiar, haunting World War II melody. A few couples stopped dancing and stood quietly listening with their arms around each other's waist, the only other sound was the slow movement of feet sliding across the floor.

Kiss me once, and kiss me twice, and kiss me once again,
It's been a long, long time.
Haven't felt like this my dear since can't remember when,
It's been a long, long time.

Carla drew back and looked up at Laird with an earnest expression on her face. "Diane must be so lonely, and she's an awfully nice person, don't you think, Laird?"

He looked down at her with his steady hazel eyes. "Yes," he said, "she's told me how much she misses Conrad."

Carla put her cheek back on Laird's chest, and neither one said anything more as they moved together through the remainder of the song:

You'll never know how many days I dreamed about you,
And just how lonely nights all were without you,
So kiss me once and kiss me twice and kiss me once again,
It's been a long, long time.

When the music stopped, the crowd was hushed, and Laird slowly lowered her hand, stepped back and smiled down into her eyes. "Thank you, Carla."

"You're welcome, Laird." She felt her face grow warm as she quickly looked away. She knew she could never, ever, let him see how she felt. It would only embarrass him, and even worse, it might ruin their sister/brother relationship. Then she'd lose him entirely.

Back at the bench, Martin Hensley was standing close to Lenore, obviously determined to stick close for the evening. As soon as Don caught Carla's eyes, he gestured with his head towards Martin; his twinkling eyes sent a clear message that Martin was an unexpected glitch in her grand scheme, and what was she going to do about it? Carla tossed her head and didn't return his smile. Lenore wasn't a key player anymore... Diane was obviously the one who interested Laird.

"Didn't I see Virgil talking to you a while ago, Lenore?" Laird looked around the room, his eyes searching for his huge friend. "He must have come back to town from his hide-out up at the lake."

"Yes, but just for a minute," Lenore said. "He said he was going outside to get some fresh air."

"Is anybody thirsty? Do you girls want a Coke?" Don asked, "or an Orange-Ade, or Root Beer, or whatever we can find?" The women ordered Cokes and settled themselves on the bench as they watched the three men walk towards the pop cooler at the far end of the hall.

Lenore smiled, her eyes sparkling. "I'm having such a good time. Aren't these great guys?"

Carla raised her eyebrows and said, "Yes, and I notice we seemed to have acquired a new one."

Lenore blushed. "Well, Martin does even up the group, and how about you? I saw you dancing up a storm with your dad out there, and with Laird, too."

Carla cleared her throat before she answered, "You know, actually, I'm not feeling very well." She stood up, "Will you tell the guys I'm sorry but I think I'll just go on home."

Diane turned grave eyes towards Carla. "But you looked like you were having such a good time."

"I was, but all of a sudden, I feel kind of sick to my stomach."

Diane nodded. She was ready to go home herself, but she lived too far away to walk, and she couldn't very well ask Don or Laird to leave early when they were having a good time. She should never have agreed to dance to *Sentimental Journey*...she should have known she'd end up blubbering, and being led off the dance floor to have a good cry. She looked down at her hands as she slowly clasped them in her lap. It was more than the music that had upset her. She was ashamed to admit that her anguish came from a fierce jealousy at seeing all the happy couples on the dance floor, and even though she told herself it wasn't Laird's fault, she resented him because he was holding her when it should have been Conrad.

Sentimental Journey had triggered the bitter knowledge that unlike those who came back alive, Conrad's journey home had been in a box.

Lenore reached over to touch Carla's hand. "Wait 'til the guys get back. I'm sure Laird or Don will give you a ride home."

Carla shook her head vehemently and said, "No, it's only eight blocks. The fresh air will do me good, all the cigarette smoke in here is probably aggravating things," and before they could protest further, she turned and hurried towards the entrance. It was probably a good thing that Martin Hensley had attached himself like glue to Lenore; now Diane could have Laird all to herself, and Don wouldn't have to take anybody home.

As she started to cross Main Street, Carla saw Laird's good friend, Virgil Nelson, and his old school mate, Harold Ferguson, getting out of Virgil's car. Harold had recently returned from working in the shipyards on the west coast and was obviously in a mood to party. He waved at Carla, "Hey, come on over and have a little drink!"

Virgil, who looked to be the more sober of the two, grinned and added, "We've got plenty left."

"I don't drink, Harold," Carla said in a disapproving voice. Anyone could see that Harold had been drinking way too much. His words were slurred and his voice boomed with the same heartiness she hated to hear in her dad's voice when he'd been drinking. "Anyway, I'm heading home."

Harold shook his finger at her and in a confidential tone of voice said, "But it's still the shank of the evening…it's too soon to go home." He reached into the car for a whisky bottle and as he straightened up, began to wobble unsteadily, but saved himself by throwing his left arm around Virgil's powerful shoulders and, leaning heavily against his solid companion, he attempted to nonchalantly cross one ankle over the other.

Carla shook her head at them. "No, and anyway, I'm not feeling very good tonight."

Virgil cocked his head, looked steadily at her and said, "Well, if you have to go home, I'm still sober enough to drive, even if this lout isn't." He took Harold's arm off his shoulders. "Let me drive you home, Carla," and, as he critically appraised her shoes added, "I know you don't live far, but it's going to be a long hike in those things."

Virgil was right. Her feet were already hurting. How often had Daddy teased her about wearing what he called those crazy high-heeled shoes? "It's not going to make you any taller," he'd say.

She looked up at Virgil and studied his broad, homely face. There was enough light from the Legion Hall to see that his eyes were focused and kind. "Are you sure you're sober enough to drive, Virgil?"

"Honest to God, Carla, as sober as a judge." He winked and said, "Well, almost." Virgil turned to Harold. "I'll be back in a flash, try to keep upright until then, will you?"

Harold straightened up and gave a facsimile of a snappy salute. "Yes, shur!"

"My car's right down the street, Carla."

Carla was relieved that Virgil had happened along, just being with him always made her feel better. She remembered Jan telling her that in high school, Virgil was the one who comforted anybody having trouble with grades, girlfriends or parents. Boys or girls, it didn't matter, everybody trusted Virgil.

He opened the passenger door, and waited for her to settle herself before he closed the door and ran around to the driver's side. He started the ignition, looked over at her and smiled, "I haven't had a chance to talk to you since I got back. I've been meaning to tell you thanks for the letters you sent while I was in the Pacific." He backed the car slowly into the street. "Letters from home meant a lot."

"I'm sorry I didn't write you more often. I thought about all of you guys and worried about you. A lot of us prayed." She sighed, "But prayers don't always work, do they?"

"No." He shifted into third gear as the car picked up speed. "Prayers don't always work, and that's the truth." He was quiet before he added, "In my case, it wasn't prayers that helped, it was blind luck to have survived a torpedoed ship, and then to be assigned to a backwater supply ship for the rest of the war. After that, the main enemy was boredom, and being cooped up below decks in the engine room."

"I guess when Uncle Sam calls you have to go wherever he sends you."

"Yah, but it's awful hard when you come home and see those gold stars hanging in people's windows, and you don't have even a scratch on you."

He pulled over to the curb outside her house and started to open his door, then stopped and turned again to face her, his eyes hidden in the darkness. "Laird and me have been to visit all seven of the Gold Star families. We got to talking about it last month up at the lake. Neither one of us had the guts to go alone, so we decided to pair up and go together. We'd get flowers from Knudsen's nursery before we'd go…Mrs. Knudsen always had some good ideas about what kind of flowers we should take."

Carla stared at him, wondering if Virgil and Laird were feeling guilty at having survived the war. She reached out and touched his hand. "Daddy says that life is a crapshoot…I think he keeps telling me that so I won't think I've done anything to deserve the polio. You mustn't feel guilty."

Virgil rubbed the back of his neck. "Well, we knew we couldn't live with ourselves until we went to see them, but it was hard. We thought they might resent us, especially Diane, but they all seemed glad we came."

"I'm sure it meant a lot to them."

"How can I ever forget those guys? Dan Tolbertson, he taught Laird and me how to sail up at Clear Lake… and Conrad Oberst, we played football against him for three seasons…he was so tough but so damn good-natured, even when he lost…and Bert Steeglemeyer, we used to go out with our twenty-twos to shoot rats at the dump." Virgil gripped the steering wheel with both hands and said, "Bert was such a bad shot… and Denny Mattson, he always helped me out when I couldn't get a math problem through my thick head." Virgil's voice trailed away. "I won't forget any of them, even Bob Hendrickson. He was one ornery guy, but I always excused him because he had such a mean son-of-a-bitch for a father."

Carla reached over to touch his hand again. "I'm so sorry, Virgil."

"I know you are, Carla."

"I see Laird almost every day and he's never mentioned any of this to me.'" Carla's voice was so quiet he could hardly make out what she was saying; the crickets were making more noise than Carla.

Virgil straightened his back and his voice took on a forced cheerfulness. "I'm sorry to be dumping all this on you, Carla. Laird's got more sense than I do…if I wasn't a little drunk, I probably wouldn't be telling you either."

He got out, came around the car and opened her door, and as he reached his hand out to help her from the car, he impulsively leaned down and kissed her on the forehead. "You're a good kid, Carla."

He stood watching her as she moved carefully in her high-heels up the cracked sidewalk towards the screened porch, and when she turned to wave, Virgil got back into the car and drove away. Carla stood quietly looking down the road long after the tail lights of his car had disappeared into the darkness.

✳ ✳ ✳

The band was still taking a break between sets when Laird, Martin, and Don came back across the dance floor carrying a cold bottle of Coca-Cola in each hand. When they reached the bench, Laird stood looking around for a moment before asking, "Where's Carla?"

Diane's eyes were somber. "She said she didn't feel well and left…we told her to wait and one of you would take her home in the car."

"But she emphatically said no," added Lenore, "and she just took off. We tried to stop her but you know how stubborn Carla is…she said it's only eight blocks and the walk would do her good."

Don handed a bottle of Coca-Cola to Diane and tried hard not to look skeptical. It was just like Carla to come up with a scheme to disappear so Laird and Diane could be alone together. Don took a long thoughtful drink of his Coke and savored the satisfying cool sizzle in his mouth. This whole thing was crazy, maybe he should tell Laird what Carla was up to. He rolled the cold pop bottle across his sweating forehead and knew he'd never tell Laird; he sure didn't want to be the one to break the news that Jan was about to marry some other guy.

Laird stood holding a Coke in each hand, then abruptly put both bottles down on the bench beside Lenore, "I'm going to try to catch up with her." He reached into his pocket for the car keys and walked toward the front doors. Why hadn't she waited to ask for a ride home? He'd noticed those high-heeled shoes she had on. She was always trying to be a little taller…wouldn't she ever learn she was fine just like she was, all four feet ten inches of her? Eight blocks wearing those shoes was going to seem like a mile.

He drove slowly down the street toward Carla's house. She'd just left the Legion Hall so she couldn't have gone far. He was sure this was the street she would have taken home, but it was odd he hadn't spotted her yet. When he approached the Swanson house Laird could see the lights were on in the living room; Carla's grandma was probably still up listening to the radio. Laird pulled up to the curb, turned off the engine and wondered if he should knock on the door to see if she'd arrived home okay. But why wouldn't she get home okay? Nothing could possibly happen to her on this small town street; maybe he'd missed seeing her.

On the other hand, the moon hadn't come up yet and it was pitch black out. Laird turned on the engine and drove carefully back down the street, checking the sidewalks on either side. Suddenly he slapped his hands against the steering wheel. Of course, her dad must have taken her home. She probably just got menstrual cramps or something, and he'd bet she was home getting ready for bed right now.

Laird relaxed and started to whistle, *"Kiss me once and kiss me twice and kiss me once again..."* and the thought came to him that he hadn't kissed any girl for a very long time.

Chapter Fifteen

Dora and Verle were still asleep the next morning when Little Grandma's sister, Flora, arrived promptly on time, at eight o'clock sharp, for Sunday morning breakfast. At sixty-eight years and a widening five-foot-two-inches, Flora was a bit stooped with arthritic legs that were beginning to bow out. She held the arthritis at bay by regularly ingesting handfuls of aspirin which she kept handy in a bottle on the middle of her oilcloth-covered kitchen table. Her twisted fingers prevented her from playing the old pump organ anymore, but she was still a determined dynamo of farm-woman-energy, and in spite of her considerable physical problems, good-humored wrinkle lines crinkled around her eyes and mouth.

This morning, like every other Sunday morning that she could make it into town, Flora was dressed for church. She wore a yellow print rayon dress, a yellow pillbox straw hat decorated with a white veil, sensible black shoes with wide Cuban heels, white gloves, and had her good white summer purse tucked under one arm. Flora loved Sunday mornings, loved having breakfast and gossiping with her sister and her granddaughters, loved going with them to the Methodist church and singing God's praises. After a lonely week on the farm with only her husband and her nephew Don to keep her company, Sunday morning was the social highlight of her week.

She opened the back door without knocking and called out cheerfully in her strong, high-pitched voice, "Good morning, Nettie. Good morning, all you dear girls."

Little Grandma hollered back, "Good morning yourself, Flora. Come on in, breakfast is nearly ready." Neither sister made any effort to be quiet during Sunday morning breakfasts. It was their not-so-subtle way of reminding Dora and Verle they should be up and getting ready for church, too.

"We're in the kitchen," Martha called back. "Grandma's fixing bacon and eggs this morning."

"It smells wonderful."

"It's bacon from your own farm, Flora. If it wasn't for you and John, we'd be eating that terrible canned Spam, like all those city folks." Little Grandma stood at the stove wearing an old housecoat and a full apron to protect her from the spattering grease.

Martha grinned at her great-aunt, "What a good looking get-up that is, Aunt Flora. I love yellow."

"Yes, you look dandy, Flora, but you need a little jewelry," her sister chided. "As soon as we're done here, let's go in my bedroom and you can borrow some of mine."

Flora's eyes twinkled as she opened a cupboard door to get herself a cup, "Well, we'll see, Nettie."

Little Grandma's persistent attempts to drape her sister in great hunks of jewelry were inevitably thwarted, although Flora did often wear the cameo pendant that had belonged to their mother. Every Christmas when the sisters went through the ritual of exchanging their mother's cameo pendant, the one whose year was ending took the necklace from her neck and placed it carefully around her sister's, adjusting it just so, then, sometimes with tears in her eyes, stepped back to survey the effect, saying, "Well now...well now, that looks real nice."

Carla came slowly down the back stairs into the kitchen; her face was somber. "Morning, everybody...you all sound cheerful."

Three pairs of inquisitive eyes turned to look at her.

"Are you feeling all right this morning, Carla?" Little Grandma asked. She glanced at Flora and explained, "Carla came home early last night from the dance, didn't feel so good. She went off to the dance all bright-eyed and bushy-tailed and I expected she'd stay 'til the last dog was hung, but no, she came home around ten o'clock, not looking perky at all."

"What was the matter, Carla? A little female trouble?" Flora asked.

"What's female trouble? Is that like the flu?" Martha asked, "Do girls have a special kind of flu?"

"Never you mind, and no," her grandmother said, "the flu's the same for everybody, boys and girls." She lifted thick slabs of crisp bacon from the sizzling frying pan and put them to drain on the flattened brown paper bag beside the stove. "How many eggs does everyone want?"

"I'll have two, Nettie," Flora said. She turned to Carla. "You do look a little peaked, honey, are you sure you feel up to going to church today?"

Carla opened the cupboard door to get herself a cup. "Oh, sure, I'm feeling fine. I didn't sleep very good, that's all." She poured herself a cup of coffee, sat down at the table and slowly stirred in a hefty dose of cream along with a spoonful of sugar. She never once lifted her eyes to look at the three pairs of eyes studying her.

Flora cleared her throat, "Well, then...Good."

Martha wanted to know all about the dance. "I've never been to a real dance. I've been to wedding dances but they're probably not like a real dance."

"Of course, a wedding dance is a real dance," her grandmother said indignantly. "And when we were newlyweds, your Grandpa's folks used to roll up the living room rug, invite everybody over and we'd have a high old time. Laird's mother was just a kid then, but she could pound out any tune on that old piano of theirs, the hired man would play the fiddle, and we'd just dance the night away. Maybe we didn't have any Big Band but we had just as much fun." She turned to her sister. "Didn't we, Flora?"

"We sure did, Nettie, we surely did."

Carla looked up from her cup, "Did you say Laird's mother used to play the piano for dances?"

"Oh, yes, she could play most any tune by ear. Just the tune and chords but she could belt them out in perfect time. Her and the hired man, Hilder was his name I think, they were a great pair for the dance music."

"I never thought they were a musical family," Carla said. "You have to prod the Nordstrom boys to sing in the car, and I don't think they even own a piano."

Little Grandma brought over a huge tray of bacon and eggs, sunny side up, and put them in the middle of the table. She sat down and started to pass the food. "Well, I imagine she and Emil couldn't afford a piano after they got married, and then maybe as the kids came along and the years went by, she kind of, you know, tucked the music memories away in a drawer."

Flora nodded, picked up her fork and looked out the window at the side yard where the blossoms on the crab apple tree were beginning to fade. "You girls will find out, as you get older, that some things, you just have to let go of…"

"Well," Martha said indignantly, "I'm never going to let go of swimming, or music, and I'm never going to let go of bubble gum either!"

This comment brought out Carla's first real smile of the morning. Little Grandma reached over and patted Martha's hand. "Good for you, Martha. You just swim and chew all the bubble gum you want to, and sing up a storm, and keep on doing it for as long as you can."

They ate in silence while the clock on the kitchen wall ticked and the upstairs toilet flushed a cascade of water down the pipe between the walls.

"I wonder if that's Dora waking up," Little Grandma said. "Maybe she'll come down and have a cup of coffee with us, although I don't know, she and Verle stayed out awful late last night." She pushed her empty plate away, picked up her coffee cup and sighed contentedly, "I do love Sunday morning breakfasts."

When she heard the next door neighbors start their car engine, Little Grandma leaped to her feet and started carrying dishes to the sink. "The Hendersons must be getting ready to leave for church…he's a deacon and has to get there early, but we better get going, too, or we'll be late. There's a clean apron for you, Flora, right over there hanging on the back of the door. I'll go put on my Sunday go-to-meeting duds and be with you in a jiffy."

It was their Sunday morning ritual; Little Grandma cooked the food, Flora and the girls did the dishes, while Dora and Verle tried to sleep late and ignore the activity downstairs.

Flora tied on her apron. "Who wants to wash and who wants to wipe?"

"I'll wash, Aunt Flora." Carla took the dishpan out from under the sink. "You might get your new dress all wet."

Flora picked up a clean dishtowel and began to sing in her quavery soprano voice,

On a hill far away, stood an old rugged cross,
The emblem of suffering and sha-a-me.
How I love that old cross, where the dearest and best,
For a world of lost sinners was sla-a-in.

Carla and Martha joined in to harmonize on the chorus,

How I'll cherish that old rugged cross,
When at last I lay down....

Upstairs, Dora quietly climbed back in bed and covered herself with the sheet as she listened to their voices drifting up the stairs. Every Sunday morning, unless there was a blizzard so Flora couldn't make it into town, they were as regular as an alarm clock at waking her up, but nothing bothered Verle. He would probably sleep through a tornado. Dora heard the girls join in with Flora on the chorus and smiled. Her Aunt Flora had the most amazing voice; Uncle John always insisted her voice could be heard out as far as their farm's south-forty section, but Dora had never believed that. They were singing the *Old Rugged Cross* today. How many times had they sung that song together...around the old pump organ out at Flora's farm, at church when she was a kid standing between her mother and Aunt Flora...doing the dishes together...how many times? Dora turned over on her side and closed her eyes. She loved to sing that old hymn, too, even if she no longer believed a word of it.

❈ ❈ ❈

By that Sunday evening, the news about the fight was all over town. People said it had happened at the Legion Hall Saturday night right after the band was packing up and people were leaving to go home. They said Laird beat up Harold Ferguson outside of the Legion Hall, and when Virgil Nelson had tried to stop him, Laird had punched him out, too.

Whatever had gotten into Laird? He'd never been one to pick a fight. Maybe it was because he was drunk, people said they could understand it if Laird was drunk. After all, he'd been in the thick of the fighting during the war and you never knew what had happened to those guys over there. Laird had earned a Bronze Star and never talked about why. You could understand why someone just back from the war might go off the deep end once in a while.

The story was that when police chief Oscar appeared on the scene, he'd told Harold to get his sorry ass into the police car so he could take him home to sleep it off, but Oscar just told Laird to simmer down and go on home. So you know Laird wasn't real drunk or Oscar would have given him a ride home, too. Laird didn't hurt Harold too bad, just knocked the wind out of him and laid him out on the pavement, but someone said Virgil was developing one hell of a shiner. Apparently Harold was so drunk he could hardly stand up, so it couldn't have taken much to knock him down. It wouldn't have been a fair fight even if Harold was sober; Harold had a big mouth but he'd never been much of a fighter, and everybody knew Laird was boxing champion in his army unit during basic training. Good thing Virgil was bigger and stronger than Laird…he'd maybe saved Harold from getting really hurt. People said Laird was crazy mad at something Harold said, but nobody seemed to know exactly what he'd said to get Laird so riled up.

Chapter Sixteen

Sunday morning after the dance, Don stayed in bed until he heard his Uncle John and Aunt Flora head out for church, the car tires of the dependable old Ford crunching along the long gravel driveway out to the main road. They'd been up since five o'clock, milking the cows, letting the chickens out to scratch, feeding the hogs, the horses, and the dog, Danny. When they got to town, Uncle John would drop Flora at the Swanson house for breakfast while John met his brothers and sister for early Mass at the Catholic church.

Don could smell coffee drifting up from the kitchen. Aunt Flora always left a pot of coffee on the kitchen stove for him. He felt a little guilty staying in bed while Uncle John and Aunt Flora did the Sunday morning chores, but ever since Don had turned eighteen years and balked at going to church, John had said that Don should do whatever he wanted on Sundays.

"Go ahead and sleep in Sundays, Don." Uncle John had told him. "You work hard around here every day. You should be able to kick up your heels on Saturday nights and not have to get up early on Sunday."

Uncle John's decisions were usually final, but that night Flora had tried to talk him out of it. "Don will never start coming to church if he stays in bed every Sunday!"

"He's a grown man now, Flora. He'll come back to church when he's ready. You can lead a horse to water but you can't make him drink. One of these days maybe he'll get over being mad at God for taking his mother and dad."

Don dressed and walked down to the kitchen to hunt up breakfast. He cut up the boiled potatoes Flora had set out for him to fry, put them in the frying pan with a few sausages, and added some bacon grease from the old Folger's coffee can Flora kept beside the kitchen stove. He checked the coffee pot and poured himself a cup of the still-warm liquid; it was strong as usual. Aunt Flora kept adding coffee grounds and water every time she made a fresh pot; she never threw out the old grounds until they filled a third of the pot. Don remembered his mother laughing about her sister Flora's coffee, "She doesn't think it's strong enough unless you can stand up a spoon in it."

Don stirred the potatoes and gave a faint groan as he remembered what a disaster last night had been. None of it would have happened if Carla hadn't come up with her crazy idea to find Laird a girlfriend. He blamed himself, too. He should never have gone along with Carla's scheme to meddle in Laird's affairs in the first place.

He sat down at the kitchen table, propped up his forehead with both hands, and closed his eyes to think. Jan was the one who should tell Laird she was getting married. Somebody should tell Jan to just leave Carla out of it. Jan could do her own dirty work. He straightened up, took a sip of the lukewarm coffee, and grimaced. The coffee wasn't quite strong enough to hold up a spoon, but almost. He got up to get some cream to smooth out the coffee, and went over to the stove to turn the potatoes and sausages.

It didn't make sense. If Carla thought Laird needed a girlfriend, why couldn't she fill the position? Anyone could see that Carla had idolized Laird ever since they were kids. Don ate slowly, staring absently at Flora's aspirin bottle in the middle of the table. No one else knew about Carla's scheme but him, so he guessed he was the obvious choice to talk to Jan. How to get ahold of Jan was the problem; a letter would take too long and the phone line out here on the farm was too public. There were twelve families on the party line, and if any one of them happened to pick up their phone to make a call while he was on the line, of course they'd stay to listen in on the conversation, and then the news would be all over town by tomorrow.

Don had been fourteen-years old when he'd come to live with his Uncle John and Aunt Flora after his parents' car accident. At first he'd been shocked to see that whenever the phone rang, Flora picked up the receiver to listen in. The Petersens' ring was three longs and one short, the Coopers' ring was two longs and two short... Flora knew them all. Sometimes she'd listen in and keep quiet, but other times she'd join right in with the conversation. Flora would sit down on the kitchen stool and relax if she was just listening in, but because the hand-cranked telephone was mounted high on the kitchen wall, she had to stand on tiptoe, crane her neck and shout in her chicken-calling voice whenever she wanted to talk. Don had never been able to understand why the telephone company had installed the phone at a convenient height for his taciturn Uncle John and ignored the measurements of his diminutive and talkative Aunt Flora.

Don soon learned it wasn't just Aunt Flora who listened in: telephone calls were a social event for almost every farm family on the party line. Early on, Don decided never to say anything personal over the telephone; as soon as he picked up the receiver to answer a call, he would hear two or three clicks as other people along the line picked up their receivers to listen in. Why they called it 'rubbering on the line' was beyond him, especially since he'd learned that the word rubbers not only described the rubber boots people wore in the winter, it was also the slang name for condoms. Probably Aunt Flora and the other farm women had never even heard of a condom. Whenever the idea crossed his mind, he shook his head and tried not to think about it.

There was nothing for it. Don knew he was going to have to go to town and call Jan on a pay phone. Her landlady was probably on a party line, too, but at least in Minneapolis, nobody would know who he was talking about. Don found the loose coin jar on the bottom cupboard shelf, and took out a handful of quarters for feeding the pay phone. After heating a teakettle of water on the stove for shaving and washing the dishes, he taped a short note on the window above the kitchen sink saying he'd back in time for supper.

His face shaved and the kitchen tidied up, Don walked out through the back porch with its sloping, linoleum-covered floor, past the gleaming stainless steel cream separator, the motley collection of dirty coveralls, assorted jackets and hats hanging neatly on hooks, and the orderly row of manure-spattered outdoor boots.

When he opened the outside door, the old cattle dog, Danny, got up from where he'd been lying in the sun by the cellar door and walked lazily over to greet him; his tail wagged slowly but his eyes were alert and intent on Don's face.

"You wonder if you're going to get lucky today; you're hoping I'll send you to bring the cows in again, aren't you? No such luck, Danny, you've herded them in once this morning. Sorry, old buddy." Don bent over and scratched Danny's head. "You'll have to wait until tonight to bring them in again."

Don climbed into the pickup and started the engine, cocked his head and listened for sounds of trouble; thank God Old Blue was still behaving herself. He sat for a minute and wondered if he dared call Jan from a Breton pay phone? Probably not…if either Charlene or Gladys was on duty at the telephone exchange, and if there was nothing much else happening, they'd surely listen in. They weren't supposed to, but everybody suspected that whenever things were slow, they listened in to keep to keep from getting bored.

"Oh, shit." Don pointed Old Blue down the driveway. He'd have to drive clear over to Aberdeen to make the call.

In Aberdeen, the telephone operator gave him the phone number for St. Mary's Hospital. One of the nurses on duty said Jan had worked the night shift and had checked out at six o'clock that morning. Don looked at his watch and saw it was almost noon. It would be at least a couple more hours before she would wake up. What a crummy way to spend a Sunday.

He waited until one o'clock, and when he called it was Mrs. Johnson who answered the phone. "I just walked in the door from church," she said in her cheery voice. "But I'm sure Janice is still asleep…she worked the night shift last night so maybe you better call back later."

"Please wake her up," he pleaded. "I'm her cousin, Don, and this is important."

"Well, I don't know about that. She's probably had only six or seven hours of sleep. I hate to wake her. She's worked three night shifts in a row."

Don tried to keep his voice calm. "Well, I've only had five hours sleep myself. She's doing better than me. Please wake her up? I'm sure Jan will want to know what I have to tell her."

"Well, you say you're a cousin of hers?"

"I'm a second cousin…her Grandma's nephew."

"Well, then, I guess it's all right," Mrs. Johnson sounded dubious, but he heard her put the receiver down, followed by the sound of her footsteps fading away across the hardwood floor.

Finally Jan's groggy voice came over the line, "Don? This better be important. I was sound asleep."

"Sorry to wake you, Jan, but it's important. You shouldn't be asking Carla to tell Laird you're getting married. Did she tell you about her scheme to get Laird a girlfriend?"

"Yes, but…"

"Well, because of that Laird got into a big fight after the dance last night, punched out Harold Ferguson and gave Virgil Nelson a black eye."

"Oh, my goodness, that doesn't sound like Laird. Was he drunk?"

"No, he wasn't drunk. We went out to the car a couple of times after Carla left and had a couple of drinks, but it didn't make much of a dent in either one of us." Don paused. "Laird was disappointed that Carla went home early without even telling him, but he wasn't drunk. We were staying sober so we could take the girls home afterwards."

"But why did Carla go home early, and without telling Laird?" Jan's voice was alert now.

"That's the thing, Jan, she went home so Laird would be free to pair up with Diane. It was all part of her scheme to find a girlfriend for Laird. Well, Lenore was a possibility, too, but then Martin came along and wouldn't let Lenore out of his sight all night. Anyhow, while us guys went to get a Coke for everybody, Carla told Lenore and Diane she didn't feel good and that she was going to walk home."

"Well, what's so bad about that?"

"But she didn't walk home. She ran into Virgil Nelson on the way out and he took her home. Virgil said he couldn't let her walk home wearing those crazy high-heeled shoes she had on, and of course Harold was there and saw Carla leave with Virgil."

"But what's the problem, and why would Laird get mad at Harold?"

"No. No. No." Don was getting frustrated, this was more talking than he usually did all day long. "Harold was drunk and Carla hates drunks, so Virgil told Harold to stay at the dance while he took Carla home."

"I still don't understand what happened."

"Just hold on a minute, I'm trying to tell you." He took a deep breath.

"So, after it all happened, I asked Virgil where in God's name he'd been after he took Carla home. And he said he went over to the football field and laid down on the grass to look up at the stars awhile, said he had to have a breather from the dance crowd because he was getting claustrophobic like he does on account of being cooped up in the engine room on that little supply ship during the war."

Jan was quiet a moment. "Things are not any clearer to me, Don."

"Well, that's because I'm not finished yet." She could hear the exasperation in his voice when he said, "So, Laird got in his car and tried to catch up with Carla and give her a ride home, because, well maybe it was because of the high heels, but I'm beginning to think it was really because he likes her a lot and wanted to be with her, how should I know?"

"Of course Laird likes her, she's the little sister he never had."

"Dammit, Jan! Oh, God, now I'm swearing at you. I'm sorry, but am I the only one who's noticed that those two might be interested in each other? But I guess you're not around to see the way the way they look at each other sometimes."

Don waited, but there was no response from Jan's end of the line. "In fact," he continued, "I think maybe Laird already has his girlfriend, but Carla doesn't know it." He hesitated, "Well, maybe Laird doesn't know it either."

"Really…" Don could hear Jan breathing out slowly, "Carla and Laird? But that's wonderful, Don. That would be wonderful!"

"Well, first someone will have to convince Carla. I think maybe she thinks no guy would ever think of her in that way."

"Oh, I see." Jan was quiet again and then asked, "But I still don't know why Laird got into a fight with Harold? And why on earth would he get into a fight with Virgil? They're best friends."

"Well, Laird didn't really get into a fight with Virgil. Virgil just got in the way of Laird's fist when he was trying to stop the fight. Virgil jumped in the middle of it because he was afraid Laird was going to kill Harold."

"But why? For Heaven's sake, Don, will you please get to the point!"

"Because after the dance, and of course by then, Harold was even drunker, the band was packing up to leave and we were all headed out for the cars, so along comes Virgil. He's getting out of his car and looking for Harold to take home because he figures Harold is probably too drunk to drive."

"So just about the time Harold sees Virgil drive up, Laird and me are with Diane and Lenore, walking out to the cars, and of course Martin Hensley is tagging along because of Lenore, and I hear Harold asking Virgil, "Where the hell have you been?" and Harold gives a little knowing smirk at Virgil and says, "It sure took you a long time to take Carla home a few blocks." Then Harold lurches over, gives Virgil a friendly punch on the arm, and says in a whisper loud enough for Laird and me to hear, "She may be a cripple, but I bet she's a nice little piece of tits and ass.""

"Oh, my…he said that?"

"He sure did! Anyhow, Laird just exploded! It's still kind of a blur to me. Harold was on the ground and Laird was trying to haul him back on his feet so he could hit him again, and Virgil was in between trying to hold Laird back."

"Oh, my goodness…"

"A bunch of us rushed over to help Virgil pull Laird off Harold. I didn't really want to save that big mouth, but I didn't want Laird to maim him either. Then Oscar showed up. You know how he always hangs around after the dances are over, and I guess someone told Oscar what Harold said because Oscar wasn't any too easy on Harold. He almost threw him into the back seat of the police car."

"What did Oscar do to Laird?"

"Well, he walked up to Laird and studied his face awhile. Laird was standing there breathing hard and kind of shaking, looking daggers at Harold. Finally, Oscar said, "You get on home now, Laird.""

"And did Laird go?"

"Yah, he walked off to his car and left. Lenore and Diane went back into the Legion Hall, with Martin of course tagging along, to get some ice for Virgil's eye while I talked to Virgil to find out what he knew. He didn't seem to hold any grudges against Laird…he just said, 'Wow, that guy packs a punch.'"

The operator came on the line. "Please deposit twenty-five cents for three more minutes."

Don groaned, "Oh God, I hate these pay phones," and inserted another quarter into the slot.

"That Virgil is such a nice guy," Jan said. "Laird is going to feel so bad he gave him a black eye."

"And none of this would have happened if you hadn't asked Carla to tell Laird you're getting married. You've got to tell Laird yourself. Call Carla right now, Jan, and tell her, so she'll stop all this ridiculous plotting to find him a girlfriend. I'm telling you, Jan, it's making her miserable. She always tries to put on a happy face, but believe me, right now, she's not a happy camper."

"I will…I'll call her today. Does she know about any of this? I mean about what Harold said about her, and the fight?"

"She'll probably hear about the fight, and all we can do is hope no one tells her what Harold said. I don't think Diane or Lenore or even Martin heard what he said because they'd stopped to gab with a couple of Lenore's girlfriends, and if Carla asks me what happened, all I'm going to tell her is that Harold made some crude army remark about someone and Laird hauled off and hit him. I'll pretend I don't know exactly what he said. Carla might not even have heard about the fight yet. Anyhow, the main thing is that you have to call Carla and tell her you're going to break the news to Laird. She obviously doesn't want to tell him." Don paused, "I guess I don't have to remind you that probably half the party line will be listening in when you call her so keep it simple."

"Don," she paused, and asked, "Can you give me any advice from a man's perspective on the best way to tell Laird?"

"That, dear cousin, is up to you." He started to hang up and thought better of it. "For God's sake Jan, he's a big boy, it won't be the end of the world."

Chapter Seventeen

The church was nearly full when they arrived. They had to take a pew towards the back of the sanctuary, which was fine with Carla because she preferred sitting at the back. She liked watching people walk in, as they greeted their neighbors, and settle into their pews. Little Grandma would rather sit towards the front because there she could hear the minister's thin voice better. "That man," she sometimes complained, "sounds like he's talking from inside a tin can."

Carla and Martha sat between Little Grandma and Aunt Flora. Carla's grandmother was resplendent in a new wine-colored felt hat and burgundy dress. On the left shoulder of her dress she wore a huge brooch set with glass rubies. On her right hand sparkled a ruby ring set with fake diamonds. Aunt Flora was a splash of bright yellow, her only decoration a small pair of pearl earrings.

Carla settled against the back of the pew and listened to the occasional sounds of people clearing their throats, the rustle of pages being turned in a Bible or hymn book, and the whispered voices of late-comers being greeted by the ushers in the vestibule. There was a hush as the church bells began to ring and reverberate through the building. When the last of the pealing bells faded away, Carla relaxed into the familiar sensation of being wrapped in a big, muffled cocoon. She loved looking at the light streaming in through the stained-glass windows and at the simple oak cross on the wall behind the altar. She often wished her parents would come to church with her some Sunday and just sit here with her, sing the old hymns, and soak in this feeling of peace. Maybe they'd like being here so much they'd quit their boycott against God.

Carla intended to use the quiet time before the service began to ask God for the strength to accept the hand of cards He'd dealt her. Mama had once said people were wrong when they called God a "he" because no God who had an ounce of humanity would allow the cruelty and suffering that went on in the world. Carla's mother believed that if there really was a God, God wasn't a "he", but an "it", a big impersonal "IT".

But Little Grandma and Aunt Flora disagreed with Mama and Daddy. They believed God had good reasons for whatever happened and just because mere mortals weren't smart enough to figure God out, that didn't mean there wasn't a divine plan. You had to have faith that you were being tested, like Job was tested. Big Grandma was fond of saying, "What doesn't kill you makes you strong." Come to think of it, the family controversy about God was one of those rare instances when Big Grandma actually agreed with Little Grandma.

"Well," thought Carla, "I've had some hard knocks and I am pretty strong; at least I try to be." A picture flashed in her mind of Diane and Laird moving so perfectly across the dance floor last night, beautiful Diane, smiling up at him, and Laird looking gravely down into her eyes. They probably had a lot to talk about; maybe Laird could comfort her about the war and Conrad. Carla sighed and studied her hands lying close together on her lap. The fact that she had this faulty body shouldn't make her ungrateful to God for all the blessings in her life. God had given her a good mind and a very special family. Having one of the best families in the whole world should be blessing enough for anybody.

After the service started, Little Grandma and Flora noticed Carla wasn't enjoying the hymn singing as she usually did; she was staring straight ahead or looking down with a serious face at the hymnal, and she barely moved her mouth during the hymns. There were none of the usual big smiles and sparkling eyes as she sang, not even when they sang *Bringing In The Sheaves,* which was one of her favorites, and they could hardly hear her voice at all during the Lord's Prayer. They kept glancing over at each other with concern in their eyes, both of them thinking maybe that girl should have stayed home in bed.

※ ※ ※

After church and a leisurely lunch with the family, Aunt Flora and Uncle John went back to the farm. Verle settled into his favorite chair to read the Sunday paper and the women were in the kitchen doing up the dishes when the phone rang.

Carla put down her dish towel. "I'll get it, Mama."

It was Jan on the line, calling collect from Minneapolis. "I won't talk long, Carla. I know it's expensive to make a long distance call, but I wanted you to know I've changed my mind. I'm going to tell Laird the news myself."

"Are you sure?" Jan detected a tremor of relief in Carla's voice.

"Yes, I'm very sure. I never should have asked you. I finally realized it was cowardly of me, and I'll be the one to tell Mother and Daddy, too. You let me worry about it now."

"Oh, I wasn't worried," Carla protested.

"Well, that's good, and thanks, Carla, for offering to help." Jan paused and then added in a soft voice, "I love you, Carla."

"I love you, too, Jan. Write us a letter soon and tell us what's happening?"

"I will...bye now."

Carla carefully set the phone back in its cradle and stood staring down at her hand still resting on the telephone receiver. Thank goodness she wouldn't be the one to tell Laird after all.

Dora walked into the dining room, wiping her hands on her apron. "Who was that, Carla?"

"It was Jan. She called collect, but don't worry, we didn't talk long."

"Any special reason? What did she have to say?"

Carla hesitated and her eyes widened. "It's a surprise. I'm not supposed to tell you yet."

"Really," Dora cocked her eyebrows quizzically. "It must have been pretty important to warrant a collect call." She looked intently at Carla, "You don't look very happy about it; there's nothing wrong is there?"

Carla vehemently shook her head. "No, nothing like that. It's a good surprise... Jan can hardly wait to tell everybody about it." Carla tried, and failed, to flash a big smile of reassurance.

"Are you sure everything's okay?"

"Yes! Everything's fine!" There was irritation in Carla's voice as she turned away. "I'm going upstairs to read for a while."

The rest of that Sunday afternoon dragged by; Carla couldn't seem to concentrate on her book and finally threw it down in disgust. She thought about calling Lenore who would surely know if there was any gossip about Laird and Diane getting together, but she didn't have the heart to talk to anyone right now. She knew Don would never call her no matter what had happened last night. He hadn't wanted to be involved in her plan in the first place. Well, at least she had the satisfaction of knowing her plan was working. Laird was probably off doing something with Diane today, maybe he'd take her to the Sunday matinee this afternoon, or for a drive in the country, or maybe out to the Gulch for a picnic.

"Carla?" Her mother's voice called up the stairs, "You're wanted on the phone. It's Laird calling."

She raced down the stairs. "I wonder why Laird's calling me on a Sunday?"

"Maybe because you weren't feeling well last night…he's probably wondering if you're okay."

Oh, of course…Carla hadn't realized he might actually worry about her. She felt a twinge of guilt. It hadn't occurred to her that saying she didn't feel good was a lie, because it was all for a good cause. She picked up the phone and tried to make her voice light and cheery, "Hi, Laird."

"Hi, Carla." His voice was even and distant, "How are you feeling today?"

"Oh, I'm fine, I just had a little stomach upset." There was silence on the line. "Did you have good time at the dance?" she asked.

"It was okay." There was more silence before Laird said, "I wish you would have told me you were leaving, Carla. I would have given you a ride home."

"I didn't want to be a bother to anybody. Anyhow, I ran into Virgil outside and he gave me a ride home, so I didn't have to walk."

"I heard he gave you a ride home." Another pause and more silence. "Anyhow, I won't be able to meet you for algebra lessons tomorrow. Dad needs me at the blacksmith shop."

"Oh, sure, we can meet Tuesday then."

"I'm not sure if I can do it on Tuesday either…I'll let you know. Well…goodbye."

"Goodbye, Laird."

She hung up the phone and stood looking down at it. Something was wrong. Even if Laird was starting to date Diane, that was no reason for him to be so stand-offish. If he was happy about getting to know Diane better, wouldn't he want to tell his kid sister all about it? No, he probably wouldn't tell Carla anything. Men didn't gab easily to other people about things like that, but at least his voice should have been more cheerful. She kept looking down at the phone, a puzzled expression on her face.

❋ ❋ ❋

Laird had no sooner finished his short conversation with Carla when his phone rang, three shorts and one long. He stared at it for a moment before picking it up.

"Hi, old buddy," Don's voice was slightly blurred by a faint crackling on the line. "I'm coming into town Wednesday to pick up some chicken feed for Aunt Flora. I should be there by two in the afternoon, how about we meet down at Dee's for a cup of coffee?"

"Sure. Okay, I'm probably going to be helping Dad at the shop all this week but I can get away for a little while."

"Maybe you should invite Virgil to show there's no hard feelings."

There was silence for a moment on Laird's end of the line before he said, "Good idea, I'll ask him." Laird sighed and ran his hand through his hair. "Actually, I plan to stop by his house later today and apologize… I don't know what got into me."

"Well, if you can't figure it out by Wednesday, I'll tell you," and before Laird could respond, Don said, "See you Wednesday," and hung up.

Laird grimaced. Oh God, he should probably go over and talk to Virgil right now and get it over with…as for Harold…to hell with Harold.

Laird went outside, sat on the porch steps, and thought about Virgil. Virgil hadn't just gotten in the way of an accidental punch, Laird had wanted to hurt him. He'd hit him on purpose. Damn Virgil for sitting out somewhere in a car all alone with Carla for two hours. Well, he might as well get his mea culpa over with. He'd have plenty of time to think what to say during the seven-block walk to the Nelson house. He hoped he hadn't hit Virgil too hard; it wasn't Virgil's fault Carla evidently preferred to spend the night with him instead of staying to dance with Laird. He couldn't blame either one of them for liking each other. Carla had such a bright shine to her, she was so sweet and so much fun, and Virgil might not sport the handsomest mug in the world, but he was big and muscular and kind, and he had an inner strength about him that people trusted. Any girl would want to spend time with a guy like Virgil.

Laird knocked twice before Virgil's mother came to open the door. Her face was stern as she said, "Oh, it's you." She was a tall, straight-backed, large-boned woman with a strong face and chin, and her unsmiling green eyes appraised him like the Valkyrie from whom she had no doubt descended.

Laird forced himself to return her accusing gaze. "Hello, Mrs. Nelson, I've come to apologize. Virgil was just trying to break up a fight and he got in the way of a punch." Laird put his hands in his pockets and looked down for a moment. "I don't know what got into me."

"Yes, well, that's what Virgil said, but I fail to understand why you young men think you can solve problems by hitting people."

"I feel pretty bad about it."

"Yes, and well you should." Mrs. Nelson turned and called, "Virgil, Laird is here to see you." Still grim-faced, she stood aside and gestured for him to enter.

"No thanks, Mrs. Nelson, I'll just wait out here on the porch."

Virgil's left eye was swollen and showing the beginnings of an angry bruise. He was holding an ice pack against the damaged eye but there was a smile on his face. "You've got a wicked punch there, Laird, and I didn't see it coming in time to duck."

"Oh, God, I'm sorry. I went kind of berserk, didn't I?"

Virgil put the ice pack back on his eye and grinned. "Yah, berserk is a pretty fair description."

"When Harold said those things about Carla, I just… reacted." Laird hesitated. "I wanted to kill him, but I didn't mean to hurt you." It wasn't totally true that he hadn't meant to hurt Virgil, but Laird decided it was too complicated to explain.

"I know you didn't mean to." Virgil gestured for Laird to sit down beside him on the porch swing. "I'd probably have hit him myself if you hadn't beaten me to it."

Laird's eyes widened…of course…he hadn't thought of that. Virgil would have wanted to defend her, too. Good thing he hadn't or the two of them might have killed the son-of-a-bitch.

Virgil leaned back in the swing and gave a little push; it creaked under their combined weight as they rocked gently back and forth in thoughtful silence.

"She's a sweet kid, you know," Virgil said, "There's something special about Carla. I noticed it when we were in high school, but you know how it is when you're in high school…three years' difference is such a barrier when you're that age."

Laird nodded. "I used to think of her as my kid sister."

"I guess a lot of us did." Virgil turned to look at Laird. "But she's not a kid anymore."

Laird looked straight into Virgil's undamaged eye and said, "Nope, she's all grown up."

Chapter Eighteen

With a resolute look on her face, Janice sat at the small desk by her bedroom window, wadded up the sheet of paper in front of her and threw it into the wastebasket. No matter how she tried, the words in her letter to Laird sounded like the same selfish rationalizations she'd always despised when she'd heard them from other people. She chewed on her lower lip, took a clean sheet of paper from the desk drawer, and tried again.

Dear Laird,

I don't know of any way to tell you except to plunge right in. I'm engaged to be married in September. I haven't told my parents yet. I'll write them a letter tomorrow. His name is Lawrence Blakesly and he's in his second year of residency here at St. Mary's. We never dated until after I returned your ring. In fact, I always tried to avoid him, but when you work together for nearly two years like we have you get to know a person really well.

You wrote that you would come to my wedding. I hope you will, but if you don't, I'll understand. We're planning to come to Breton next week so Lawrence can meet the family and I'd like you to meet him too, if it won't be too uncomfortable. You'll always be a very special person in my life, Laird. I hope you can forgive me for taking so long to know my own heart.

Jan

Janice carefully folded the fourth draft of her letter to Laird and sealed it in an envelope. She hated telling him by letter, but there was no good way to tell him. It was too bad the wedding would happen so soon after they'd broken up, but Lawrence was right, there would probably never be a good time to tell him. Besides, Lawrence had already waited for nearly two years, and Don's words echoed hopefully in her mind, "For God's sake, Jan. He's a big boy. It won't be the end of the world."

* * *

On Wednesday, Laird stopped to pick up the mail before he met Don at Dee's Café. There were two letters in the PO box for Laird, one from Janice, and one from the University of South Dakota. Laird waved at the Postmaster, and went outside to sit on the bench in front of the post office to open his mail. He wondered why Jan was writing. It was strange, but he hadn't thought much about her for the past few weeks. He opened the envelope and read her letter, then folded it slowly, put it back in the envelope and slid it into his shirt pocket. The other letter was from the registrar's office at South Dakota State, saying they would be happy to have him enroll in the fall. Laird put the letter from the college in his back pocket and sat staring down at the sidewalk for a full minute before he took Jan's letter out of his shirt pocket and read it a second time. Finally, he stood up and started walking toward Dee's Café and the meeting with Don.

Bert Jamison and Max Pratt drove by and waved to get Laird's attention, but he didn't respond. "That boy is deep in thought today." Max commented.

"Appears to be." Bert laughed. "I wonder if he's planning who he's going to punch out next?"

* * *

Don was waiting in a back booth, holding his ever-present cigarette in one hand, and a cup of coffee in the other, oblivious to the cloud of cigarette smoke he was producing.

Laird greeted Mavis at the counter and ordered a cup of coffee before he walked over and slid into the booth opposite Don.

"Hi, Laird, good to see you. Is Virgil coming?"

"No, he said he's going out to his Uncle Charlie's farm today, said they needed someone with a strong back and a weak mind to help them muck out the barn."

Don laughed, "Well, he's got a strong back anyhow."

"I went over and talked to him on Sunday and tried to apologize." Laird shook his head. "I gave him a real shiner. Can you believe he smiled at me and said he'd have hit Harold himself if I hadn't done it first?"

"I believe it. Virgil is a heck of a good guy."

"I could take a few lessons from him."

"So," Don took a drag on his cigarette and peered at Laird through the haze, "is that why you're looking kind of down today?"

"Not entirely." Laird pulled the letter out of his shirt pocket and laid it on the table. "I just found out Jan is getting married in the fall."

Don carefully tapped the ash off his cigarette against the rim of the ashtray. "Pretty big news." He studied Laird's face and said, "No wonder you're feeling down."

Laird ran his hands through his hair, "Actually, I'm not sure how I'm feeling; mostly kind of stupid, I guess, that I thought she loved me all this time, when for the last two years she's been trying her best not to own up to the fact that she loves this other guy."

Don took another puff on his cigarette and continued to study Laird's face.

"The funny thing is," Laird added, "I don't feel much of anything about Jan right now, except I'm a little embarrassed to have been so gullible."

Mavis came over and put a cup of coffee in front of Laird. "Do you boys want something to eat with your coffee?"

"No."

"No thanks."

They both watched Mavis walk off before Don said, "Sounds like Jan didn't exactly have things figured out either."

Laird stared into his cup of steaming black liquid. "Three years is a long time. To tell the truth, after a while, she was kind of like a dream to me, kind of like a Betty Grable poster." He was silent a moment before he looked over at Don, "No, she was more than that, but I can't blame her for falling for someone who was flesh and blood and working right beside her every day. It's the old story, he was there and I wasn't."

"So," Don hesitated, "You going to be okay with this?"

"I'm amazed myself, but, yes, I think I'll be fine. Actually, I was feeling low before I got Jan's letter."

Don raised his eyebrows. "That thing at the dance?"

Laird clenched his jaw and nodded, "I totally lost control of myself, I really wanted to kill him." His eyes darkened. "I'm not kidding Don, I wanted to kill him. If we'd been alone, and if Virgil and the rest of you hadn't stopped me, I don't know what I would have done…I couldn't seem to stop." He picked up his cup and Don noticed a slight tremor in Laird's hands.

Don sat in silence before he said, "Maybe it's a hangover from the war, all the stuff you went through during the war."

"Maybe, but during the war, we had to kill to keep them from killing us. Harold wasn't going to kill anybody." Laird propped his elbows on the table, and began to massage small circles on his forehead above his eyes…Sophia used to massage his forehead like that.

He looked up at Don. "It was like he shit on everything decent and fine. I'm sick and tired of bastards like Harold shitting on people like Carla."

"Well, at least Carla won't know what he said. Only a few people heard and nobody would ever repeat it to Carla."

"Carla…she's another reason I've been feeling down."

"Why would you feel down about Carla?" Don flashed a puzzled look across the table.

"Well, it's really about Carla and Virgil. I guess I didn't realize how much she means to me until she went off and left the dance without even telling me, and then spent half the night with him. She couldn't have been feeling too sick if she felt good enough to go off with him." He sighed, "Not that I blame her, any girl with half an ounce of brains would want to be with Virgil."

Don straightened up and stubbed out his cigarette in the ashtray. He put his hands flat on the table top in front of him and cleared his throat. "Laird, you don't know diddly-squat about any of this." He cleared his throat again and said, "In the first place, Virgil took her right home and then he went off to the football field to lie flat on his back and look up at the Milky Way for a couple of hours. He told me he was getting claustrophobic at the dance…you know how he's been lately whenever he gets to feeling closed in."

Don noted with satisfaction that Laird's mouth had dropped slightly open.

"And the second thing is, you stupid son-of-a-gun, I think Carla has a crush on you…at least, I'm pretty sure she does, but she tries to hide it because she thinks you'll never see her as anything other than a kid sister. There. I've finally said it." Don leaned back, gave a huge sigh of relief and lit up another cigarette. "Carla would be so pissed at me if she knew I told you."

※ ※ ※

The rest of the day went by in slow motion for Laird. He stopped by the blacksmith shop to see if his dad needed any help, but work at the shop was slow and Emil said he'd be closing up early. Next, he walked over to the swimming pool where Diane was teaching a class of kids how to do the butterfly stroke. His two younger brothers and Martha were in the group, all diligently watching Diane demonstrate. The kids were too busy thrashing through the water to notice him, but Diane surfaced, smiled at him and waved. Laird waved back and walked on. Too bad Diane was busy; he'd been hoping she'd have some free time so they could talk a while. He wondered if she would agree with Don, or just laugh at him for taking Don's idea seriously.

Laird couldn't see that Carla treated him any differently than how she treated everybody else, and, just as important, he wasn't sure how he felt about Carla. Would he have reacted the same way if Harold had said those things about Lenore or Diane? He probably would have grabbed Harold by the collar and made him apologize, he might even have hit him, but would he have exploded into killer mode like that? What had made him so fierce about wanting to protect Carla? Was it her lovely deep-blue eyes, her laugh, or her mysterious, firm breasts hidden away under those cover-up blouses that attracted him? Was it her sunny disposition, or just that she was like a kid sister, or maybe his sudden interest in Carla was part of a rebound process to compensate for losing Jan? But why would he rebound to Carla, with her physical handicaps? It didn't make sense that he would rebound to Carla instead of to perfect, beautiful Diane, but dancing with Diane last night had been like dancing with a friend, while dancing with Carla had triggered a flood of tenderness, and, he had to admit, sexual attraction.

Was there something about Carla that reminded him of Jan? No, it couldn't be that. The two sisters weren't anything alike. They were both warm and loving, but they were entirely different in appearance and in personality. Jan had that thick, wavy, perfectly groomed auburn hair, while Carla, like Martha, was always fighting with her mass of curls. They had totally different eyes: Jan, with green eyes and olive skin, and Carla with blue eyes and fair skin. Jan had a more reserved and measured way of dealing with people, while Carla was spontaneous and open, with a quick-silver mind always playing around with ideas. Maybe the one attribute they had in common was the smile. They both had the same warm, brilliant smile.

By bedtime, Laird was exhausted from thinking about everything that had happened that day. It was still hot upstairs so he took all his clothes off except his shorts before climbing into bed. He pulled the sheet up, then threw it off again and lay looking up at the ceiling, listening to the sounds of his brothers using the bathroom and doing whatever boys do before they settle down for the night. He turned and looked toward the drawer of the bedside table where he kept Carla's letters. He hadn't finished re-reading them yet; he'd been savoring one or two each night before he went to sleep. He wished he had more of her letters. It was too bad so many had been lost…

April 7, 1946

Dear Laird,

I went to the regional speech contest over at Sisseton High School today. I was entered in the narrative poetry category and recited the "Cremation of Sam Magee" by Robert Service. (I got a number one rating, probably because I've heard Daddy recite it so often, it seems almost like a real happening to me!) Anyhow, there were also a couple of Indian kids competing, and I noticed again how slow and unhurried their speech is. Don gave me a ride over to Sisseton so we got to talking about it on the way home.

Did you know that the Indians used to call my Grandpa Swanson "Honor Heart" because he always kept his word? You probably know that lots of people cheated the Indians. Daddy says that before the government gave away the Indian lands during the Reservation Run when Grandpa Swanson homesteaded his 160 acres, they first gave 160 acres to every Indian man, woman and child, but farming wasn't what Indians were good at because they were used to a nomadic life. Anyway, most of the Indians kept borrowing from the store owners and the banks and eventually lost all their land.

And besides that, some white people even sold them watered down whiskey laced with strychnine. The strychnine gave it a kick and hid the fact it was watered. Can you imagine putting poison in their whiskey? It made them even crazier than regular whiskey did, and regular whiskey makes people crazy enough, but that's not what I meant to tell you about.

Anyhow, Don and I got to talking about the way Indians speak and Don said his Uncle John and a lot of the old farmers talk that way, too, kind of slow and deliberate. We wondered if maybe it's because farmers and Indians spend a lot of time outdoors. It's quiet outside usually, and especially when you're alone, you don't need to do any talking, and you notice things you don't notice when you're inside a house. Outside you notice natural things, like the sound of wind blowing through the grass or the cottonwood trees, horses blowing and stomping their feet, and that good smell horses have, and the change of light just before a lightning storm. We decided maybe noticing those things slow you down a bit, and is a part of what makes people good farmers and Indians. What do you think, Laird? Well, I'm afraid I'm rambling, I'd better close. We all miss you.

Love, Carla Rae

Laird remembered the discussion this particular letter had engendered among his fellow workers during a slow night shift at the Frankfurt decoding headquarters. Three of the guys had grown up on farms, and one of them who had grown up on a farm in the midst of the Flathead Indian tribal lands in Montana had agreed about the slower, more measured speech you hear in both farmers and Indians.

Laird had always loved reading Carla's talkative letters, even before he came home and realized the person writing them was no longer Little Squirt. He picked up her last letter, and held it in his hand. It was the one he'd received just before shipping out for home.

May 26, 1946

Dear Laird,

Well, graduation is over. A lot of us girls stood around outside and cried afterwards. Who knows where we'll all end up, and it makes me wonder how you and Jan must have felt when you left for the army during the war. I ran into Mr. And Mrs. Emory in Dee's Café the day after graduation. Mrs.

Emory looks just the same as when you left, tall and beautiful with her milky skin and red hair, and Mr. Emory is just as short and stocky as ever. I went over to their booth to tell him how much I appreciated him for being such a wonderful music teacher and they invited me to sit down with them and tell them all about my college plans.

I noticed Mr. Emory was kind of quiet and then I remembered he'd been on a leave of absence because his mother was sick. I asked him how his mother was and he said she had passed away, and they were leaving for the funeral in Aberdeen the next day. Then he started talking about his mother...she was a brilliant pianist, did you know that? Anyhow, he said that the night before she died, he was sitting holding her hand, and she said to him, "I'm coming to the end of my song, Dwight, I hope I didn't make too many mistakes reading the notes along the way." Mr. Emory had tears in his eyes, you know how it is when you're trying not to cry. He said he told her that as far as he was concerned, she got every single note exactly right...I'm crying right now just thinking about it. (Mr. Emory once told our class we were going to have to mostly sight-read our way through life because there are some things you just can't practice beforehand. I bet his mother taught him that.)

Did I tell you I got the Orion Music medal (for vocal achievements) and a math scholarship at the senior awards ceremony? Jenny Congers was valedictorian for the class, she got straight A's all four years of high school!! What a girl!!! She gave a good talk about being brave enough to risk and not being so ambitious you didn't take time to care for other people, so you can see she's smart in more ways than one.

I'm so glad you have a safe job at the command headquarters in Frankfurt, but aren't you getting close to your 85 points yet so you can come home? I hope you know we won't be really happy until we see you again in person!!

Love, Carla Rae

Laird put both letters back in the drawer, reached over to turn out the bedside light, and lay on his back thinking about Carla. He remembered what Don had told him, that Carla didn't have a chance to be valedictorian of her senior class because she could never get an "A" in physical education. Carla hadn't written one word explaining why she hadn't been chosen valedictorian like Jenny Congers, not a word.

Chapter Nineteen

It was Friday afternoon and the Swanson household was in an uproar. Everyone was rushing to get ready for Janice and Lawrence's arrival the next day. They'd decided to put Lawrence in Martha's tiny bedroom and move Martha to the living room davenport. The two bathrooms needed to be scrubbed, in fact every room in the house had to be cleaned, but even more important than a clean house was the food. Lawrence needed to find out what good cooks the Swanson women were.

After the initial stunned reaction to Jan's letter about her new wedding plans had died down, Martha enthusiastically volunteered to write Big Grandma, tell her the news and ask her to start sewing the flower-girl dress.

Dora had looked up from Jan's letter, arched one eyebrow and looked at Carla. "So," she said, "this was Jan's big surprise, and you managed to keep it a secret."

"You knew? You knew and you didn't tell us?" protested Martha.

"Well, it wasn't something that I wanted to talk about, because I kept thinking how bad Laird would feel when he found out about it."

Dora's forehead wrinkled in concern. "Oh, of course... Laird. Does he know?"

Carla nodded, "Jan wrote to Laird the same day she sent a letter to you. He mentioned it at our last math lesson."

Little Grandma sat down in the dining room rocking chair and started to rock back and forth rapidly, her brows drawn together disapprovingly. "Jan didn't waste any time finding someone else...poor Laird. This wasn't a very kind thing for Jan to do. Couldn't she have waited awhile?"

No one said anything, but silently they were all thinking the same thing, all except Carla, who was remembering what Jan had written, "We're like the opposite poles of two magnets."

※ ※ ※

Dora sat at the kitchen table, her forehead furrowed in concentration as she made up her menu list for Saturday night dinner. Verle had suggested she fix her famous Swiss steak smothered in onions and gravy, everyone loved that, especially with mashed potatoes. Little Grandma had volunteered to bake a fresh batch of bread and use some of the dough to make her special doughnuts. Carla planned to bake a chocolate cake Saturday morning so it would be fresh when Jan and her boyfriend arrived. In spite of having no current sugar ration coupons on hand, Dora had had the foresight to put away some extra sugar for a special occasion, so Carla would be able to frost the cake with the frothy whipped egg-white and boiled sugar frosting Jan loved. Dora was sick and tired of rationing. Almost everything was rationed: meat, tires, gasoline, sugar, butter, nylon stockings, shoes, coffee, even Martha's beloved bubble gum was almost impossible to buy. At least Dora no longer had to save kitchen fat for making explosives, or tinfoil for making bombs. Feeling a bit ashamed, she reminded herself that rationing was nothing compared to what some people in the world had had to endure during the war.

Dora put the tip of the pencil between her teeth and bit down. They'd probably arrive in mid-afternoon so they'd need a snack. Cheese was always good, and she could slice some of the cold roast beef Aunt Flora had brought in from the farm. At least she wouldn't have to serve them Spam; someone was sure to groan if she put Spam on the table again. She could serve home-made bread and maybe some home-canned peaches, that should hold them till supper. Then, of course, there were the doughnuts Little Grandma was already starting to stir up. Dora shook her head in amusement at the realization that she was starting to think of her own mother as Little Grandma.

Dora planned to get up early Sunday morning to make sure everyone had a good breakfast before they left for church. Aunt Flora was always happy to bring fresh eggs and butter from the farm. Dora wondered if maybe Don would want to come along to meet Lawrence, but probably not. Don was about as likely to put his foot inside a church as Dora was.

Dora put down her pencil and took a sip of coffee. Jan and Lawrence would probably leave for Minneapolis right after church, if they went to church at all, although Jan would no doubt go to church in order to make her Grandma and Aunt Flora happy, and at this stage of the game Lawrence would probably do whatever Jan wanted. Dora smiled, thinking of how pleased her mother and Aunt Flora would be, parading down the aisle with Jan and her new doctor boyfriend in tow.

Carla was busy upstairs. She first set out clean sheets in Martha's room so she could quickly change the bed linen in the morning and then started to clean the bathroom. She knelt by the claw-foot porcelain tub, generously sprinkled on the Bon Ami and began to scrub, but her mind was on Laird, who must be feeling terrible about Jan while the Swansons were all so happy and chipper. Carla stuck out her lower lip and tried to blow back a stray curl that had flopped down across her face, and when that didn't work, she sat back on her heels and tried to push her hair back with her forearm without dripping water on her face.

Laird had insisted he was okay with Jan and her marriage plans, but Carla didn't believe him. She was still puzzled about Laird's recent behavior. Why had he avoided getting together for his morning algebra lessons for three whole days after the dance? He'd said he had other things to do, like working at the blacksmith shop or helping Don out at the farm, but when she'd talked to him on the phone, his voice had been disturbingly cool. If it had been anyone else, she would have thought he was avoiding her, but why would he want to do that?…unless maybe he was embarrassed about getting into a fight with Harold and didn't want to talk about it.

Lenore had dropped by on Tuesday after the dance, her green eyes shining with excitement at having a good story to pass along, and told her about Laird's fight with Harold.

"We looked around and there Harold was, flat on the ground and Laird was trying to get him back on his feet so he could hit him again, and then Laird accidentally hit Virgil right in the face when Virgil tried to stop him."

"That doesn't sound like Laird," Carla said. "What on earth did Harold do to get him so mad?"

Lenore glanced uneasily away and shook her head. "I heard he said something insulting about some girl, and it must have been something really bad, because nobody will tell us what he said."

Carla shrugged, "Well, Daddy always said Harold's big mouth was going to get him in trouble someday."

Lenore darted a mischievous side glance at Carla. "Well, it sure got him in trouble this time."

"So," Carla tried to sound matter-of-fact, "I guess Laird didn't take Diane home after all."

"No, Don took Diane home." Lenore gave Carla a small smile, "and I went home with Martin."

"Do you think Diane and Don might be interested in one another?"

Lenore shook her head. "No, well, maybe Don is interested in Diane, for all I know, but Diane evidently doesn't care much about anybody in this town because at the dance she told me that she's decided to move out to the west coast. Says she wants to get away from all the sad memories around here. Diane's sister out in Oregon told her she'd get her a job in the same telephone company she works for."

"Are you sure? You mean Diane's leaving Breton?"

"That's what she told me, said there's nothing to hold her here."

Carla stared at Lenore. Don had been right after all. She shouldn't have tried to meddle in other people's lives, and here she'd been feeling so smug about her grand plan working out so well. The whole thing had turned out to be a total bust.

Carla smiled brightly and asked, "Would you like some lemonade, Lenore? There's a fresh batch in the frig."

❋ ❋ ❋

When Laird called on Thursday, his voice was as upbeat as ever," Hi, teacher, how about we get back to our lessons before I fall too far behind the curve?"

The next morning, while they were going through a set of practice problems, he'd stopped and turned to her. "I guess you know Jan plans to marry somebody named Lawrence." Carla nodded. Well, now he knew, and he was putting up such a brave front.

"What shall I do with her letters, Carla? Is there some kind of a protocol about what to do with old love letters?"

Carla put down her pencil and studied his face. His eyes were questioning, not much different than when he was asking her a question about a math problem.

"I'm not sure, Laird, how many letters do you have?"

"I don't know…it's a pretty good-sized stack. I didn't save any of the early ones because things were pretty chaotic, but once the war was over, I kept quite a few."

Carla nodded, "Jan saved all your letters. She told me she has three shoeboxes full, one for each year."

Laird looked away and groaned, "Oh, God, I hope she burns them. Will you ask her to burn them, and I'll do the same with hers if that's what she wants. I can't imagine she'd want them back."

Carla met his troubled eyes and nodded, "I'll ask Jan when she comes home this Saturday. I guess you know she's bringing him home to meet the family." She reached out and lightly touched his arm. "I'm so sorry, Laird."

He sat back and looked at her appraisingly. "Don't worry about me, Carla." He reached out and put his hand on hers. "I'll be fine. Jan was something that happened a long time ago, she's kind of like a good dream that's over."

Carla eyes widened. "Are you sure, Laird?"

"Very sure, Carla…now, let's get back to work."

He pulled his chair a little closer and, as they bent their heads together over the paper, she felt the warmth of his muscular arm touch hers. The mysterious, sun-warmed scent of him made it hard for her to concentrate. She was thankful she knew the mathematics so well she didn't need to focus on the lesson. She was thinking instead about her own partial shoebox of Laird's letters tucked away in the bottom drawer of her bedroom dresser.

Later, while she sat reading the novel, *Gone With the Wind,* waiting for Laird to finish some practice equations, she looked up and caught him studying her, his head slightly tilted, his deep-set eyes grave and thoughtful. When their eyes met, she tried to ignore her own flushing face and said severely, "Are you ready for me to correct your problems, Laird?"

"Not quite yet, teacher." He grinned at her and went back to solving the equations.

Chapter Twenty

Martha was waiting on the screened front porch when Lawrence's old grey Studebaker pulled up to the curb and Janice leaned out the open car window to call, "Hi, Martha."

Martha turned to open the front door and shouted, "They're here! They're here!" before slamming the porch door behind her and racing down the sidewalk.

Little Grandma was the first one on the porch, eyes guarded and wary. Dora came out and stood behind her mother as they watched a tall young man with thick glasses get out of the car and go to open the car door for Jan. Little Grandma breathed in sharply through her nose and smoothed down the front of her dress with both hands. "I bet he can't hold a candle to Laird."

Dora took off her apron, tossed it onto the porch swing and flashed a warning glance. "Now, Mother... Let's give him a chance."

Verle came out onto the porch and hurried down the steps. "Welcome home, kids!" He grabbed Lawrence's hand and pumped it vigorously. If Jan loved him, he'd do his best to at least be polite to the guy. "I'm Jan's dad. Glad to meet you, Lawrence."

"Good to meet you, too, sir."

Verle shook his head as he reached for one of the suitcases. "No sirs around here, Lawrence, that's for the army...just call me Verle."

Janice held protectively onto Lawrence's arm as she steered him up the sidewalk and introduced him to the rest of her family waiting on the porch. She scanned their faces anxiously. Would they like him? Of course they would, who wouldn't like him?

Lawrence was uncomfortably aware that all eyes were on him, friendly, but not too friendly. He hoped he was passing whatever kind of test they were giving him; he suspected the criteria for passing was how he measured up to Laird, something he wondered himself.

Janice beamed as she reached out and took Carla's hand. "And this is my sister, Carla."

Lawrence was struck by the familiar brilliance of Carla's smile. "I'm glad to meet you, Carla." He paused a moment while he looked at each sister in turn. "Wow, you can sure tell you two are sisters, you both have the same wonderful smile."

Verle nodded his approval, "They sure do…they're a couple of peas in a pod."

Martha looked up at Lawrence, her green eyes serious. "How about me? I'm a sister, too, you know."

He turned serious eyes downward and studied Martha's upturned face. "Oh, I can definitely see the resemblance…you have hair like Carla's and eyes like Jan, I could see that right away."

Martha nodded, satisfied, "Yes, that's what people say. They say that when I'm their age, I'll be a beauty, too."

Dora felt some of her tension beginning to evaporate. Jan's tall, lanky, future husband was unassuming and direct, his magnified eyes were warm and open. She glanced over at her mother, but there were no signs of thawing in that direction. "If you girls will show Lawrence where he's going to sleep," Dora said, "I'll put on the coffee."

"Come on, Lawrence," Martha raced ahead towards the stairs. "You get to sleep in my bedroom, Jan sleeps with Carla, and I get the davenport."

"Oh, oh," Lawrence picked up the suitcases and followed her into the front hall. "Am I in trouble with you for taking your bedroom?"

Martha stopped halfway up the stairs and faced him, her eyes serious, "Oh, no, you're in no trouble with me; you're the reason I'm going to be a flower-girl and get a new dress!"

Lawrence and Jan started to laugh. Martha laughed too, not quite sure what was funny but happy that things were going so well.

Once back downstairs and seated around the dining room table for lunch, the getting-acquainted ritual began in earnest. Verle discovered Lawrence knew a lot about cars so conversation flowed smoothly at that end of the table, and Little Grandma began to relax when Lawrence complimented her on the doughnuts by eating three of them and protesting he couldn't manage another bite.

Carla was in her quiet mode, following the conversation with her eyes but saying very little. She helped Dora wait on the others, poured second cups of coffee, took away the dirty dishes, and when Janice jumped up to help, shook her head firmly and said, "No, Jan, you just sit with Lawrence and visit."

She observed Lawrence out of the corner of her eye as she walked around the table. It was apparent he was a nice enough person, and good looking in a gangly kind of way, and she imagined he must be smart enough since he was a doctor. She sat down again at her end of the table and took a slow sip of coffee. She couldn't fathom why Jan would rather marry Lawrence. Was it because he was older? But he didn't act any more mature than Laird; maybe Jan chose Lawrence because Laird was just beginning his education, and Lawrence was already on his way to a good career. Carla frowned. It wasn't fair. Lawrence didn't have to go serve in the war, he didn't have to lose three years out of his life.

She looked up to see Lawrence watching her, his eyes warm but questioning. She looked away, pretending to be engrossed in her father's explanation of his most recent invention, using dual brakes in cars instead of the present single-brake cylinder.

Little Grandma said, "Well, dual brakes make a lot more sense than your automatic toilet seat."

After lunch, Little Grandma insisted on bringing out the family photograph albums to show Lawrence. Verle escaped by excusing himself to go outside for a smoke, and Martha soon followed to play with Mac. An hour-and-a-half later, Lawrence had heard more about both sides of the family than he'd probably ever wanted to know, and Carla grudgingly had to admire him for showing no visible signs of boredom in spite of having to listen to Little Grandma's convoluted stories about parents, brothers, sisters, aunts, uncles, grandparents and cousins.

When Little Grandma finally closed the last photo album with a satisfied sigh, Lawrence leaned back in his chair and said, "Thanks for sharing the family history with me. I know Jan even better now."

Little Grandma beamed, "I thought you should know that Jan comes from good stock." She stood and picked up the photo albums, "Well, of course, every family has a few scallywags in it, but I always say those kind of people are best forgotten."

Lawrence grinned at her as he stood up from the dining-room chair and stretched his long arms towards the ceiling. "Someday I hope my folks can show you our family albums...as far as I know, we don't have too many deadbeats."

Carla was exasperated to see Jan look up at Lawrence adoringly, like he was some stupid Greek god. Carla leaped to her feet and said, "Let's go for a walk, we need to move our muscles after all this sitting. Who wants to come with me?"

The afternoon was heavy with heat, but they were protected from the direct glare of the sun by the dense shade of the old elm, oak and maple trees that lined the sidewalks. They strolled in pairs, Carla and Martha in front, Lawrence and Janice in the rear, not talking much except when one of the girls pointed out a local landmark to Lawrence.

Jan said, "Let's stop in and see the Hollidays. They live only a couple of streets over… but maybe we should have called them first."

Martha said, "Oh, good, let's go see Mrs. Holliday. She always has good cookies in her cookie jar." Martha turned around and walked backwards while she talked to Lawrence, "Dr. Holliday offered Jan a job you know, as soon as she graduates."

"I've heard that," said Lawrence.

"I don't think they'll mind if we drop by for just a few minutes. Dr. Holliday might be at the hospital, but I'll bet Mrs. Holliday will be home." Jan looked up at Lawrence, "I really want you to meet him, Lawrence, I just know you'll like each other."

Martha skipped ahead, being careful not to step on cracks in the sidewalk. "You can both talk doctor talk so that's good." She stopped skipping and said thoughtfully, "Of course, Mrs. Holliday doesn't talk doctor talk." She turned around to face Lawrence and said, "She likes birds. Do you know anything about birds?"

Lawrence shook his head and gave her an apologetic smile, "Not much."

Martha resumed her skipping. "That's all right. Mrs. Holliday will like you anyway."

The Hollidays were both home, and Jan was radiant as she introduced them to her future husband. Lawrence squirmed uneasily in his chair when Janice insisted on giving detail after detail of brilliant surgeries Lawrence had performed. "Even cranky old Dr. Crowley admitted Lawrence did a miracle job on the Baker boy when he came in with a ruptured appendix," Jan said proudly.

Lawrence looked uncomfortable and said, "I'm sure no one wants to hear all the details, Jan. I'd rather hear more birding stories."

Martha was pleased that Lawrence and Dr. Holliday did indeed talk doctor talk. I was right about that, she said to herself, as she chewed on the peanut butter cookie Mrs. Holliday had given her.

Home again, Jan was relieved to see that the tension emanating from Little Grandma had evaporated, and the conversation around the supper table flowed easily. As Verle had predicted, Dora's Swiss steak and gravy was a big hit, and when Dora and Carla stood up to clear the dishes from the table, Little Grandma pushed back her chair and leaned over to whisper to Janice, "I like your young man. He's a regular old shoe. Do you think he'd come to church with us in the morning?"

Janice whispered back, "I bet he will. Why don't you ask him?"

A fresh pot of coffee was perking on the stove, wafting its aroma into the dining room, and Carla was putting pieces of cake on the good Fostoria glass dessert plates when Martha heard a knock at the front door.

"I'll go see who it is," Martha said as she leaped out of her chair and ran to the front door. They heard her pleased voice saying, "Oh, Laird. It's you. Come in and meet Lawrence. Carla's just about to serve dessert and you can have some, too." She took Laird's hand and walked him through the front hallway into the dining room.

Lawrence and Verle pushed back their chairs and stood up. Verle walked around the table and held out his hand. "Come on in, Laird, you're just in time for dessert." Verle's voice was hearty and welcoming … a little too hearty, thought Laird…oh well, he'd known this meeting wasn't going to be easy for anybody.

Verle gestured at Lawrence, "This is Lawrence Blakesly, Laird. Lawrence, this is Laird Nordstrom." The family watched intently as the two men shook hands and studied each other. Laird was only a few inches shorter than the tall, gangly Lawrence. His shoulders were wider, his build more powerful, and he held himself with an athlete's natural grace. Lawrence's looser body had a relaxed air, as though he intended never to hurry, but would eventually get things done, and get them done right. They seemed different in every way except for their intelligent, penetrating eyes. They shook hands, each man noticing approvingly that the other's handshake was firm, but not too firm.

"I'm glad to meet you, Laird."

"Same here, Lawrence." Laird turned to Dora who was bringing another chair to the table, "I didn't realize you'd still be at the table, I better come back later."

"No. No." Dora patted the back of the chair she'd squeezed in between Verle and Martha. "You sit right down. Carla and I are just about to serve up the cake and coffee." Seven other voices chimed in urging him to "Please stay," and "Sit down, Laird."

He sat. He might as well get this over with. Jan was directly across the table from him and was watching him with anxious eyes and a hesitant smile on her face.

Laird cleared his throat, "I thought I'd just drop by for a few minutes to meet the bridegroom." He felt his shoulders begin to relax as he looked around the table. This wasn't as hard as he'd imagined it would be. There she sat, the one who'd been the girl of his dreams, and he felt only a quiet fondness for her. He looked directly at Lawrence and said, "I'm kind of the big brother in this family, so I thought I'd better check you out."

Lawrence nodded slowly, "I can understand that, I've got two sisters myself." He looked up to thank Carla as she placed a dessert plate in front of him, and when he turned back to Laird, his eyes had dropped their guarded look. "I hope I'll pass inspection."

Martha blurted out, "Oh, he's already passed inspection. We all like him a lot, don't we Mama?"

Dora poured coffee into Verle's cup and gave Martha a small smile. "Yes, Martha. We like him a lot." She hoped Martha's enthusiasm for Lawrence wouldn't make Laird feel bad, but how else could Dora respond in front of Lawrence? Besides, it was true, they all did seem to like him, except maybe Carla. Carla was in one of her inward moods, and when she was in one of these moods, it was impossible to know what she was thinking.

Laird finished his cake, which he praised profusely, and turned down a second cup of coffee. "I better get going. I promised Don and Virgil I'd meet them downtown tonight. You know Don, he can never resist a Saturday night in town."

He looked around the group and said, "Don't get up, I'll see myself out the door." He turned affectionately to Janice, "I'm glad to see you looking so happy, Jan." He gave Lawrence a slight smile, but his eyes were serious, "You be good to her."

Carla jumped to her feet. "I'll see him out," she told her father, who was halfway out of his chair. Verle sat down again, and joined in the chorus of goodbyes that followed Laird and Carla as they headed towards the door, "Bye, Laird," "Bye," "Say hi to Don and Virgil for us."

Out on the screened porch, where Mac was dozing on the doormat, Laird and Carla stopped and looked at each other. It was still light enough to see Laird's face clearly. Carla stamped one foot in frustration, "Oh, Laird, this is all so rotten for you. You are so brave to come over to meet him."

His face lifted in surprise. "Brave?" He laughed, "Brave, you think?" His amused eyes studied her face. "Carla, will you quit worrying about me?" He took her by the arm and led her over to the porch swing. "Let's sit awhile."

Mac slowly got up and walked over to look up at them.

"I'll admit I had some qualms when I was walking up to the front door tonight, but once I sat down at the table and looked into Jan's face, I knew it was all right."

Carla gave the swing a push with both feet. "How could it possibly be all right to see them together?"

"Because, when I actually saw them across the table, sitting together, all I felt was fondness for her, and I realized she was right: at this point we are kind of like brother and sister."

"Well, I don't believe you. You're just rationalizing." Carla's voice was almost angry, "You know darn well you and your whole family are a bunch of stoics, and you wouldn't think you had the right to complain if your house burnt down."

Laird stopped the swing. "Carla...I wish I could make you understand." He leaned back again and started to rock the swing gently back and forth. "When you're away from someone for so many years, that person kind of fades...the Jan I saw tonight is not the same girl I said goodbye to, and I'm not the same person either."

Carla shook her head, "But you wrote each other so many letters. How could either one of you fade away when you shared all those thoughts?

You wrote three shoeboxes full of letters to her, and I bet she wrote even more than that."

Laird stopped swinging and bent over to pet Mac who was patiently standing in front of them, looking up with one ear cocked to the side. "I don't know, maybe neither one of was a very good letter writer."

Exasperated, Carla started the swing going again. "That's not true, Laird, I got to know you even better after you went away because of your letters, and you didn't send me nearly as many letters as you did to Jan. I've only got half a shoebox full."

Laird raised his eyebrows, "You saved my letters?"

Oh, darn, she hadn't meant to tell him that. She nodded, "Yes."

Neither one said anything for awhile. They rocked slowly back and forth, listening to the crickets and the steady creaking of the swing. Laird broke the silence by saying, "I saved some of your letters, too."

Carla turned to look at him, her eyes bright with surprise, "You did? Why would you save my letters?"

"Oh, I saved quite a few letters after the war was over and I was stationed in Germany. I saved some from Mother and Don, too."

"Oh." Too late, she noticed the disappointment in her voice.

Laird heard it, too. "I loved your letters, Carla…they sounded almost like you were with me in person, and sometimes you trusted me enough to talk about situations when you were working through a serious decision of some kind." He grinned at her, "Like the night at the slumber party when you gave in and looked at Miss Colton's English test."

She felt her face flushing and was glad it was getting dark.

He reached over and closed his big hand gently around hers. "I felt kind of like I was there with you, watching you grow up."

"Oh," she said in a hushed voice.

"Why did you save my letters?" Laird asked quietly.

"Well," she paused, "after all, you're like my big brother… you're like my own family. Why wouldn't I save them?"

"Of course," he said and stood up. "We're like family…Well, it's time for me to go meet Don and Virgil."

"Okay," she said, "I'll see you Monday morning at 9:00 am sharp. We're almost finished with Algebra II. I'm sure we'll have time to review some geometry before you go off to school in the fall." Laird had proved to be remarkably quick at learning. By the end of the summer, he wouldn't need her help anymore.

He grinned down at her and gave her a sloppy salute, "Okay, teacher, whatever you say… see you on Monday."

She stood and watched him favoring his left leg as he walked away down the sidewalk. She wondered if his leg hurt him when he walked; he hadn't brought his car so probably the leg didn't hurt too much. Maybe he'd parked his car on Main Street earlier to use as headquarters tonight.

Suddenly Laird stopped, turned around and came back. "How would you like to go the movies tomorrow night? There's a double feature on with Clark Gable and Claudette Colbert and I hear both films are pretty good."

"Oh, Laird, I'd love to go. Ask your brothers if they'd like to come and I'll ask Martha."

Laird pushed open the door to the screened porch and walked back inside where Mac stood beside Carla, looking up quizzically and wagging his tail lazily back and forth.

Laird reached out, took both of Carla's hands in his and lightly kissed each hand in turn, her strong left hand and the soft, paralyzed right one. He looked into her eyes with quiet warmth, "No, Carla, if it's okay with you, how about just you and me this time?"

Laird saw her eyes widen in bafflement. "Just you and me?"

He kissed each hand one more time before releasing them and grinned at her, mischief sparkling in his eyes. "Yup, just you and me."

Her smile was tentative, "What time should we go?"

"I'll check the movie schedule tonight and call you tomorrow. It'll probably start about 6:30." He quickly turned and left, letting the screen door bounce shut behind him.

She listened to him whistling *Chattanooga Choo Choo*, and watched him until he was out of sight. In spite of his bad knee, his walk had taken on an almost jaunty air.

Carla bent over to scratch Mac behind the ears and asked, "Mac… did he just ask me out on a date?"

❋ ❋ ❋

Lawrence helped clear the dishes, and, after grabbing a dishtowel to help wipe them, the final seal of approval came from Little Grandma when he joined in harmonizing to *The Old Rugged Cross*. "How can someone so tall and skinny have such a deep, bass voice," she said approvingly, "and you wipe dishes, too!"

After the dishes were done, Martha convinced them all to play a game of Hearts. When they'd finished the card game, Verle invited Lawrence to join him outside for a smoke, saying, "Dora won't let me smoke inside. She doesn't care how many doctors recommend Lucky Strikes, she won't have us smoking up her house. I think she's unreasonable, but there's not much you can do when Dora sets her mind to something."

Lawrence smiled, "Reminds me of my mother."

On the way out the back door, Verle grabbed the pencil and tablet that always sat beside the telephone. "I'm going to draw you a diagram to show how the dual brake system will work. It's really quite a simple idea, and it should be fairly easy to manufacture."

The two men sat down on the back steps, and when Verle offered Lawrence a cigarette, Lawrence shook his head, explaining he'd never taken up smoking. Verle stuck the pack of cigarettes back into his shirt pocket and quickly began to sketch a diagram of a brake drum with two cylinders instead of one. Lawrence studied it for a while, nodded his head and said, "It looks to me like it's a practical idea, and it would sure be a great safety feature."

Verle grinned his lopsided smile, "Yup. I think this one will work." He shook his head ruefully, "I know a lot of my ideas sound crazy. Maybe they are crazy. You heard Dora's mother laugh about my automatic toilet seat and my perpetual-motion machines. I suppose the battery-powered windshield wiper to keep eye glasses dry in a rain storm was the worst." He gave a self-deprecating chuckle, "At least it got the most laughs."

Lawrence smiled, "I don't know, Lord knows I could use something like that for my glasses." He took off his thick wire-framed eyeglasses, pulled a clean handkerchief out of his pocket and started cleaning the lenses and squinting as he held them up to the light. "You know what I think, Verle? I think ridicule is an occupational hazard of having a creative mind. An inventor is an experimenter and most experiments fail. Look at all the failures in medicine, aviation, and the automotive industry. We're still experimenting in every field, having failure after failure, and probably always will. But, sometimes, an experiment succeeds." Lawrence pointed with his long elegant finger to the drawing, "Like this one maybe, and that one success will make it all worthwhile."

"Why, thank you." Verle reached out and clasped Lawrence's shoulder, "Thank you, son."

Dora opened the back door. "I think it's time for us to head off for bed, Verle, so these folks can get enough sleep, and not be late for church in the morning."

"Will you help me make up my bed on the davenport, Mama?" Martha asked.

"Never mind, Mother, I'll do it," Janice said. She headed for the linen closet and called back over her shoulder, "Who wants to use the upstairs bathroom first?"

Dora said, "Why don't you go ahead, Lawrence. Just holler when it's ready for the next person."

Verle came in from the porch and looked around the room. "If my mother were here she'd say, 'Tack for dagen.' So I'll say it for her, 'Tack for dagen'."

Lawrence looked inquiringly at Verle, "Which means?"

"It's Swedish," Martha volunteered. "It means…Thanks for the day."

Lawrence smiled, "I've never heard that expression before." With a big grin on his face, he repeated, along with everyone else in the room, "Tack for dagen."

From the kitchen where she was putting away the last of the dishes, Carla could hear the conversation, and she told herself grimly that probably Laird wasn't a bit thankful for the day.

Later, upstairs in their bedroom, Janice and Carla undressed in silence, put on their summer nightgowns, and lay down on their beds. The open window let in an occasional welcome whiff of night air, and moths fluttered frantically against the window screen, powerless to resist the mysterious attraction of the bedside table light. Janice reached over and turned off the lamp.

Listening to a far-off chorus of barking dogs, Carla pulled the sheet up to her waist and said, "Thank goodness Mac isn't a barker."

"Mac's always been such a good dog."

Carla turned over on her side to face her sister, "Mac's getting old. The only time he perks up is when someone walks with him downtown, then his ears and his tail stand straight up and he bounces along like a puppy."

Janice laughed, "I know, and then the minute he gets back home, he collapses in a heap." She turned on her side to face Carla. As her eyes adjusted to the dark she could make out Carla's shadowed features opposite her. "You were so quiet tonight, Carla. What do you think of Lawrence? Isn't he wonderful?"

Carla answered slowly, carefully measuring each word, "He's very nice…and the family seems to really like him."

"But what about you? I do so want for you to like him, Carla. He'll be like a big brother to you and Martha."

Carla rolled over on her back, her face set in stubborn lines. "I don't want another big brother, I've already got Laird. I'm sorry, Jan, but how can I like someone who's giving Laird so much heartache?"

The room was quiet except for a lone mosquito that kept buzzing over their heads. Finally Janice said softly, "But tonight Laird seemed to be okay with Lawrence. He obviously made it a priority to come by the house to tell us so."

When there was no response from Carla she added, "And not long ago, he wrote me a letter telling me I was right to say we were more like a brother and sister. He said he hoped I'd find someone to marry one day… he even said he wanted to be invited to the wedding."

Carla yanked the sheet up over her head, her voice muffled and indignant, "And you believe him?" She threw back the sheet and looked over at Jan, "No, I'm the one who's like a sister, and you're still the one he loves."

Janice bit her lip in exasperation. "Is that what Laird told you on the front porch tonight? Was everything he did and said to us when we were eating dessert, was all that a lie?"

"No, that's not what he said on the porch tonight, and of course he's not lying, not on purpose anyway, he's just trying to make the best of a bad situation."

Suddenly, Janice sat up, reached over to turn on the bedside light, stared at Carla and started to bite her thumbnail. Biting her nails was something Carla hadn't seen Jan do in years. Startled, Carla sat up, too.

Janice stopped chewing her thumbnail and began to crack the knuckles of her right hand, another habit she'd given up long ago. When she finally stopped, she heaved a big sigh, pulled the sheet up and carefully smoothed it across her knees. "All right, Carla. I'm going to tell you something Don told me. I suppose I shouldn't…but Don's a pretty astute guy, don't you think?"

"Absolutely…yes."

"He told me he thinks Laird has already found a girlfriend."

Carla stared at Jan, her face an unreadable mask. "Who?" she asked weakly.

Janice stabbed her finger at her sister, "You, Carla… You."

Chapter Twenty One

Sunday afternoon, after Janice and Lawrence had left for Minneapolis, Carla pulled out the organ stool and spun the seat down a few turns. The higher adjustment for the organ stool indicated her mother had been playing the organ while the rest of them had been off at church. Carla absentmindedly riffled through the stack of sheet music on top of the organ, hoping that music would help her forget this morning's church service and the coffee hour afterwards.

When they'd entered the church that morning, Little Grandma had spotted an almost-empty pew down front in the third row. Curious eyes and murmuring voices had followed them as they strolled down the aisle, Little Grandma and Aunt Flora beaming left and right to their fellow Methodists, aware they were making quite a splash accompanied by Janice and her new boyfriend. After the service, people clustered around to be introduced, and people said they were so pleased to meet him. They were all smiles and good cheer, but Carla could see the wheels turning in their heads. She knew they were thinking that Jan had found someone else pretty quick after dumping poor Laird. It took all her self-discipline to keep on smiling at them through the coffee-hour, pretending that everything was just hunky-dory.

When Carla plopped down on the organ stool and crashed out an ear-splitting sequence of A Minor chords, Verle looked up from the overstuffed chair where he was reading the Sunday paper, feet up on the hassock, and protested, "Whoa there, girl, how about something soothing for your old Dad?"

"Sorry, Daddy." She chose a book of music from the stack on top of the organ and began to leaf gloomily through the pages.

Verle studied his daughter over the top of his reading glasses; it was evident something was bothering her. Dora told him in bed last night she thought Carla resented Lawrence on Laird's account, but Verle couldn't for the life of him figure out why Carla would still feel that way today. After all, Laird stopped by last night and everything seemed fine with him. Maybe the problem was that it was her time of the month. He'd lived with women long enough to know that during certain days, a man better just keep his head down. Verle nodded, "Thank you, darlin'," and went back to reading the funnies section.

Carla felt herself begin to calm down as she opened *Hit Parade Favorites of 1945*, a gift from Janice on Carla's eighteenth birthday. She read again what Jan had written on the inside cover, "The only good thing about the war is the music." Jan was right, there had been so many lovely songs written during the war years. Carla decided to focus on playing and singing her favorites, and when she finished the last satisfying chords of *When the Lights Go On Again All Over the World*, she sighed and put her hands in her lap. She sat quietly, reflecting on all that had happened during the past few days.

Thoughts of Laird's strange behavior last night continually flitted through her mind. He'd kissed both her hands, even the paralyzed one, and looked so mysteriously into her eyes. Carla moved the back of her left hand slowly across her lips and wondered what her hands felt like on Laird's lips. She picked up her paralyzed hand and kissed it; it felt softer than her good hand. Why don't you admit it, she asked herself crossly, you absolutely melted inside when he did that, and now tonight they were going to the movies together, like on a date. She ought to be feeling happy but she couldn't bring herself to believe Laird thought of her as a possible girlfriend.

She stood up to leave and carefully placed the *Hit Parade* book back on top of the organ. Realization hit her at the same moment she lifted her hand from the book. She finally understood Laird's puzzling interest in her. It was suddenly so obvious, so clear to her that, for a moment, she felt unable to move or to breathe. "I resemble Jan," she thought. "He sees Jan in me."

Verle put down his paper and looked up. "I think it's almost time for *Fibber McGee and Molly*. I'm going to go ask your mother if she wants to listen, want to join us?"

Carla looked uncomprehendingly at her father, "What?"

Verle regarded his daughter with interest, "You're deep in thought today."

"Oh, do you think so?" She turned slowly and left the room, her quiet footsteps echoing on the hardwood oak stairs leading up to her bedroom.

"Yes, you are, my darlin,' deep in thought," Verle said quietly, to no one in particular.

Upstairs in her bedroom, Carla opened the door to her closet, trying to focus her thoughts on something ordinary, and wondered what would be a good thing to wear to the movie tonight. She took her lavender dimity dress with the long, full sleeves from the closet and laid it carefully on the bed. For shoes, she chose the tan slip-ons and the white anklets with the little ruffle around the cuff. It would be wonderful when nylon stockings were available again, but until then, she'd resigned herself to wearing anklets. Like their mother, Carla and Janice refused to use leg makeup and the gadget needed to draw a straight seam down the back of your leg. After one hilarious attempt to paint a straight seam down the back of Jan's leg, they'd all decided to wait until the war was over, when the factories would gear up once more to make nylon stockings instead of parachutes.

Maybe she'd wear her silver charm bracelet, the one with a special charm for every year of her life since she'd started kindergarten, the one Daddy and Mr. Dillon, down at the jewelry store, had designed with a band of silver beads threaded on a stretch cord so that she could slip the bracelet off and on herself. Mama had told her that the eighteenth birthday charm would be the last addition to the bracelet, because now she was entering the adult part of her life. Daddy, too, had let her know this would be the last charm when he'd attached the tiny silver graduation cap complete with a filigree tassel and said, "This old charm bracelet is getting loaded down, darlin,' time to move on to something else."

Carla sat on the edge of her bed and placed her hands in her lap. This would be her first real date. At all other social events, she'd been surrounded with friends, both boys and girls, and this past couple of months, wherever she'd gone with Laird, they'd taken along his brothers or Martha. Tonight it would be just her and Laird. "Just you and me," he'd said. She breathed in a tremulous intake of air and realized she'd been holding her breath. She had no doubt that choosing her as a girlfriend was a way Laird had unconsciously figured out to keep from feeling hurt about Jan and Lawrence. It made sense he would choose her as a substitute, she thought, because even Lawrence had commented on the similarity in their looks. She repeated Lawrence's words aloud, "Someone with the same beautiful smile." Saying the words out loud solidified the truth for her, rooted it in reality, and made it inescapable. Somehow, in spite of her polio, when Laird looked at her, he saw Jan.

She went over to her dresser, opened the drawer and carefully inspected the two silver candleholders she'd bought for Jan and Laird's wedding present. They didn't need polishing, they were still bright and shiny. She wrapped them up again and closed the drawer.

If making her his girlfriend was how Laird needed to handle the pain of breaking up with Janice, Carla would go along with it. Besides, if she was really honest with herself, she would have to admit she wanted it, too, even if it was only going to be temporary. In six more weeks college would start and they would both go their separate ways. Laird would fall in love with someone at college who would be a real replacement for Janice, and Carla would fade away in his memory. Eventually, when he looked at Carla, he would see just a kid sister again.

She straightened up, took her bathrobe off the hook and started towards the bathroom, pausing on the landing to shout down the stairs, "I'm going to take a bath. Anybody need to use the bathroom first?"

※ ※ ※

Laird parked the car and came up the walk at 6:00 pm. He checked his watch and smiled as he remembered his father's advice, "If you can't be on time, be early."

Martha flung the door open even before he got to the stairs leading up to the porch. "He's here!" she called excitedly over her shoulder. "He's here!"

Verle came to the door with an outstretched hand. "Good to see you, son. So you two are going to take in a movie, are you?"

'Yup, I'm trying to catch up on all the movies I missed in the past three years." Laird shook Verle's hand, and, as always, was fascinated by the man's energy, Something about Verle was always in motion, his mobile face, his restless hands, his shifting feet.

"Carla told us you're going to see *It Happened One Night* with Clark Gable. Dora and I saw that last fall, it's pretty good." He winked at Laird, "Dora loves Clark Gable."

Dora came into the front hall, wiping her hands on a dishtowel, "Oh, Verle, it's not just me, half the women in town love Clark Gable."

Little Grandma bustled into the hallway wiping her hands on her apron and smiled affectionately at Laird as she said, "I'd say it's more like ninety percent of us."

"We're just finishing up the supper dishes," Dora said. "Carla will be right down. She ran upstairs to get her purse."

Verle's smile was huge as he turned to watch his daughter coming down the stairs. "You're a pretty picture tonight, darlin'."

Carla hesitated and stared at her family all clustered around Laird, so excited they could hardly stand still, trying hard to pretend they were nonchalant about her first ever date. She felt her face flush.

Laird grinned at Carla's discomfort, he'd known he'd have to run the Swanson gauntlet tonight. He'd done it many times before with Jan.

"Try to get home by eleven, kids," Verle called after them as they went out the door, and a chorus of good-byes followed them down the sidewalk.

Still grinning, Laird opened the car door for Carla and waited while she gathered her skirt around her, then he closed the door and leaned down to say through the open window, "Your dad is right, you are a pretty picture tonight."

Carla flushed as she watched Laird get behind the wheel and close the door. He turned to look at her as he started the car, "They love you, Carla."

"I know they do." She looked straight ahead and put her hands in her lap. "The reason they're acting so giddy is because this is my very first date."

Laird put the car in gear and pulled away from the curb. "That's pretty hard to believe…a beautiful girl like you?"

Carla shook her head, "No, it's true , I've only been out with groups of friends." She turned to look at Laird's relaxed, chiseled profile and felt her throat tighten, "It's easier to go places when you're part of a group."

Laird glanced sideways at her, his eyes held a teasing glint. "I've noticed that you're usually in the middle of a crowd."

"That's because I'm lucky to have lots of girlfriends, and the guys think of me as a sister."

Laird steered the car slowly down the tree-lined street with his left arm casually leaning on the open window frame. The motion of the car made a slight breeze of warm air against their faces. "Well, I certainly don't think of you as a sister," Laird said, and his eyes were dark as he turned to give her one of his unfathomable looks.

"You don't?" She looked out the window away from him. "You always used to say you were like my big brother."

He shook his head emphatically. "That's when you were a kid." He continued to give her that mysterious look she found so baffling and said, "No, Carla. Now I think of you as a lovely woman." He put both hands on the wheel and looked out at the road again, "And I'm honored to be your very first date."

She looked down at her hands; the left hand was placed firmly on top of the paralyzed one. Carla had only to close her eyes to see Jan's laughing face, her undamaged body. She bit at her lower lip, thinking about all the times Laird had gone on dates with Jan, and even after she opened her eyes, Jan remained a steady presence somewhere in the back of her mind. It felt almost like Jan was there in the car with them.

Laird parked the car a block from the theatre, switched off the key and turned to look at Carla, his eyes questioning. Something was bothering her...maybe if he'd had a sister he could understand better what she was thinking.

Carla looked back at him with a solemn and a somehow determined look on her face, but her voice was bright and cheerful, "Well, we're here. Let's go find out if I want to join the Clark Gable fan club."

Chapter Twenty Two

The next morning at the Nordstrom house, Ellen was dishing up a breakfast of scrambled eggs and fried potatoes when she heard Laird come bounding down the stairs whistling *String of Pearls,* one of her favorite Glenn Miller tunes. He came cheerily into the kitchen and sat down in his accustomed place by his father. "Morning everybody." He flashed a smile round the table and said, "Sorry I'm late. I've been working on my math assignment. I don't want to get in trouble with my teacher."

Emil studied his eldest son and thought that Laird was acting more like his old self lately. He hoped Laird was finally leaving memories of the war behind him, or, maybe it was due to Carla cheering him up and helping him get over his disappointment about Janice Swanson. Ellen told him last night that Laird had taken Carla to the movies.

Duane grinned at Laird, "You and Carla must have stayed out pretty late if you didn't get your homework done."

David swallowed a half-chewed mouthful of fried potatoes and asked, "Was it a good movie? We didn't want to see it because it sounded kind of dumb."

Johnny nodded seriously, "We mostly like cowboy movies." The other two boys nodded their heads in agreement.

Laird reached for a piece of bread, began to spread butter on it and grinned at his brothers, "Yes, it was a good movie, although I doubt if you guys would have liked it. There were no horses in it and nobody got shot."

Ellen set the last plateful of food on the table and began to pour glasses of milk and cups of coffee. "Did Carla like it?"

"Yup, she says she is now a full-fledged member of the Clark Gable fan club. Her Grandma told me that ninety per cent of the women in this town are members. Does that include you, Mother?"

Ellen smiled as she sat down to join her men at the table, "Oh, I guess I am." She glanced over at Emil, a sparkle in her eyes, "But I'm not a serious fan."

There was a companionable silence at the table as the family settled down to the business of eating breakfast. Everyone was thinking how wonderful the food tasted, but no one thought to say so.

Laird's thoughts drifted to Carla. She'd acted like she'd had a good time, she'd been bright and cheery as usual, but not really herself. A part of her kept skittering away from him. Maybe she'd been uneasy because it was her first date, but that didn't make any sense, not for him and Carla. They'd known each other practically since she was born, and how could anyone be nervous about going out with someone you've known for years? Laird chewed slowly and took a sip of coffee as he looked across the table at his mother. Maybe if he asked his mother, she might have an idea what the trouble was. Maybe it was just that Carla was worried he would want to take her out to the golf course after the movie and start necking, but Carla must surely know he wouldn't pressure her to do anything like that, not so soon anyway. Last night, when he'd walked her up to the front door, he'd given her just a light kiss on her forehead. God, she'd smelled so sweet.

After Emil wiped the last bit of egg off his plate with a piece of Ellen's homemade bread, he pushed back his chair, took a cigarette from his shirt pocket and asked, "How're the math lessons going?"

"Actually, pretty good, it's easier the second time around, and Carla's a good teacher. We're almost ready to start reviewing geometry next."

Duane got up to check the frying pan for second helpings. "When will you know what college you're going to?" he asked.

"I'm still waiting for a letter from one more college. I know I can go to South Dakota State. I haven't heard from Northwestern or the University of Minnesota yet."

Ellen sat sipping coffee from one of her rose-bud china cups. "Better not wait too long to enroll, Laird. School starts in only six weeks or so, doesn't it?"

"I know, but don't worry, I'm keeping track of the deadline dates. Anyway, Mr. Seglie says I've still got time. He thinks the schools are slow to respond because there are so many vets applying."

"Well, I'm sure you know what you're doing, and as for me, I better get to work." Emil stubbed out the last of his cigarette, oblivious to the fact that Ellen followed him around the house, emptying his ashtrays. He looked at Duane and David and said, "I could use a little help today on Bert Thompson's granaries. One of you can put the bolts through from the outside and the other one fasten from the inside."

"Sure, Dad." Emil always paid his sons wages for working in the shop, and both boys were eager to earn a little money. In Sweden, Emil's father had hired him out to the neighbors and kept the wages for himself; Emil had vowed he would never do that to his own sons. During the war, there hadn't been many men available to hire for part-time jobs in the blacksmith shop. Emil had tried hiring old Nestor Gladdley, but he was usually too drunk to remember he'd promised to show up, and, if he did remember, he often found a corner where he could lie down and sleep most of the day. Laird knew Emil was grateful that he could depend on his sons.

Laird looked around the table at his brothers and impulsively said, "You're all good kids, and I'm proud of you."

No one said anything. There was an uncomfortable silence at the table, but his brothers' faces shone with pleasure. Finally Duane said, "Thanks, Laird. I'm proud of you, too."

"Yeah, me, too, Laird," David and Johnny both said at the same time, and, not knowing what else to do, all three boys leapt to their feet and raced from the room.

Laird looked at his mother, "In the army, the guys I fought with were like my brothers. I did everything I had to do to keep them safe." He looked at his father, "I give you my word, Dad. I will always do the same for my real brothers." His jaw was set as he looked as his mother, "I give you my word." He stood up abruptly. "Well, Carla will be here soon, I'd better get my homework in order."

After Laird left the kitchen, Emil reached across the table and gently put his hand on Ellen's. She met his eyes through a mist of tightly held tears, "Well..." she said softly... "Well."

✳ ✳ ✳

Laird hurried up the stairs, passing Duane coming back down. Laird reached out and ruffled his hair, "Have a good day at the shop, Duane."

"You, too, Laird, and tell Carla I said hi." Duane's face lit up with a smile as he turned and watched Laird go up the stairs.

Laird went into his bedroom, walked over to the window and saw that Johnny was outside in the back yard playing with the Swansons' dog, Mac. Old Mac often wandered the three blocks over to the Nordstrom house whenever Martha was at the pool or busy inside the house. Johnny was determined to teach Mac to fetch sticks, but Mac refused to learn, and although everyone else was convinced it wasn't in Mac's genes to fetch and carry, Johnny was stubborn and insisted that one day Mac would catch on.

Laird sat down at the small desk in the corner of the room and idly wondered why the folks hadn't gotten a new dog to replace old Mayberry. Mayberry's death had been bad news, even in the midst of the senseless human deaths surrounding Laird during the war. Maybe old Mayberry was just a blip on the buttocks of the world, but it had hurt like hell to find out he was gone.

Laird had only one more set of problems to work out before Carla came. He put his hands behind his head, leaned back in the sturdy wooden desk chair, and stared absently at the old National Geographic world map tacked to the wall over his desk. Where had that emotional outburst down in the kitchen come from? He knew he'd embarrassed his brothers; he smiled and thought that a little embarrassment wouldn't hurt them any.

We few…we happy few…we band of brothers. The familiar verses from Shakespeare ran through his mind. God bless Miss Colton for making him memorize so many pieces of poetry. There had never been an occasion to recite the introduction to the *Canterbury Tales*, although he could still do it, but many times in the past three years those lines from *Henry V* had run through his head and brought him comfort. *We few… we happy few…we band of brothers…for he today that sheds his blood with me shall be my brother.* How many times had he recited those words in a drunken toast to his equally drunken buddies during the rare intervals of relative safety behind the front lines? Laird guessed at least half of them were dead now…maybe in a few years, he could find out who was left. They'd all done what they could to keep each other safe. Not all, of course, you couldn't expect that of everybody. A couple of the guys had simply turned around and quietly walked away. He sometimes wondered if they'd gotten away with their disappearing acts. But most of the guys had stuck it out, as he had. The things Laird used to think soldiers did for love of their country, and because they were brave, he now knew had nothing to do with bravery or patriotism. Soldiers did what they had to do to keep themselves and each other alive.

A picture of Charlie Greer flashed through his mind. What a mean son-of-a-bitch Charlie was, but when he'd ended up with two bullet holes in his shoulder, he tried to fight off the medics who'd come to take him to the aid station. "You God damn, fuckin' sons of bitches," he'd screamed at them. "Let me be. I don't need an aid station." It took three men to hold him down while the medic gave him a shot of morphine, but he was still awake enough to reach for Laird's hand when they lifted his stretcher onto the back of a jeep, pleading softly, "Laird, God damn it, don't let them take me. You guys need me."

Laird never saw him again. It happened. If you didn't get wounded too bad, they patched you up and tried to put you back in your old company, but if they couldn't locate your old bunch, they rotated you into a new company and a new platoon. It wasn't the same as being with the original bunch, but if you managed to live through enough hell together, you bonded with the new guys. Eventually, you were willing to kill… maybe die…for them, too.

Laird sat up straight and tried to clear his head. Better not to think about it. He remembered what the chaplain had said, "Nobody wins in a war."

He picked up a pencil and began to check through the sheet of math problems. He told himself to stop thinking about it, for God's sake, the war was over…and Carla would be here soon.

When Carla knocked on the door promptly at nine o'clock, he was there to open it, and to smile down on her upturned face. She looked up at him through a puzzling veil of reserve, and he noticed she was wearing a short-sleeved tangerine and white dress that set off her creamy skin and shining curls.

"You look good enough to eat," Laird said.

"Only in a metaphorical way, I hope." Carla tried to brush off the compliment, but she flashed a smile at him.

Laird stood aside to let her in and said, "Well, you know what Miss Colton always said, 'Metaphors are lies that help to tell the truth'."

Carla walked over to the study table and laid her book down. She sat and patted the seat of the chair next to her, "Come on, let's get to work, Laird…if you give me any more compliments, I'll think you're fishing for a good grade."

He sat down, propped his chin against his hand, and regarded her steadily. His deep-set eyes held a mischievous twinkle. "Nope, I'm fishing for something more important than grades."

Carla looked away and opened her math book. "Well, it's no use trying to bribe me with compliments," she said firmly. "You should know by now, I'm incorruptible." She lowered her eyes as she suddenly remembered that she'd written to him about cheating on Miss Colton's English test. "Well, almost incorruptible."

Laird grinned at her and turned to open his own book. "Okay, I guess I'll just have to think up a different tactic."

Carla ignored that remark. "Okay, let's go over these last problems together. You seem to be understanding matrices really well, but we'll do some reviewing today anyway, and I think tomorrow you can take the final exam. Then Wednesday we can start on geometry…" She stopped and said, "That is, if you want to."

"Of course I want to." Laird smiled, "I bet you're just as good at geometry as you are at algebra."

She glanced over at him and admonished, "You're doing it again, Laird."

"No, I'm not…I'm not talking metaphors here. I'm just telling the unvarnished facts. If facts turn out to be a compliment, you'll just have to live with it."

Carla admitted, "It's true, I am pretty good at geometry. Mr. Adams and I used to talk about math sometimes…in fact, he told me something about geometry you might be interested in."

Laird turned his chair to face her and said, "Fire away."

"Mr. Adams said there's a theory by a guy named Einstein that says space is curved, and not only is it curved, it changes over time, kind of like the ocean with waves and ripples, and," she said, leaning forward excitedly, "there was another man, and believe it or not, his name was Nordstrom. Maybe he's a relative of yours?"

Laird shook his head, "I doubt it."

"Well, anyhow, Nordstrom said light always goes in a straight line, that's like Euclidean Geometry." Carla paused to be sure Laird understood, "That's the kind of geometry we'll be learning, Euclidean Geometry."

Laird watched her, fascinated. She loves this stuff, he thought.

"But Einstein said light bends…for example, if two straight lines are parallel and they go by a star, they'll curve and bend back towards each other, but Nordstrom said, no, the light has to continue along parallel lines. Isn't that interesting?"

She stopped and sat back. "A few years later they did an experiment during an eclipse of the sun and, sure enough, light from the stars bent around the sun just like Einstein predicted."

So," she added with an air of finality, "Einstein was right. It means there must be another kind of geometry that varies over time and space. Physicists are still trying to figure it out."

Laird grinned, "Are you telling me I have to have an opinion about non-Euclidean geometry in order to pass this course?"

"No, of course not," Carla looked down at the open text book and gave a small self-deprecating laugh, "I guess I get too excited about these things."

Laird was surprised to see a hint of sadness in her eyes.

"But I don't have anybody to talk to about mathematics," she said. "Only Mr. Adams, and he's just a teacher."

Laird reached out and put his hand over hers. "Don't worry, Carla. You're going to find lots of people in college who'll want to talk about science and math."

"I'm hoping that too, Laird." She looked down again and pulled her hand away, "We better get to work."

He put his completed homework assignment on the table in front of her and wondered what went on in that head of hers. Sometimes he could swear Don was right, that maybe she did care about him, but other times she seemed withdrawn, almost cool. He ran his fingers through his hair and tried to listen as she began to explain the math problems. Evidently he'd gotten them all right. Oh, God, he hoped the acceptance letter from the University of Minnesota came soon. If they didn't accept him, he was seriously thinking about getting in the car, driving up to Minneapolis and pounding on their doors until they did.

Chapter Twenty Three

Dora had just spread a clean dishtowel over the fragrant bread dough rising in her mother's ancient crockery bowl when she heard a knock on the back door. "Come in!" she called. As she turned on the kitchen faucet to wash her hands, she was surprised to see Laird walk into the kitchen.

"Hi, Laird, come on in, what a nice surprise! I'm sorry Carla isn't home yet. She's down at the swimming pool watching Martha graduate from Diane's advanced swimming class. I guess you know that Martha's latest career choice is to be a life guard."

Laird hesitated at the doorway of the kitchen. "Yah, I knew about Martha, and I know Carla's not here. That's why I stopped by." His face was somber. "Can you spare a few minutes?"

"Of course I can. Mother's gone to a Ladies' Aid meeting at the parsonage, and Verle's at work, so it's just you and me. Would you like a cup of coffee, or some lemonade?"

"Lemonade would be good, thanks. It's a little too hot today for coffee."

Dora laughed and opened the refrigerator door, "I think so, too, but there are always people like my mother who insist that hot coffee cools you off on a hot day."

"No kidding. How does she figure that?"

"I've never been able to understand it." Dora took a pitcher of lemonade from the refrigerator and set it on the table. "Someday, you'll have to ask her to explain her theory." Dora smiled, "She does have a theory."

She took two glasses from the cupboard and watched Laird out of the corner of her eye. His face was impassive, but the tenseness of his body was palpable as he silently pulled out one of the kitchen chairs, and turned it around to straddle the seat, his long legs on either side, arms folded over the back of the chair.

She took a few peanut butter cookies out of the cookie jar and sat opposite him. "What is it, Laird?"

He cleared his throat uneasily. "I got my acceptance letter from the University of Minnesota yesterday."

"That's wonderful! You and Carla will be going to the same school." She studied his face and her smile faded. "You don't seem very happy about it."

"I'm happy," he ran one hand through his hair and shifted in his chair, "but Carla isn't."

"Are you sure? Why wouldn't she be delighted to have you with her at the University?"

"That's what I came to ask you about, and please be honest with me. Why doesn't Carla want me to go to school with her? If she doesn't want me to go to the same college she does, why is she always willing to go out with me?" Laird suddenly stood up and began to pace back and forth across the linoleum floor. "Maybe she doesn't want to hurt my feelings… sometimes I think she feels sorry for me because of Jan, but I've told her several times that doesn't matter anymore. Or does she feel sorry for me because of the war? Maybe she senses the emotional shrapnel I'm carrying around…maybe it scares her…" He stopped pacing and said, "Well, maybe she's right to be cautious about that, sometimes I think I'd be better off with pieces of metal in me, like Oscar …"

He stuffed his hands in his pockets. "Maybe she figures the only way she can get rid of me is for us to go to separate schools this fall…what do you think? I trust your opinion, Mrs. Swanson. If you think that's what Carla wants, I'll leave her alone."

Dora sat stunned, unaware that her mouth had come slightly open.

"Tell me the truth and, if you think I shouldn't, I won't bother her again."

Dora closed her mouth and asked, "First of all, what makes you think Carla doesn't want you to go with her to the University of Minnesota?"

Laird turned the chair around, sat down, leaned his elbows on the table, and looked at her intently, "Because when I showed her the letter, she got this odd look on her face and said in a tight little voice, 'Oh, that's wonderful, Laird,' but anyone could see she didn't mean it. You know Carla, she can't tell a lie to save herself."

"Oh, my." Dora picked up the pitcher of lemonade and poured them both a glass.

Laird's eyes narrowed as he watched various fleeting expressions dart across Dora's face. "You do know something, don't you? Please tell me, don't worry about my feelings, I just want to know the truth."

Dora stared at the sugar bowl in the middle of the table. "I've noticed she's been troubled about something lately, but I didn't know what." Dora looked at him abruptly, her hazel eyes intent on his face. "How serious are you about Carla, Laird?"

He looked straight into her eyes and his voice was grave, "I love her, Mrs. Swanson, and someday, when she's ready, I want to marry her."

Dora looked out the kitchen window and took in a deep breath. She could see Laird was telling the truth that he loved Carla, at least as much as any young person knows what love is. Dora turned and met his eyes again. "Have you told her that you love her?"

"Not in so many words, but I've sure given her plenty of hints." He ran his hand through his hair again and said, "I've been waiting for a few hints back from her, but I haven't been getting any."

Dora took a sip of her lemonade. "Maybe part of the problem…" Dora hesitated… "I'm almost sure Carla wouldn't want me to tell you this, but maybe part of the problem is that some years ago, Carla decided she would never marry."

"But, why would she decide that? What's she got against marriage?"

"Because of her polio, because she doesn't have a perfect body she thinks no one will ever want to marry her." Dora's voice broke… "You know how independent Carla is. So, if she's the one who decides never to marry, she'd be the one in control of the relationship."

Laird raised his eyebrows and nodded. "A good offense is the best defense."

"Yes," Dora said. "I think she's afraid if she takes you too seriously, and if she allows herself to love you, she'll end up abandoned and hurt."

He cradled the moist glass of lemonade in his hands. "So, how can I convince her otherwise?"

Dora ignored his question, and asked him one of her own, "Have you noticed Carla has started to wear short-sleeved clothing when she goes over to your house for the morning math session?"

"Sure, it's been hot, why wouldn't she wear short sleeves?"

"Laird, Carla never wears short sleeves away from home."

He studied her face, a puzzled expression on his own. "That's a good sign, isn't it? She must feel at home at our house now."

"No, Laird," Dora shook her head patiently, wondering how such a smart young man could be so dense. "I think she's reminding you she has a paralyzed arm. I think she's trying to tell you she's not someone you'd want to marry."

Laird suddenly straightened and gave a little grin. "More offensive tactics, right?"

Dora smiled and nodded, pleased that he finally seemed to understand. He abruptly leaped to his feet and started to leave the room, then turned around again and said, "Thanks, Mrs. Swanson, you don't know how much I appreciate you…is there anything else I should know?"

Dora hesitated, "There is one more thing I'd like to say, Laird, about that emotional shrapnel you mentioned. Do you know that every piece of shrapnel that comes out through Oscar's skin is encapsulated in a coating? His body protects itself somehow, by coating those hard pieces of metal." Dora looked up into Laird's questioning eyes, "I'm absolutely convinced that those who love you, as well as your own good sense, will find a way to protect you from any emotional shrapnel. I know from personal experience, Laird, that time…and love…are great healers."

He stood looking down at her, his face somber. "I hope you're right." He turned and ran down the steps, the screen door banging shut behind him, and she heard his tires squeal as he drove away. Clearing the table, she began to hum, *Sweet Georgia Brown*.

When Verle dropped by for a coffee break later in the day, he commented, "You're sure in a good mood."

"Yes, I am," she said, giving him a small, Mona Lisa kind of smile, "In fact, I'm in a very good mood."

※ ※ ※

Laird was almost at the swimming pool when he spotted Carla walking back home under the thick shade of the elm trees. He noticed that in spite of it being a hot day, she was wearing a long-sleeved blouse. He made a quick U-turn, drove up beside her, leaned over and yelled out the open window, "Hey, Carla, want a lift?"

"No, thank you, you don't have to bother, Laird. I'm nearly home," she smiled at him and kept on walking.

Laird stopped the engine, got out of the car and fell in beside her, "I'll walk you home then."

She noticed the mischievous glint in his eyes, "Oh, all right, you can give me a ride, if you insist." She tossed her head, and tried to make her voice sound impatient, but it was hard not to smile.

"Good decision," he said, as he took her by the arm to steer her towards the car. Once in the car, Laird made another U-turn and grinned at her, "I offered you a ride, not a ride home."

She looked sideways at him, under raised eyebrows.

"I'm taking you someplace we can talk, and Frostie-Freeze is the only place I can think of where we can have some privacy. We can sit in the car and order a malt or something."

Carla sat back and looked straight ahead, her lips pressed firmly together. "Okay, if you say so," she said darkly, "You've got me in your power." Their eyes met and they both started to laugh.

"You didn't have to kidnap me, Laird. I'd have gone if you'd have asked nicely."

"Maybe…maybe not."

He drove down Main Street, made a left-hand turn at the grain elevators onto Highway 26 and turned in at the Frostie-Freeze Drive-In. He parked in the shade of the restaurant canopy as far away as possible from the one other car outside the drive in. He turned off the motor as Mavis came out the door, her little white Frostie-Freeze waitress cap slightly askew on her fly-away hair.

Mavis looked in the car at them with kindly eyes and said, "Hi, there, what can I get for you two?"

"Boy, you give fast service," Laird said. "I didn't even have time to turn on my headlights."

"What are you doing here, Mavis?" asked Carla. "I thought you were working at Dee's."

"Oh, both of these jobs are just part-time," Mavis said. "I kind of like a change of scene anyhow."

As soon as Mavis left to get their chocolate malts, Laird leaned back against the door and draped one arm over the steering wheel. "I wonder if we could talk awhile, Carla, if that's okay."

"Of course it's okay." She settled herself against the other door and studied his face...he probably wanted to talk about the University of Minnesota. She'd felt a confusing jolt of happiness mixed with pain when he told her he'd been accepted there. Of course she was delighted they'd be attending the same school, but she dreaded being there and having to watch the inevitable relationship that was bound to develop between him and some other girl.

"I don't know much more than you do about the university, Laird. Daddy and Mama are going to take me to Minneapolis when it's time to register and sign up for a dorm room...do you want to go with us?"

Laird blinked in surprise. "No, I didn't want to talk about school, maybe we can do that another time.'

"Oh, I just assumed..."

Laird ran his fingers through his hair. "No, it's something else. I don't know exactly how to start." He shifted uneasily and said, "Maybe I should have waited for some moonlit night." He impulsively reached across the seat and took both her hands in his, "I love you, Carla, and I'm asking you to marry me."

Carla sat very still, her eyes fixed on his face, her lips slightly parted.

"Carla?" He lifted each hand to his lips and kissed them, one at a time. "I love you, Carla."

Her voice was faint, "I don't know what to say."

"I would sure be relieved if you said you love me, too," he looked questioningly at her.

"Oh, Laird," her voice was anguished, and she bit her lower lip, never taking her eyes from his. "It's not me you love...you only think you love me because of Jan."

Laird sat back and let go of her hands, "What on earth are you talking about?"

Just then, Mavis came back to the car with their chocolate malts, fastened the tray to the open car window and asked cheerily, "Anything else, kids?" As she looked into each of their faces, she realized something important was happening here. She immediately turned to leave and said over her shoulder, "Just blink the lights when you're finished."

Carla looked away, "Jan and I resemble one another, don't we, Laird? Everybody says so."

Astonished, he protested, "But you don't look anything alike!"

"Sure we do! People always say we have the same smiles, and Daddy sometimes says we're like two peas in a pod."

"Well, you don't look anything alike, but even if you did, what does that have to do with me loving you?" he demanded.

Carla eyes began to shine with tears, "I'm sure you see Jan in me, and you've transferred your love for her over to me because of that." Her voice was so soft now, he could hardly hear her, "It's Jan you love…not me."

Laird gripped the steering wheel in frustration, "You actually think I still love Janice?"

Carla could see he was incredulous at the idea, but she also knew it was because he'd hidden the truth from himself. "I'm sure of it, Laird. It all makes perfect sense, Jan is such a wonderful and beautiful person, how could you fall out of love with her so soon?"

He looked at her for a long minute. "The thing with Jan is in the past. Three years was a long time for two kids to be apart, we didn't even know what real love was. It's over."

"You know very well you didn't know it was over until just a couple of short months ago, and how could you possibly think you're in love with me if it wasn't because I remind you of Jan?" She looked away from him and added, "Why else would you think you loved someone like me?"

Laird's eyes softened as he turned toward her again, "But don't you see? You're exactly the someone I love."

They sat in silence for a moment before Carla tried again to make him understand. "Look, Laird…what's your favorite flavor of ice cream?"

He raised his eyebrows and said, "It's chocolate, it's always been chocolate, but what does that have to do with anything?"

"Well, don't you see? Jan is chocolate, the flavor you'll always like the best. Right now you think I'm chocolate too, but I'm really not, and once you discover I'm only strawberry or pistachio, you won't be so interested in me." She looked away from him and said, "Well, I hope you'll always like me…but I'll never be Jan, even if right now you think I am."

Laird stared at her and said, "You can't be serious." He reached out to hold her hands again, "Please, look at me, Carla…you're a very smart person, but you're wrong." She continued to avoid his eyes and steadfastly looked out the car window.

"Carla, do you remember the day you asked me what I believed in? And I said something about the clouds and the red-winged blackbirds?"

"And the mosquitoes," Carla added with a little smile as she turned to look at him.

"Of course," he grinned, "the mosquitoes…but I should have told you that you're at the top of my list." He shook his head in exasperation, "I'm not saying this very well. There is no list."

Carla tilted her head and frowned slightly, "I'm trying to understand, Laird."

"Everything is a circle. All the parts of the Universe make up one big circle, or maybe it's a big ball, but you're there, Carla, at the very center. There's no God outside of the circle, Carla. There's no God you can pray to out there somewhere who can stop wars and illness and cruelty. God is the whole process, it's the cause and effect and the interrelationship of all those clouds and blackbirds and mosquitoes, and you and me. You're with me right here at the center of it all…that's how close I feel to you."

"But what does that have to with whether or not you love me, just me, with all my imperfections?"

He rubbed his forehead and sighed, "Well, I just told you how…how could I not love you? I can't imagine my life without you." He reached over and gently pushed her curls back from her face. "I love you at a level way beyond looks, Carla. Even though you're so beautiful, and the most wonderful girl I've ever known, I love you way beyond those things."

As silent tears begin to run down Carla's cheeks, Laird took a deep breath and asked, "How about me, Carla? I've got my own imperfections, a lot of them aren't visible like my limp, but I've got my share, more than you know. Can you love me in spite of them?"

She sniffled and asked, "Do you have a hanky?"

His eyes never left her face as he reached into his back pocket and pulled out a clean, pressed handkerchief. She took it from him with a small laugh, "You're the only man I know who could produce a clean handkerchief at a time like this." She wiped her eyes and blew her nose. "You don't have any imperfections, Laird." She blew her nose again and smiled at him. "But, even if you did, I'd still love you, you're at the center of my universe, too."

He tried to move closer across the seat to pull her towards him but the stick shift got in the way, "Damn this stick shift, it's as bad as having a chaperone."

Carla laughed and moved towards the center of the seat as Laird's arms closed around her and his lips lightly touched hers. He kissed her eyelids, her forehead, and then placed another light kiss on her parted lips before he drew back, put a finger under her chin and tilted her head so he could look directly into her eyes. "What a lucky guy I am." He leaned forward to kiss her again, this time with a passion he was trying hard to control.

Carla was not prepared for the sudden rush of melting sensations that burned down her body and between her legs. She pulled away, flustered, and looked up at him... this must be what Jan meant when she said she was attracted to Lawrence like the opposite poles of a magnet. "Oh, my goodness, Laird, I don't think we can wait until we graduate from college to get married."

He started to laugh and hugged her close, "I don't think we can either." He drew back again and his eyes were suddenly serious, "But even after we're married, don't worry, you'll finish college, and you'll meet all kinds of people like yourself who love science and math. It'll be just like you planned." He grinned, "Well, not exactly like you planned. You'll be a married lady and we'll have our own place. Married vets get special housing arrangements at the university."

"Imagine! Our own place..." Carla raised a quizzical eyebrow at him, "Do you like eating supper by candlelight?"

"I haven't had much practice but I'm sure I'd learn to like it."

"I hope so, because all I have in my hope chest are two candleholders."

Laird drew his finger along the line of her chin and bent to kiss her lightly on the nose, "I didn't know you had a hope chest."

Carla closed her eyes and lifted her face to be kissed again, "Neither did I," she said.

"You didn't?" Laird wanted to look into her eyes to see if she was joking, but her eyelids were still closed.

"Nope," she answered, "I didn't have a clue."

He gave a little laugh, "Want to enlighten me?"

She opened her eyes and gave him a mysterious glance, "Not really."

Suddenly her face clouded and the sparkle left her eyes. "But what if I get pregnant? It seems like the minute people get married, they get pregnant. How can I go to college if I have a baby to take care of?"

He cocked his head and regarded her seriously. "There is that," he said.

They looked at each other in consternation before Laird smiled and said, "Not everyone has a kid right away. There are ways to prevent it you know. Don't worry, we'll figure it out."

She reached up to touch his hair and kissed him softly on the lips, "Do you think so, Laird? Do you really think so?"

"Yes, I do," he whispered huskily, "I really do."

❋ ❋ ❋

The only two people inside the Frostie-Freeze drive-in were Mavis, busy shredding cheese at the counter, and an elderly woman with greying hair and bright lipstick who sat at one of the back tables munching contentedly on her order of hamburger and French fries. They were both enjoying the peace and quiet of the mid-afternoon lull; the only sound filtering through the pleasant stillness was the voice of Frank Sinatra singing *Million Dollar Baby* on the juke box. Mavis glanced out the window to see whether Laird's car headlights were turned on. "For goodness sake!" she said out loud in a surprised voice, "Those two are necking in broad daylight out there."

The elderly customer got up and walked slowly over to the window to see for herself. "I don't know about this younger generation," she said with a disapproving frown, "They don't seem to have any self-restraint at all."

Mavis gave a slight smile and, turning to look at herself in the mirror, carefully adjusted her waitress cap. "I thought something important was going on with those two."

The grey-haired woman returned to her booth and began to finish off her plate of French fries. "Well," she said, "It's probably just because of the war and all."

This is the poem Jan's psychology professor assigned to the class for a discussion topic:

I Love You

You said you loved me just now.
A complex and fizzy sort of proposition,
Love…

A sharp bowel-constricting delirium.
A deep sunk shaft of nourishment.
An outstretching of welcome.

Love is building a fence and telling someone
"You'd be safer in here for a little while."
Other times love is opening the gate,
saying, "Go ahead and try your wings."

Love is a pat on the shoulder,
and a helping hand.

Love is giving in joy until the joy and the giving
become a fuel that feeds itself until
you are expanded and absorbed into the world,
but hardly anyone ever loves that much.

Love is like ice cream.
It comes in assorted flavors.

I love you, too.

Made in the USA
Charleston, SC
15 December 2012